...PIRES

...ritten
...UR
...es'

Phil Earle, bestselling author of
When the Sky Falls

'DELICIOUSLY DARK,
fangtastically feisty and gloriously gothic!
Brilliantly dangerous and funny.
A delight for the senses!'
Laura Ellen Anderson, author of *Amelia Fang*

'BRILLIANT. It's a deadly funny, twisty,
gothic romp with the loveliest vampire.
Sara Ogilvie's illustrations are the perfect match'
Jenny McLachlan, author of *Land of Roar*

'WICKEDLY FUN, with
a wonderfully strong girl hero'
Cressida Cowell, Children's Laureate

'Wonderfully atmospheric,
HUMOROUS and TOUCHING'
Radiya Hafiza, author of *Rumaysa*

'Had me LAUGHING with
e...

ALEX FOULKES

RULES for VAMPIRES

GHOSTS BITE BACK

ILLUSTRATED BY
SARA OGILVIE

Simon & Schuster

First published in Great Britain in 2022 by Simon & Schuster UK Ltd

Text copyright © 2022 Alex Foulkes
Illustrations copyright © 2022 Sara Ogilvie

1 3 5 7 9 10 8 6 4 2

Simon & Schuster UK Ltd
1st Floor, 222 Gray's Inn Road, London
WC1X 8HB

www.simonandschuster.co.uk
www.simonandschuster.com.au
www.simonandschuster.co.in

Simon & Schuster Australia, Sydney
Simon & Schuster India, New Delhi

A CIP catalogue record for this book is available from the British Library.

PB ISBN 978-1-4711-9957-8
eBook ISBN 978-1-4711-9958-5
eAudio ISBN 978-1-3985-1736-3

Typeset in the UK
Printed and bound by CPI Group (UK) Ltd, Croydon, CR0 4YY

MIX
Paper from
responsible sources
FSC® C171272

For Oldfields.
May your creativity lunge from
the shadows like a swiftly striking
beast, in pursuit of all your best ideas.

CONTENTS

Human, come closer,
and listen well:

This tale may give you a fright.
For while you are tucked up
safe in your bed,
There are creatures who lurk
in the night . . .

THE EIGHT VAMPIRIC LAWS

Tips and tricks for being the MOST POWERFUL vampire, according to Leo von Motteberg!

1. The Vampire will not enter uninvited. *Unless you've practised your Vampiric Will like me – then you can use hypnotism to get your invite!*
2. The Vampire will not stand in the light of day. *Would YOU like to be turned to stone?*
3. The Vampire will not touch the purest silver. *Ouch!*
4. The Vampire will not partake in the foul bulb, flower or stalk of the garlic plant. *Yuck!*
5. The Vampire will not gaze upon Holy artefacts. *But the graveyard is a fun vampire hang-out spot. A good place to play chess.*
6. The Vampire will possess no reflection. *Who needs a silly reflection when you can run up walls and glide like a bat?*
7. The Vampire will consume the blood of the Living, thus sustaining their immortal unlife into eternity. *Handy tip: ask your butler to warm up the cup for maximum tastiness!*
8. The Vampire will undertake their first Hunt on

the dusk of their one hundredth vampiric year. *Unless . . . everything goes disastrously wrong and you accidentally create two GHOSTS who are at war with each other. And THEN you have to team up with one of them to defeat the other, before he can destroy the forest . . . and before your evil vampire mum finds out . . .*

Can you keep a secret?

ONE

TARGET PRACTICE

The Ghost-Hunter's Companion is an ancient book from a time forgotten by history. It is also so rare that only one copy exists in the known world, stashed in the labyrinthine library at Castle Motteberg, high up on Mount Moth.

Presuming you survive the trek through the Dreadwald – a dank, dismal and deadly forest, as vicious as it is vast – a terrible trial will then await you. To read the book you must brave magical warding spells, a telekinetic baby, an enchanted suit of armour and the single most evil, most horrendously bloodthirsty VAMPIRE there has ever been, amongst other horrors.

This is a pity, because the book contains expert advice on an oddly specific but worthwhile topic: HOW TO KILL A GHOST. It includes even more information than *The Novice Hunter's Murder Manual*, a popular title found in all good libraries today (which is to say, every library).

Ghosts, according to the *Companion*, are some of the most difficult creatures to kill. They cannot be staked like vampires or burned up in sunlight. Nor can a ghost be slain by silver bullets like a werewolf or cut down by iron or steel like the fey folk. Not only this, though they themselves cannot be touched, a powerful ghost is undeterred from interacting with our world. Ghostly tactics may include dropping a heavy book on your head, throwing you off a cliff or squashing you flat against the ceiling. Few have successfully banished a ghost. Even fewer live to tell the tale.

Leo the Vampire – a natural enemy of ghostkind – already had quite the story. The question was: how long would she survive to tell it?

Dropping to her knees, Leo ducked behind a lopsided tree stump, snow soaking through to her skin. The impact made her wooden right leg groan beneath her, but she was too busy *listening out* to pay it any mind. All around her, the Dreadwald forest was abuzz with familiar sounds of the night. Winter insects whirred sleepily in the thorny brush. Pines stretched and sighed. Malevolent laughter approached, winding through the branches overhead—

'Leeeeoooo! Where, oh *where*, did you go?'

Eerie light emanated from the canopy, casting a sickly

glow. Leo hissed and crouched lower, mindful of her wild hair poking out.

It was here, wasn't it? This was where Leo had left what she was looking for? It was definitely this stump; she had hopped over the River Mothling to the north, turned left at the clawed-up beech tree and then snuck beneath the bowed willow. Her wayfinding in the forest was second to none and she would need it to escape unscathed. Leo scrabbled in the dirt with both hands, reaching through a hole in the bark to nudge aside the mushrooms that grew inside.

'Are you . . . HERE?' A branch shuddered directly above her. Leo's skin prickled at the sight of pale toes drifting through the pine needles. 'Oh, come ON now – you know you can't hide from me!'

The ghost-killing ritual – good for spirits, spectres, phantoms, wraiths and all manner of apparitions – is complex. It demands the total destruction of the bond between the ghost and the world of the Living. Leo knew this ritual very well, having learned every component by heart. The list had been stuck in her head for weeks, replaying over and over in her mind.

To kill a ghost, you needed salt. You also needed sulphur. And smoke. If they weren't difficult enough to come by, there was also twice-blessed water and the glow of a sunrise – good luck getting hold of those. Finally, perhaps trickiest of all, you needed a weapon of intent: something to actually *wield*. Leo gritted her teeth and stretched, reaching deeper into the stump . . .

Yes!

Her questing fingertips found no weapon of intent. Nor was there salt, sulphur or indeed any of the ghost-killing items. Rather, there was the thick coil of rope she had previously stashed, its rough fibres stiff with frost. Leo hurriedly unwound it. She could feel her black heart pulsing, strong enough that her usually dormant vampiric blood began to rush in her ears . . .

'HEY!' she shouted. A thrill knifed through her as the pale light drew closer. 'Who said anything about hiding?'

Throwing her weight backwards, Leo tugged the rope with all her strength.

A shrub rustled violently. From the tangle of twigs sprang three circular targets. Each had been cut from wood, then crudely painted with white rings and a red dot in the centre for—

'BULLSEYE!' someone yelled. There was an almighty CRACK as the first target burst into splinters. 'Ha! Too easy!' The second target was swiftly snapped in two; the broken half ricocheted off a tree trunk and clattered out of sight.

Zooming overhead, brandishing a shimmering poker like a sword, was a girl who looked about Leo's age – she could have been no older than perhaps eleven or twelve. Unlike Leo, however, she was floating in mid-air. Her long colourless hair fanned outwards as if she was underwater. Her ratty nightgown was cast in the same peculiar translucent white colour as her body. She could be made of misty glass all the way down to her bare toes.

The *ghost*.

Perhaps Leo should have been afraid. The *Companion* detailed more than three hundred different ways unlucky souls had fallen victim to ghost attacks. They were alphabetically listed from ABSORB'D BY A GHOSTLY FOG to ZIPP'D AWAY THROUGH AN OPEN WINDOWE AND UNTO THE AWAITING JAWS OF THE NIGHT.

But . . .

'Hey! You missed one!' Leo called out, hopping up on top of the stump. The ghost girl wheeled round, a young tree bending as she swept past it.

Before Leo could react, the ghost sailed straight through her in a freezing rush.

'I know, I know!' the ghost's voice snapped in Leo's ears. 'Give me a chance!' She jabbed with the poker. A ragged circle was punched through the centre of the third target. The deadly prong gleamed sharp through the hole.

A shower of splinters rained down on Leo's head.

'There!' the ghost exclaimed haughtily. She flew down, brushing her hair away from her face and adjusting the see-through hairband she wore.

Jumping down from her perch, Leo's feet hit the icy ground. Inside her scruffy winter boots, one foot had grey flesh and clawed toes. The other was a heavy prosthetic, whittled from oak. Thin and spindly and easily six feet tall, Leo loomed over her ghostly companion as she drew herself up to her full height. She grinned her needle-toothed grin. Her black eyes, deep and dark and unsettling, curved happily.

Leo and Minna made an odd pair. Vampires and ghosts, despite both being technically Undead, were as different as night and day. There was a reason the two factions had been SWORN ENEMIES for as long as unliving memory, ever since the very first vampire-ghost war.

The vampires needed the blood of the Living to survive . . . and an unfortunate side effect of the vampiric diet was that the Living tended to die. The ghosts blamed the vampires for their deaths. The vampires thought the ghosts should stop complaining and continue about their business. And so it had been for ever, back and forth, locked into a never-ending cycle of hatred. In some corners of the world it was now a *sport* for each side to hunt their enemy, inflicting harm with increasingly creative cruelty.

A vampire and a ghost being friends was unheard of. Worse still, it went against everything Leo's family stood for. The Von Mottebergs were a proud noble clan. Their ancestry could be traced back to the first aristocratic vampires. Their ferocity was unmatched, as was their cunning. They had the *Ghost-Hunter's Companion* in their library, after all.

'Your aim is getting *scary*, Minna!' Leo said cheerily, brushing shards of the broken target from her tattered cape.

The ghost called Minna tossed her head. 'What do you mean, *getting* scary? I've been a great shot for ages! *You* haven't been paying attention!' She paused to push the sharp end of the poker through her own shoulder, sheathing it through her body.

'Bleurgh . . .' Leo looked away. Despite all the times she had seen Minna do this, it still made her feel squiggly inside. 'I-I was just trying to say, you're clearly improving! I'm sure that was dead-centre on all of them this time!'

'I appreciate your help with my training, Leo – I do – but I don't need your approval,' Minna said. Her chubby cheeks and the gap between her two front teeth didn't make her expression any less stern. 'This is a . . . a ghost thing, after all. You wouldn't really understand. All you have to do is keep the targets coming. Or, I don't know, throw me some rocks again, so I can practise making my hands solid.'

Leo pinched the bridge of her nose, feeling a headache coming on.

Though she considered Minna to be her most precious friend, Minna remained a mystery to Leo in many ways. Her temper was one such conundrum, as it rivalled even the moodiest vampire Leo knew: her sister, Emmeline. On top of this, for weeks now Minna had insisted on meeting in the forest at night for ghostly combat practice, for reasons she wouldn't explain. If only Leo could see into her brain and spy on what she was thinking . . .

Last autumn, only a few months ago, both of their unlives had been turned upside down. In fact, Minna had LOST HER LIFE entirely, in what Leo now privately referred to as, 'the incident'.

It hadn't been Leo's fault, not really, but she still felt guilty. On the night Leo turned one hundred and eleven years old, she had stalked the human town of Otto's End, seeking her prey on her very first Hunt. A fire had broken out at the orphanage, St Frieda's Home for Unfortunate Children. Two humans had needlessly died in the process, their precious blood wasted. One of the humans was a

Living girl called Minna, now not-so-Living but just as fierce in personality.

And the *other* human who lost their life that night, well . . .

The thought of HIM was like losing your footing in the dark and hurtling down into an endless pit, your screams echoing as you tumble for ever.

The Orphanmaster. Their fight with Minna's former guardian had been the peril of all perils, a potential disaster epic enough to rock the Dreadwald down to its very roots. Leo had almost died (again) and more than once at that. The lives of Minna's human friends had been on the line and so had the fate of the forest. When you went through something like *that* together, you should trust each other completely, Leo was sure.

'Leo? Did you hear me?' Minna was asking, peering curiously up at her. 'Oh, don't sulk! You've been an enormous help, you have. But it's hard for me! You'll never know what it's like to be . . .' She gestured vaguely up and down her own translucent body. 'Like this.'

'You're strong, Minna,' Leo said earnestly. 'And fast.'

'Not strong or fast enough . . .' Minna muttered.

Not strong or fast enough for what? For who? Leo wanted to ask, despite knowing that Minna wouldn't tell. She'd already tried.

'H-hey, there's still hours left until sunrise,' Leo pointed out instead, to distract Minna from her brooding. She hopped nimbly up on to a fallen tree, making her cape billow dramatically behind her. Catching rocks was nice, but she knew what was better. She held out a clawed hand in a 'come on, then!' sort of gesture.

'Think you can take me one more time, Minnow?'

Whatever ghostly growing pains Minna had, there was one thing that never failed to cheer her up: sticking her poker through the interfering vampire who had (however inadvertently) killed her not so long ago.

'I told you not to call me "Minnow"!' Minna snapped. 'And I think the question is,' she added, with a gappy grin, 'can YOU take ME?'

Minna's hand flew to her poker. There was a *swoosh* past Leo's cheek as she dipped to one side in the nick of time – she bent low to avoid the swift backswing, dropping into a crouch. An inch from the top of her head Minna swiped again, slashing with her weapon. Its hooked tip gleamed and whirled in Minna's hand, slicing back and forth with lightweight ease.

Minna was quick, but so was Leo. She rolled forward and beneath Minna's dangling legs, coming up to deflect the next solid blow with her claws. Leo showed her fangs in victory. On top of building hideouts and researching the flora and fauna of the Dreadwald, sparring was now one of her favourite hobbies. It made her feel powerful. Invincible. As though even if *he* came back, she would be ready to—

'*Vaaaampire* . . .'

Leo froze, her ears twitching. Hot and cold flashed up her spine to make her scalp itch, before the freezing bite of the poker through her belly jolted her back to reality. She blinked hard.

She thought . . . She thought she heard . . .

'Wow, haven't got you like THAT in a while!' Minna said smugly, nodding at where the poker felt like a shard of ice between Leo's ribs. The sight of it might have been shocking, sunk to the handle in Leo's stomach and angling up through her most vital organs – but when Minna withdrew the weapon, it came away harmlessly. Leo's shirt was intact, as was her grey skin. All that was left was a residual chill.

Minna tossed her hair snootily. 'You're going to have to be quicker if you're ever attacked by the REAL DEAL! Not every ghost is as forgiving as . . . Leo? Are you listening?'

Leo was listening indeed, but she was listening *out*. She pressed a claw to her own mouth, flapping her other hand to tell Minna to keep it down.

'What's up with you?' What's wrong?' Minna hissed,

now somewhere between annoyed and spooked.

'I thought I . . . heard something, just now.'

'*VAMPIRE!*' a voice wailed again, winding through the trees. The log beneath Leo's feet shook as the sound vibrated through its hollow centre. Leaves rustled on a foreboding wind.

'Okay,' Minna said, now gripping the poker tight. 'THAT'S definitely something.'

'You hear it too?' Leo's eyes, with their pupils that were usually catlike slits, were now completely black. She scanned the shadowy trees around them, studying every shape in the darkness. This was the hour of the Undead – no Living person was roaming the forest at night. It was a time only for vampires and ghosts and creatures of the dark . . .

While a thousand possibilities jostled for position in her brain, a looming, hulking shadow was slowly cast across her mind's eye. Leo swallowed. 'What if it's . . . What if he's . . .'

'He's dead, Leo. The Orphanmaster is dead.'

'S-so are we?'

'You know what I mean!' Even through her unease, Minna still managed to be surly. 'We defeated him. We *banished* him, with the sulphur and smoke and everything. There's no coming back from wherever he is, you know that! He's deader than me, and I'm *extremely* dead.'

It was the first time Minna had spoken about the Orphanmaster in the months since his defeat. Hearing his name out loud made Leo's skin crawl.

'R-right!' She braced her feet on the fallen tree. Her wooden leg creaked, the knee joint locking into place and ready to jump. 'This is just . . . a mystery voice!' She huffed out a high nervous laugh. 'Happens all the time! Perhaps it's friendl—'

A great gust of freezing air rushed from beneath them, blasting out of either end of the hollow log. The force of it blew a hole in the weak bark directly beneath Leo's feet. Her cape flew up and caught around her head, blinding her. She felt for a moment as though *something* was closing in around her, like the hand of a giant . . .

'Let's be going, then!' she heard Minna squeak.

Wriggling her head free of the raggedy fabric, Leo leapt from the log. She didn't chance a look back, but her vampiric senses were zinging and she could feel a presence close, TOO CLOSE, behind her. Her feet connected with the frozen earth and she was away.

Panic seized Leo as she ran. She stumbled, dodging tree trunks and crashing through the shrubbery, thorns stinging through the sleeves of her shirt. The Dreadwald swelled and morphed in the dark, familiar pathways tangling up in a confusing knot. It was only made worse by the snow, which smothered every shape. Minna flew alongside Leo, sailing through the foliage.

'What do we *do*?' Leo cried, finally glancing back at where the pines were bowing, bending out of the way of the invisible force barrelling towards them. Orphanmaster or not, Leo was now certain it was a ghost. All the signs were there: disembodied voice, bitter wind, horrible chill . . .

One ghost was enough for Leo. Other than Minna – maybe Minna's parents at a push – Leo would be grateful if she never saw another ever again. She had encountered a grand total of zero ghosts in her eleven years as a human. After that, her century as a vampire had also been ghost-free.

She wasn't precisely sure what had changed, but lately she had become some kind of ghost magnet.

'Can you talk to it?' Leo shouted. 'Ask it what it wants! WHAT DO YOU WANT?'

There was a long mournful creak from behind them, followed by a CRASH that rattled Leo's fangs.

Leo gasped. 'That was a *tree*! It's going to pull down the whole Dreadwald!'

'You should go home!' Minna called back, sounding far too breathless for someone without the need of lungs. The point of her poker jabbed up at the sky; the three-pronged shape of Mount Moth was emerging beyond the thick canopy. 'We'll split up to confuse it!'

'But—' Leo's wooden leg creaked and she almost fell on her face, barely catching herself in time. 'But, Minna, what about you?'

'Leo. GO HOME. I'll be fine. I'll come and find you as the sun's coming up!'

'I . . .'

'In your bedroom at sunrise! Don't you dare be late! I know what you're like!' And with that final scolding Minna veered away in a swooping arc, the tips of her toes the last part of her to vanish into the darkness.

TWO

FINE ART

Leo couldn't believe her misfortune. Only a few short months since her battle with the Orphanmaster and here she was again: being chased by what seemed to be *another* furious ghost. There was something about her that drew trouble like the castle candelabras attracted stray moths. Leo kept running, and running, and the list of ghost-killing ingredients flashed across her mind.

Unfortunately, while racing through the Dreadwald towards the sanctuary of the mountain . . . Leo found the pockets of her cape somewhat emptier than she would prefer.

Yes, she was unprepared. And, yes, she had been caught by surprise.

But she wouldn't be outpaced.

Leo rushed up the mountain path, breaking free of the Dreadwald's piney cover. Above her, the night sky was clear and dotted with faraway stars. A solemn moon framed the highest point of Mount Moth. Of course, Leo understood, it wasn't really part of the mountain at all. Dad's wards meant that any Living onlooker would see three snowy peaks pointing towards the heavens. But the vampires who lived there knew that the summit was, in fact, the severe and stony Castle Motteberg.

Risking a glance back, Leo felt her insides lurch. A breathy blue-white mist had gathered at the thinning treeline. The ghostly cloud shifted and wavered as though uncertain of its path, rearing up to watch the fleeing vampire go. Leo allowed herself a grin – she was safe for now. There weren't many enemies of vampirekind brave enough to face Castle Motteberg. Perhaps the ghost should be *especially* afraid, considering the fearsome Von Motteberg reputation.

The castle loomed as Leo drew near. Moonlight glinted off the gargoyles, highlighting the spiked arches and silvery tips of the towers. Slitted windows studded the weathered stone, wrapped here and there in creeping vines. Sliced in two by the grand stone bridge that stretched towards the castle entrance, the mountain lake reflected the white moon. Leo skirted the water's edge, hopping on stones well worn from a hundred years of sneaking.

Leo scrambled up on to the castle ramparts, sending a rain of dust pattering down below. Holding her arms out for balance, she tiptoed nimbly along the wall. When she peered down at the slumbering Dreadwald, stretching off for miles to reach the horizon, the ghost-cloud was nowhere to seen. Her shoulders slumped in relief.

Straightening her cape, smoothing her hair, Leo tried to make herself presentable. Her hair lay flat for three seconds before springing up again. She put on her best smile: the one with a lot of shiny teeth. Her meetings with Minna were still new enough that Leo couldn't help but worry every time she returned home to the castle. Having a secret ghost friend wasn't exactly befitting a distinguished, devious and deadly Von Motteberg.

It felt far safer for Leo to slink back to her room, high up in the western tower, than risk unwanted interrogation in the foyer. She braced her flesh-and-blood foot on the wall of the tower.

With her wooden leg Leo pushed off. Leaning precariously backwards, she took a flying step into nothing and then up on to the side of the tower.

Her cape spiralled behind her as she began to run horizontally up the tower. Higher and higher, Leo put one foot in front of the other, every muscle in her body working to propel herself onwards. The frost-tipped trees below fell away, while the black sky above felt like it could envelop her, as though she might take off and swim in it. At the tower's pinnacle Leo's bedroom window beckoned . . .

Her room was always lovely and quiet, somewhere for her to relax and recharge. She would check in with Minna later, to figure out the whole *mysterious ghostly attacker* issue before it could cause any more trouble and—

Above Leo's head, the shutters exploded open. The windowpanes rattled in their wooden frames as they too were flung wide, and a pair of huge iron-gauntleted hands reached out into the open air.

Oh, pustules! Leo had time to think, pinwheeling her arms to try to slow down – but it was too late.

'MISS LEO, where HAVE you been?' a shrill voice cried, and the gauntlets snagged her by the shoulders and yanked her inside.

A young vampire's bedroom was personal. A private place, where they could escape the expectations of upper-class unlife. Leo loved spending time up here, high above the rest of the castle.

Her plush four-poster bed was cosier than the fanciest of coffins. Her various collections (rocks, fossils, fossils-that-looked-like-rocks, rocks-that-looked-like-fossils and so on) were proudly on display. Her giant mural map of the Dreadwald – hand-painted across one of the walls – made Leo feel like a piece of the forest was here with her, keeping her company. It was peaceful. It was calm. Usually . . .

'Marged, I'm *sorry*. I didn't mean to forget!' Leo protested, perched on the edge of her bed where she had been unceremoniously plonked. She fiddled with the blanket between her claws, spinning a thread loose. 'I didn't realise it was tonight!'

Chased by yet another ghost and now *this*. Perhaps she was cursed. It would certainly explain a lot.

'Well, Miss Leo, tonight it is!' From inside Leo's open wardrobe there was the metallic glint of a wiggling bottom as Marged the butler rooted around for something. 'I've been looking for you for *hours*. As you know, patience is not exactly one of Lady Sieglinde's qualities!'

I do know, Leo thought queasily. Mum could be described in a lot of ways: commanding, mighty, bloodthirsty, vicious . . . But patient?

Leo swallowed. 'Th-this is all unnecessary!' she said. 'I don't *need* a painting. Mum has plenty of portraits of me!'

It was true. There were renderings of every Von Motteberg lining the castle hallways, in the parlour, in the dining room . . . Eleonore 'Leo' von Motteberg – youngest daughter of the Great and Terrible Sieglinde – was no exception. It just so happened that Leo's portraits tended to be on the small and smudgy side, especially compared to her sister's. Emmeline always demanded the most wall space, despite her small stature.

'You are to have a *family* painting, like Miss Emmeline's,' Marged said. There was a rattling noise as she wrestled with something. 'Lady Sieglinde commands it, and so it will be done. Aha!'

With a victorious clatter, a knight clad in iron armour emerged from the wardrobe. On top of her helmet, a red feathery plume bobbed. In one giant gauntlet was a sagging bundle of powder-blue fabric, weighed down by the sheer amount of frills and lace attached seemingly at random.

It was THE DRESS.

Leo gasped, betrayed. Perhaps it *would* have been better if the ghost-cloud had caught her, after all. 'Marged, no!'

The knight nodded grimly. 'Oh yes.'

'You can't do this to me!'

'Come now, Miss Leo!' Marged caught Leo as she tried to flee for the bathroom. There was a brief struggle. Leo's wiry limbs flailed wildly, but Marged wouldn't be deterred. 'It's Lady Sieglinde's favourite – she insisted you wear it, just this once!'

'Just this once!' Leo griped, half smothered in fabric. It had the texture and smell of old wallpaper. 'It's *always* this dress! It's the only dress in my wardrobe!'

'Oh, but it does make you look so *smart*, little one.'
Marged heaved the fabric down and Leo's disgruntled
head popped through the neck opening. The fabric bulged,
rustling dangerously, and then with a powerful POOF the
ruffled collar burst outwards like a sad-looking flower.

'There now!' said Marged cheerfully. 'Oh, don't you
look nice?' One metal-clad thumb scrubbed over Leo's
cheek.

'It's *so bad*,' Leo groaned to herself, looking down at
the misshapen monstrosity. It somehow managed to be
both tight and baggy at the same time, with an abundance
of bows that would put even Emmeline to shame. The
puffy pleats made it impossible to run in. Defeated, Leo
let herself be steered over to the desk. She slumped into her
chair, the voluminous skirt inflating around her.

Against the wall, the chest of drawers rustled curiously.
The uppermost drawer slid open enough for something
brown and furry to peek out. A glare from Leo was enough –
the drawer slid closed again with a muffled 'meep'.

'It is VERY PRETTY,' Marged said firmly. 'But
perhaps next time the seamstress visits, you should ask
for something more . . . you.' In her giant hand she held
a dainty comb, which she dutifully tried to work through
Leo's nest of hair.

Leo tried to turn her head to look suspiciously at the knight, but Marged held her still. 'What do you mean, next time? Is the seamstress coming?'

The tiny imp-like woman, with her pointy fingernails and pointier pins, was not Leo's favourite person. The feeling was mutual.

'No, no. I meant, some time in the future!' Marged's chuckle sounded a tad nervous.

Sighing, Leo winced as Marged tried and failed to loosen a particularly stubborn knot. 'You're supposed to tell me these things. You're my butler.'

'Nanny,' Marged corrected, under her breath. 'And, Miss Leo, you know I am always here for you. I always keep you to your schedule. Is there anything *you* wish to tell *me*?'

Leo dug her claws into the edge of the desk and tried to hold as still as possible. Marged could always tell when something was wrong.

Marged knew all about Minna. She also knew about the Orphanmaster, which was a whole other level of trouble. But if not for Marged, Leo probably wouldn't be here. After Leo had defeated the Orphanmaster in lethal sunlight, her battered body had been scooped up moments before she'd have turned permanently to stone. It was Marged who had come to find her. She really was an excellent butler.

Things had been quiet at Castle Motteberg ever since. Leo wanted so desperately to keep it that way. Even though Marged had tentatively agreed it was best not to tell Mum and Dad about the battle with the ghost, she also had a troublesome tendency to *fuss*. Hearing of another ghostly attack in the forest would surely send poor Marged spiralling.

'I just . . . I don't understand why Mum even wants another portrait of me!' Leo complained, changing the subject. 'She should have another one of Emmeline – Em LOVES being painted!'

'Miss Leo, I know you're frustrated.' Marged gently laid her metal palm flat against Leo's scalp, so the pulling wouldn't hurt quite so much. 'It's a small thing, and it will keep your parents happy. They are proud of you! They want a reminder of this special time!'

'Special . . . ?'

'You won't always be young, little one. Your mother wants . . . She wants to treasure her memories of her daughters. A portrait is a lovely memento. You know how Lady Sieglinde feels about fine art!'

The comb clicked on to Leo's desk, its quest abandoned. Leo spun in her chair, peering up into Marged's visor. As she lifted her chin from its ruffly bed, she felt her hair spring straight back into its usual tufts.

'What does Mum *really* want?'

Marged patted her kindly on the shoulder. 'We should make our way downstairs. Your parents have been waiting. Let's not leave it any longer.'

Dread filled Leo's belly, as heavy as a stone.

She thought, as she looked back to the window, that she saw a whisper of a blue-white cloud – but when she blinked, it was gone.

Flames smouldered in the fireplace and atop the waxy candelabras, casting a foreboding glow over the Castle Motteberg parlour. It was the most lavish of rooms, with the fanciest furniture, the shiniest crystalware and a sprinkling of spiderwebs.

In a high-backed chair Leo was the unwilling centrepiece. She had managed to stuff the folds of the enormous dress round herself, so that she was now propped up on multiple layers of skirt and velvet cushion. Her legs stuck out at awkward angles from the frills, one grey and one wooden. She tried not to frown.

She never dwelled too much on her missing leg – lost in an unfortunate GRIMWALKing accident. The GRIMWALK, where a vampire would turn into bats and then reappear in their vampiric form, was an important power for every young vampire to master. Sadly for Leo, when GRIMWALKing for the first time, some of those bats had decided to fly away, leaving her with a limb missing. It typically didn't bother her, since Dad had done such a good job on her prosthetic, but she was keenly aware of it as she had her portrait painted. Perfection was everything to the Von Mottebergs.

'That's it, Miss Leo – remember to keep still!' Marged chirped, half hidden behind the easel. Slowly, with painstaking precision, she ran the tiny paintbrush across the canvas, adding another black hair to the subject's head. If it happened to be less messy than in real unlife, who was to complain?

'Oh yes,' Marged said approvingly, 'that's looking rather splendid!'

Leo sighed. Marged – a knight of many talents – had been working diligently away on her masterpiece for hours. Meanwhile, Leo's bottom was numb and her mind had long since wandered. It wasn't every night you were forced to run from a wrathful spirit – and this was now *two* ghosts in the space of only a few months.

Without moving her head Leo's eyes darted in their sockets, looking left and right around the room. No sign of any ghostly activity. Nothing was out of the ordinary, aside from the crimes committed against vampire fashion.

'Excellent work, Marged!' said Dad on Leo's left. 'You *are* getting my good side, aren't you?' He stood a little straighter, his chin lifted proudly. On his head the lenses of his goggles had been shined to a gleam. There was a sharp TWANG as one of his waistcoat buttons suddenly pinged off his round belly, flying away across the room. 'Oh my . . .'

'That's quite all right, Lord Dietmar – stay where you are. I'll paint it back on!' Marged assured him with a flourish of her brush.

To Leo's right Lady Sieglinde sniffed. She was a long, thin shard of ice in Leo's peripheral vision, outfitted in her signature stark grey dress. Leo kept her gaze forward. As usual, being sat next to Mum was both a terror and a thrill. Leo hoped she would one day be as intimidating as her.

There was no one more fearsome. The cruelty and power of the Great and Terrible Sieglinde was legend – there wasn't a single vampire who didn't know her name. It was Leo's destiny to be exactly like Mum when she grew up, if Mum didn't eat her first.

'Really, Dietmar. Is this the impression we want to give to guests?' Lady Sieglinde – *Mum* – rumbled, eyeing the fallen button. Her low voice was punctuated by the click of her claws against the back of Leo's chair. Each slow *tick* made Leo sit up a little straighter, until she was practically leaning forward in the chair to get away from the sound.

Dad laughed, adjusting his pristinely pressed lab coat. 'I'm sure our guests will be more than impressed, my love. This painting will look perfect at the end of the banquet table! After all –' he made lovey eyes at Mum – '*both* of our daughters have completed their Waxing Moon! What more could a father ask for?'

Unnoticed, Leo's claws punctured the armrests and sank deep into the downy cushioning inside. Staying completely still, she met Marged's metallic gaze from across the room.

'Yes, the Waxing Moon,' Mum rumbled. She might have been smiling smugly, but it was hard to tell. 'Another generation of formidable Von Mottebergs, completing the Hunt on their first try.'

Leo looked at Marged. Marged looked at Leo. Leo had suspected as much, but it still stung; this was no ordinary portrait. Rather, it was to mark her Waxing Moon. The set-up was almost identical to the enormous painting of her sister Emmeline that hung above the fireplace, her wicked stare piercing all who entered the parlour.

The Hunt of the Waxing Moon was certainly the most important night of a young vampire's life. It was the number-one hallowed milestone, the first solo Hunt, THE Hunt with a capital H to match. Off into the world alone, to bite and drink from Living prey, as adults did. It was right there in the Vampiric Laws: *The Vampire will undertake their first Hunt on the dusk of their one hundredth vampiric year.*

But there was nothing in the Vampiric Laws to say that the Hunt had to be perfect. Many young vampires met failure on their first outing – especially if fighting (Leo swallowed nervously) HUMANS.

Unpredictable humans. DANGEROUS humans.

Like the Orphanmaster, Leo's brain supplied, making her shiver.

The Vampiric Council did not demand first-time success. Leo hadn't burst into flames herself, after the catastrophic disaster of *the incident*.

But perfection was a Von Motteberg thing. It was a *Mum* thing. As far as Leo's parents knew, Leo had completed her Waxing Moon on her first try, just like Emmeline, just like Mum and Dad, just like the countless Von Motteberg ancestors buried in the castle crypt.

Von Mottebergs who failed the Hunt were never heard from again. They disappeared, mysteriously vanished from the family records, as though they had never even existed. So far, Leo mercifully hadn't been caught out and Marged was keeping her secret . . . but how long could that last?

'Leo!' Mum snapped. 'Sit still, child. What are you doing?'

Leo looked round before she could stop herself. The sight of Mum's face, gaunt and severe, her grey lips curled down in distaste, turned Leo's blood to ice.

The black eyes glimmered, sucking Leo in.

If Leo stared for too long, she was sure Mum would realise that she hadn't *actually* completed her Waxing Moon on her first try. In fact, she hadn't completed it AT ALL after what had happened in Otto's End on her one hundred and eleventh birthnight. She had been too anxious to try again, and besides, she had Minna's ghost-training to think about—

There was a CRASH. The paintbrush skittered across the floor. The palette clattered after it, flecks of paint splattering on to the ornamental rug, and attached to it was . . .

Marged's metal arm, from the gauntlet right up to the pauldron that protected the shoulder.

Leo stared forward again, the spell broken, returning her hands hastily to the armrests of the chair.

'Whoops!' Marged said brightly, clanging to her feet. 'Clumsy me, my sincerest apologies . . .' When she bent down to retrieve her fallen arm, the hole in her shoulder revealed her hollow insides.

Deflating in the chair, Leo's throat bobbed against the itchy ruff. That was a close call. Not everyone was fortunate enough to have an enchanted suit of armour as a butler. Marged's knightly timing was spot on, as were her detachable limbs.

'Dearie me,' Dad was saying, bustling forward to help

Marged reattach the arm. 'I'm not exactly an armour-smith, Marged, but I'm sure I could do something about this!'

'Not to worry, my lord. I am used to it,' Marged replied, pushing the shoulder back into place. There was a click and she wiggled her fingers. 'See?'

'Are we ALL moving now?' Mum interrupted, displeased. 'Need I remind you all that the Banquet is in TWO NIGHTS' TIME! There is no room for dallying and even less for RIDICULOUS SHENANIGANS!'

Ban . . . quet?

Amidst the flurry of activity around her, Leo's mind was quiet. She searched every dark nook of her memory, feeling as though she had forgotten something. She could probably be forgiven, considering the ghostly commotion of late, but there was definitely *something* going on . . .

The dress. The portrait.

The mention of the seamstress with her pointy pins.

Shooting out of the chair in an explosion of frills, Leo gasped.

'The Blood Moon Banquet!'

THREE

MADAME KINKATCH

The pale winter sun rose behind a blanket of heavy cloud. As the morning drew in, flakes began to fall, coating the Dreadwald pines in crisp white snow.

High on Mount Moth, inside the western tower with shutters closed and curtains drawn, Leo really should have been asleep.

'I don't get it!' she whispered urgently, buried beneath the extra blankets Marged always piled on at this time of year. 'Why wouldn't she warn me? Making a fuss is . . . it's Marged's favourite hobby, b-but she hasn't mentioned any banquet. This is a BIG DEAL – all the noble vampire families will be here! In two nights!'

She was propped up on her elbows in bed, the top of her head forming the peak of her makeshift blanket tent. In her hand was a dagger shaped like the tooth of a huge beast. It was Minna's dagger: the one Leo had stolen during their first meeting at St Frieda's orphanage. After Minna's accidental death, she hadn't had much use for it, so Leo had hung on to it.

Besides, its reflective surface was excellent for long-distance emergency conversation. Moving through mirrors, and mirrored surfaces, was one of Minna's most useful ghost powers. The polished metal glowed with white light, filling the blanket tent with such brilliance that Leo had to squint, her pupils turning to slits.

The spectral scene reflected in the blade was almost entirely obscured by Minna's round, gappy-toothed face – now showing her trademark frown.

'Is it really Marged's job to remind you? You're not a baby, Leo. If there is an important vampire thing coming up, you shouldn't need to be told more than once!'

'It actually is Marged's job,' Leo said, feeling defensive. 'She's my butler, after all. That's what butlers do. Did you hear the part where I said ALL the noble vampire families? Here! At Castle Motteberg!'

The Blood Moon Banquet, held once a year, was usually something Leo looked forward to. It was a rare opportunity to see other vampire children, who knew what it was like to grow up with the pressures of an immensely evil, powerful lineage behind you.

There would be music and dancing and the finest

delicacies from the castle kitchens. While the children played secret games, their parents would swan around with blood wine and pretend to be charmed by each other, all the while plotting ways to strengthen their own hold on the vampire world.

Lady Sieglinde von Motteberg, host of this year's banquet, would certainly be looking to make an impression. She had schemed for centuries to become Head of the Vampiric Council – a position currently held by Lord Ayman, who she utterly despised. As far as Mum was concerned, she would want to see total perfection in everything from the décor to her daughters.

Including, Leo thought with a sinking feeling, the daughter who had been chased through the forest by YET ANOTHER ghost earlier that night. If the spirit crashed the party . . .

Minna didn't reply, but there was a judgy look on her face that said it all. She really didn't understand how it felt to be a vampire. She leaned back, folding her arms across her chest.

Behind her, the snowy forest beamed into view. It was luminescent in the eternal half-light of the Ghostly Realm: Minna's home, the place where she went when she wasn't training with Leo. The place where all ghosts went after seven moons had passed since their deaths. The place

Minna had been so shy about discussing.

It was a rare glimpse into Minna's world. Leo peered closer.

In the background were two spectral figures. A tall man was standing ramrod straight, his back against a tree and his gloved hands at his sides. Between his gappy teeth was an apple. A few paces away, his shorter, plumper companion held a shimmering bow with an arrow primed to fly. Her long hair was coiled into two buns to keep it out of her face. She would have been the picture of concentration, if not for her mad grin.

'Your family is doing well, then?' Leo ventured. She tilted her head to get a better view of the Ghostly Realm, but all she could see was endless trees and snow. She couldn't help but be reminded of the first time she had seen Minna's parents – from afar, just like this, peeking in on their little world that felt so far away.

'They are.'

'Have you told them about the . . . the *you-know-what*?'

Minna wrinkled her nose. 'You can say GHOST, Leo. *I'm* a ghost. It's okay.'

'Fine! The g-ghost, then.' Leo winced as she stammered. 'You know what I mean – has it . . . is it . . . ?'

'No. It didn't follow me back to the Ghostly Realm.' Minna's face filled the blade again as there was a TWANG of the bowstring from behind her. Raucous laughter rang out. She sighed. 'It must have given up after you made it back to the castle. Ghosts aren't supposed to behave like this, Leo – you have your rules and we have ours.'

'You have rules? Ghost rules?'

'Well, yeah. We're not meant to start interfering with . . . you know. The *other* world. Your world. If it's here, coming after you, then it's probably up to no good.' A sudden dark look came over Minna as she narrowed her eyes. 'I shouldn't have run away. I could have taken it; I know I could. I'm ready to fight. My technique with the poker is a lot better than before.'

Leo buried herself deeper into the blankets, curling her leg up beneath her in case she was suddenly grabbed from the bottom of the bed.

'Can you stop that?' Minna grumped. 'I can see right up your nose from this angle.'

'Sorry!' Leo propped the dagger against her pillow again. 'I . . . I have CONCERNS, Minna! We were absolutely right to run! This ghost knows what I am! A-and the timing COULD NOT BE WORSE, I promise you – if it climbs the mountain, I'll be absolutely done for—'

'*You'll* be done for!' chimed in a voice, and the dagger shook as Leo's pillow wriggled. 'Oh! I see! It's all about you, isn't it, Leo?'

From beneath the downy cushion popped a furry brown face dotted with eight beady eyes. A skinny leg covered in fur emerged, feeling its way across the mattress, and then another, and another, until eight limbs were waving around and poking Leo in the face.

'Rodri!' Leo gasped through one of the legs, which was squashing her lip up towards her left nostril.

'You need to start being a better roommate!' the newcomer nagged, clicking his fangs. 'What's this about ANOTHER ghost? Is one not enough?' He turned towards the dagger, his sightless eyes swivelling. 'Yes, I know you are here, Ghost Girl.'

'Hello, Rodrigo,' greeted Minna flatly. 'Nice to see you, too.'

Unimpressed, Leo batted the legs away. 'Rodrigo! How many times do I have to tell you? No spiders allowed! The bed is vampires-only. You have a whole drawer to yourself!'

The oversized spider – Rodrigo – sighed huffily. 'Vampires-only . . .' he muttered. 'Vampires-only! Yes, until you need a sneaky sleepover with your secret ghost friend!'

'Minna isn't *here*. She's in the Ghostly Realm.'

'So? A-and what about the wretched weasel, hm? *He's* allowed on the bed!'

As it was, Button the cat was nowhere to be seen, but

that wasn't out of the ordinary. Any sighting of Minna always sent him scarpering. Leo was sure he would be back to terrorise Rodrigo again by nightfall. They were sworn enemies.

'I'm worried about you, Leo!' Rodrigo continued. 'If Lady Sieglinde finds out, well . . .' His fur bristled all over, from the tips of his legs to his fluffy bottom. 'Listen, one ghost is enough. One ghost is TOO MUCH, in fact – you need to rethink your choices! What will happen to ME if—'

'If Mum turns me to dust, I know, I know. You won't be homeless, Rodri. Nothing will happen to any of us. We . . . w-we have the situation under control.' Leo was trying to reassure *herself*. She caught Minna's stare in the dagger. 'We defeated an evil spirit once. We can do it again if it comes to it.'

Minna touched a hand to the poker through her shoulder. 'This is precisely why I've been honing my fighting technique,' she said curtly. 'You're right – *if* it comes to it, we can defend ourselves. We don't even know what this ghost wants! It could be anything . . . but judging by the way it came at us, we should prepare for the worst.'

Leo stared. Her suspicions about Minna's training had been correct, after all. Minna was expecting to fight *more* ghosts.

'And this fancy-pants banquet?' Rodrigo piped up before Leo could reply. 'What about that? The castle will be crawling! Someone's *bound* to notice if you're . . . YAH!' He made a chopping motion with one of his legs: a mimicry of ghostly karate. 'And then it will be bye-bye to me AND to you AND also to Ghost Girl—'

'Aw,' interjected Minna with no hint of sentimentality. 'You thought of me.'

'Well.' Rodrigo sniffed. 'You seem okay. For a bringer of death and destruction.' He shook himself. 'Leo, promise me you'll be careful! You need to stop getting mixed up in these things – remember what happened last time!'

Leo didn't need reminding. Outside, beyond her window, the sun's eerie presence made her nerves prickle. She was hyper-aware of it, even safe inside her bedroom – it was a vampire's survival instinct to be wary of the sun.

'I promise,' Leo said. 'And while we're on that note, *you* need to keep this to yourself. Marged is busy with the preparations. She doesn't need to be worrying about me.'

'Hmph! I think you mean you don't want her nosing in on you while you're off doing something dangerous!'

Leo scooped Rodrigo up; he was about the size of her fist. The blankets fell around them, disturbed by the wriggling.

'AH! Ah, Leo, no!'

'You need to promise! We'll figure it out – but if we're going to be roommates, then you need to learn to keep a secret!'

'But—'

'I wonder where Button is . . .'

'*Ack!*' Rodrigo choked. He didn't fancy being chased by the cat. 'Okay! Okay, fine!' He glowered up at Leo in the snowy dagger light. 'But don't say I didn't try! Back in—'

'Back in Argentina this would never happen,' said Leo and Minna, perfectly in unison.

Rodrigo gave a defeated huff.

Leo detangled herself from the blankets, hopping across the chilly floorboards. She returned Rodrigo to his drawer, setting him inside with her winter socks. 'You stay here,' she told him sternly. 'And not a word to Marged! We've got everything under control.'

Sort of, she thought to herself, looking back at the bed. Inside the dagger blade, Minna had drawn the poker and was swishing it back and forth. Leo indulged in a deep, calming breath, right from the bottom of her skinny ribs.

The hostile ghost hadn't dared venture beyond the treeline – they were safe up on the mountain. The guests would be none the wiser. *Mum* would be none the wiser. The Blood Moon Banquet was all about making Lady

Sieglinde look impressive before the Council. Leo could focus on being the picture-perfect vampire daughter and leave the ghost-battling for later. She had kept her family and Minna mostly separate so far, there was no reason why it all had to come crashing down now . . .

Was there?

Somehow, Leo couldn't quite push down the sick feeling that squirmed in her guts.

'I still think—'

'*Good day*, Rodri.'

Rodrigo squeaked, rolling around inside the drawer as Leo pushed it shut.

The new night saw a flurry of activity at Castle Motteberg. Suits of armour gleamed. New candles adorned the candelabras, only half melted with dripping wax. The tapestries had been shaken of dust and the family crest – a winged insect, poised in mid-flight – glinted menacingly above the grand entrance, ready to welcome their guests.

There was no mistaking the Von Mottebergs. Every inch of the castle was a testament to their powerful history, from the ancestral portraits to the relics

they had won from their
enemies. Marged had been
up all day, clanging around
like a knight possessed, but
she showed no sign of tiring.
In fact, her grip on Leo's
hand had been as unshakable
as ever when she had whisked
the youngest lady out of bed.

'Come now, little one!'
she had chimed, while Leo
shuffled along and rubbed
at her tired eyes. 'Only one more night and day left!
There's much to be done!'

As it was, Leo had only one job: to refrain from bolting
as rattling chains announced the lowering drawbridge and
the arrival of an early guest.

It was how she found herself stood atop a wooden stool
in the dining room, enveloped in a cocoon of violently
green velvet.

'Green is VERY on-trend for the winter,' declared
Madame Kinkatch – the seamstress – from somewhere
outside the prison of fabric. Leo could just about hear her
voice and it was as scratchy as her pins, two of which were
jabbing Leo in the hip.

Madame Kinkatch was tiny and heavily bejewelled and had a great puff of fluffy hair that doubled as a pincushion. Her rows of identically sharp teeth were not unlike those of a Venus flytrap. Her eyes were small and shrewd, her hands pointy-tipped and mean, and her ears were long and delicate where they stuck out from her head at right angles.

'Would you stand still, girl?' she snapped. 'And straighten your back! I've seen three goblins stacked on top of each other with better posture than you!'

Leo stood dutifully straighter. Slowly, avoiding Madame Kinkatch's ire and her pins, Leo turned her head to free her face.

The dining-room table was an eruption of buttons and bows, with fat spools of thread and rolls of fabric stacked to the ceiling. In the doorway the head of an enormous green-blue rhinoceros beetle poked through, as big as a horse. Its long smooth horn was currently draped with various measuring tapes, and the beetle held patiently still as its mistress selected one.

'Thank you, dear,' Madame Kinkatch said.

'You're . . . welcome?' replied Leo, not wanting to be impolite, then jumped when something pricked her bottom. 'Yowch!'

'Not you!' the seamstress snapped. 'I was talking to Socrates.'

The gigantic beetle let out what was probably a gentle sigh, but enough to make the candlelight flicker and the mountain of fabric wobble dangerously.

Leo pinched her mouth firmly shut before she could get into any more trouble. She spied the top of Madame Kinkatch's pin-studded head as she whirled round her on a floating stool, the measuring tape flowing from her hands by some kind of dark tailoring magic. Leo could feel the fabric cocoon shifting, no doubt becoming something equally as hideous as the blue dress. She sighed, remembering what Marged said about requesting something more 'her'.

Madame Kinkatch would probably use *Leo* as a pincushion if she questioned her work.

'Looking good, Leo!' someone crowed.

Leo jerked round to see a bundle of white frills shoot up behind Socrates' shell. A flying toddler sailed into the room on a wave of telekinetic power, chubby hands outstretched. Everything about her looked perfectly angelic, from her curls to her matching bonnet and booties.

It was all an act, of course.

'Hi, Emmeline,' Leo sighed, hooking her chin over the swaddling velvet.

'Ohhh, that really is your colour! Very *swampy*.'

Emmeline landed unsteadily on the rug, her floppy

little body fighting for balance. The haughty tilt of her chin and the way her red eyes flashed, however, was far from babyish. Her sneer was positively teenaged.

Any newcomer to the castle would be likely get the two of them confused, since Emmeline's physical form was so young and helpless. In fact, she was actually the *older* Von Motteberg sister, having been turned into a vampire roughly fifteen years before Leo. Of course Emmeline had been a baby, and Leo had been eleven years old when Mum had given her the CHOMP, as Minna called it. To be made a vampire, you had to first be bitten by someone with vampirism. It was a painful honour.

An eternity as a small limp creature had certainly given Emmeline a sour attitude, though she had almost everyone wrapped round her pudgy little finger.

'Hmmm?' Madame Kinkatch popped up from where she had been rummaging through the ruffles behind Leo. Her face lit up. 'Oh, if it isn't Miss Emmeline!'

'Madame Kinkatch!' Emmeline smiled sweetly. 'This colour is SO charming on my sister!'

Marged, Leo silently moaned, *where are you?*

But Marged couldn't save her. She was down in the kitchens, working herself up into a culinary frenzy. Mum had demanded a hundred different hors d'oeuvres for the party tomorrow, (which was apparently French for 'many fancy bites of food'), and Marged was the knight for the task.

'I was just talking to our mum – to *Lady Sieglinde*,' Emmeline said. She looked up into Madame Kinkatch's face, making her eyes adorably round. 'She was saying that she wants Leo's new outfit to be a real statement at the banquet. She mentioned something about a train . . . ?'

Leo stared. If *she* had critiqued Madame Kinkatch's handiwork, she would have been thwapped around the head. A protest crawled up her throat and stuck on the tip of her tongue. She couldn't decide which was worse: a hideous dress made even *more* hideous and cumbersome, or making Madame Kinkatch angry . . .

'Why, yes – hmmm!' The seamstress tilted her head, considering the fabric mountain. 'I believe a train would work.'

Leo squidged her eyes shut with a tiny moan of despair. The last thing she wanted was to drag around an annoying trail of velvet all night.

'Something DRAMATIC!' Emmeline insisted, glaring gleefully at Leo while Madame Kinkatch's back was turned. 'The heavier the better, Mum said. She wants all eyes on Leo. She *has* recently completed her Waxing Moon, after all.'

'Emmeline,' Leo said desperately, 'what about you? You *are* the older sister. It can't be *all* about me; it's the Blood Moon Banquet!'

'Ah yes, Miss Emmeline – on the subject of YOUR gown . . .' All too eager to abandon the gangly scruff of a youngest daughter, Madame Kinkatch flew to the ornate chest balanced on Socrates' shiny back. 'I've been adding the finishing touches; it will look positively splendid, I'm sure . . .'

'Um . . .' Leo tried. 'Should I get down?'

'We should have another fitting!' Emmeline exclaimed, as though she hadn't been exactly the same size and shape for one hundred and fifteen years.

'What a delightful idea!' Madame Kinkatch pulled a diminutive dress from the trunk, covered in Emmeline's favoured frills. Chattering away, the pair of them disappeared behind the wooden modesty screen, leaving Leo stood like a lonely tree.

'*Pssst! Leo!*'

Someone was calling her. Leo tried to turn, but the stiff fabric rustled dangerously. She stilled, trying to see out of the corner of her eye.

'*Leo!*'

'W-who's there?' she whispered back, arms pinned to her sides.

On the mantelpiece one of the candles caught her gaze. It was burned down to a squat stump, dripping wax. Its flame, now a vibrant blue-white, was scowling at her.

'What do you mean, who's there?' it grumped. 'For goodness' sake, Leo!'

Minna!

Minna had truly become a master of sneaking around, squeezing her ghostly form into all sorts of things to avoid detection. The candle flame, however, was new.

'We have a problem,' Minna told her. Her round face bobbed, curls of black smoke wisping off the top of her head. 'Out in the Dreadwald. You need to see this!'

'I'm kind of busy . . .' Leo wriggled, trying to get the velvet to sit more comfortably. It only became even tighter, squeezing her organs.

'Busy!' The candle flared, sputtering more smoke. 'Well! I'm sorry – I'll leave you to it, shall I? You can deal with the FURIOUS GHOST once it's here on your doorstep!'

Jerking round, Leo made a frantic shushing noise.

Behind the screen, Emmeline had said something uproariously funny, judging by Madame Kinkatch's scratchy laughter.

'What do you mean, on our doorstep?' Leo hissed, feeling her hair begin to stand on end. Inside her velvet prison, her skin roiled with goosebumps. 'It can't . . . it can't reach the castle! It can't get through Dad's wards! When I saw it b-before, it got stuck at the edge of the Dreadwald . . .'

Saying it out loud now, Leo realised that this couldn't be true.

The Orphanmaster had attacked her at this very castle, after all, in the library and the armoury and the gallery that led to the servants' quarters. There was nothing to stop a ghost from invading Castle Motteberg if it was powerful enough. Worse still, everyone was distracted by the impending banquet. Dad's protective wards needed near-constant upkeep and if he was taking a break from his laboratory . . .

'Leo, come on!' From out of the top of the candle Minna began to emerge, her long hair spinning out. 'There's no time for . . . for . . .' She blinked, gesturing up and down Leo's body. 'For whatever's going on here. What even is this?'

Leo groaned. 'Minna . . .'

'No, seriously. Are you a roll of carpet?'

'Please—'

'Are they going to unfurl you at the banquet so everyone can walk on you?'

Enough was enough. With a great heave Leo's arms punched through the fabric either side of her, seams splitting with an incriminating CRACK. Madame Kinkatch's fluffy head appeared round the screen, gawping at her.

'LEO!' she shrieked, aghast, as her young client hopped down off the stool. Minna disappeared swiftly into the wall, taking advantage of the commotion as Leo lolloped clumsily to the door.

'I'm sorry, Madame Kinkatch!' Leo called back, ducking apologetically past Socrates. 'It's an emergency! I'll be back as soon as I can!'

The enormous beetle sighed.

'YOU GET BACK HERE AT *ONCE*!' was the seamstress's shrill cry, the sound chasing Leo out of the dining room and down the stony passageway. Leo paid it no mind, tearing at the smothering cowl of fabric to free her face, leaving a flapping trail behind her.

'Minna!' she gasped, running as quickly as her bound knees would allow. The result was an awkward gallop. 'Where are we going?'

'Back to your room!' Minna sailed in and out of the stony wall, emerging from a portrait of Cousin Luisa and disappearing back into one of Great-Aunt Henrika. 'We need to get up high to see it!'

The stairs of the western tower proved challenging. The constricting dress forced Leo to jump up each step, hoisting herself up the stony spiral using the narrow handrail.

Up and up they flew, Minna shouting encouragement until they burst into Leo's bedroom—

'Leo! The window!'

Tugging back the heavy curtains, Leo fumbled with the latch on the windowpane. The shutters banged against the stonework as she thrust them open, too, leaning out into the night sky.

'There!' Minna cried, pointing down at the forest far below them. 'Do you see that?'

Amongst the trees, a sinister, supernatural fog had gathered. It wound itself sinuously through the pines. It swelled and shrank in an unsettling mimicry of a Living beast, taking breaths of wintry air.

It was enormous, Leo realised, feeling her stomach flip-flop beneath her pounding heart. Visible even from this high up – the top of the tallest tower of Castle Motteberg – the ghostly mist seemed to reach for miles. Whatever phantom was down there, it had power unlike anything Leo had seen before, beyond even the Orphanmaster with his terrifying telekinesis and oily, rotting hold on the forest.

Worse still, the thing was on the move, rearing up as though it could see them staring. Like a terrible tide, it began to draw back, growing brighter as its mass built up amongst the faraway trees. It was coiling itself like a snake preparing to strike.

'You get it NOW?' Minna burst out, flying past Leo and out into the night. 'This is bad! This is REALLY BAD!'

'Okay. Okay.' Leo tried not to panic. 'What do we do?'

Should they run? *Could* they run? Leo considered simply pulling the shutters closed. It was childish, she knew, but maybe they could hide under the bed where it couldn't find them. She had hidden there from Marged plenty of times.

Far away, the trees began to shake and bend, snow puffing up in an icy cloud. The ghost was taking a running leap. Closer and closer, the Dreadwald pines began to tremor in an alarming chain reaction, the shaken trees cutting a green line through the white-tipped forest, zeroing in on the mountain—

'COME ON, THEN!' Minna roared, drawing her poker.

'Wait!' Leo cried as Minna's pale feet disappeared up and on to the rooftop above her. 'What are you DOING?'

'This is it, Leo!' Minna's voice called back. 'THIS is why we've been practising! GHOSTLY BATTLE! We're ready! There *won't* be another Orphanmaster getting the best of us!'

'What? Minna, hang on!'

Before Leo could think, one of her feet was up on the window ledge. There was a loud RIP as another seam in the green dress broke, and then her other foot was up there, too, her wooden leg creaking.

She dug in desperately with her claws, tearing off swathes of fabric. Freed up to the knees, the green velvet fluttered away and Leo clambered up to join Minna on the tower rooftop. She must have looked like some sort of deranged caterpillar, half crawling across the uneven tiles. At the tower's peak, a bent weathervane gave a rusty squeal as it spun one way, then the other, rotating wildly.

'Minna!' she shouted. The wind was deafening – Minna's name had barely left her lips before it was snatched away. 'We need to get inside! We can't fight like this!'

The ghostly mist advanced towards them, multiple arms reaching from its shapeless form to propel itself up the cliff. Leo thought she saw Dad's magical wards flash purplish-blue for a split second, but the ghost sailed straight through them with barely a pause.

'Minna, we have to GO! NOW!' Leo staggered back from the edge of the roof as the ghost rushed up the tower.

'LOOK OUT!' Minna yelled into Leo's ear, barging in front of her. Her elbow sank icy-cold through Leo's chest. Minna brandished the poker as the misty form emerged over the edge, washing out the black sky.

It spun down, reshaping itself. A pair of boots stomped from the fog. A curved sword hung from a belt with a large ornate buckle. The very tip of a bushy beard led to . . . even more beard still, plaited here and there and topped with an impressive moustache. Bulging eyes flashed beneath bristling brows. Finally a three-cornered hat appeared, perched on a shaven head.

'AAARRRGH!'

Minna charged the ghost man but was swept harmlessly aside in an instant. There was a familiar glassy screech: the sound of two ghosts clashing. Minna yelped in surprise as the poker fell from her grasp and bounced on the tiles.

'WAHAHAHA!' the man bellowed, his mouth opening in a wide grin that revealed several missing teeth. He pressed forward, cheerfully undeterred as Leo leaned away from him. 'SO *THIS* IS LEO THE VAMPIRE!' he shouted. 'I EXPECTED YOU TO BE . . . BIGGER!'

Bigger? Leo was offended. She tried to draw herself up, larger and more fearsome, readying her claws for attack. She showed her fangs, far longer and sharper than the ghost man's.

'I am! I am Leo the Vampire! W-what of it?' She pushed the flapping green fabric from her face. It was somewhat ruining her terrifying performance, but she wouldn't let it stop her.

'WONDERFUL!' He reached a broad hand to his belt. Leo tensed. She saw Minna out of the corner of her eye, staring at her in horror. 'I HAVE *SOMETHING FOR YOU*, VAMPIRE!'

Eyeing the curved sword, its sharp edge glinting menacingly, Leo backed up a step. A loose tile threatened to trip her. She hissed.

'LEO!' Minna scrambled for the fallen poker.

'HERE IT IS!' The ghost man threw his head back and laughed, right from the bottom of his belly. His hand whipped out, clutching . . .

It's . . . a letter?

Between his thick fingers was an envelope with a wax seal, cast in the same spectral glow as the ghost himself. It fluttered gently in the breeze as the wind finally calmed.

Beaming, the ghost man leaned into Leo's stunned face.

'SPECIAL DELIVERY!'

FOUR

THE SUMMONS

'I . . . don't understand . . . a letter?'

Maybe it was a trap. Perhaps the letter would explode, blowing the top off the tower and taking Leo and Minna with it.

'You're trying to kill me!' Leo blurted, blinking incredulously up at the peculiar ghost man. 'Aren't you? That's why you're here?'

The ghost man blinked at Leo in return. Then he let loose another uproarious laugh, this time so hard he bent double, tears springing to his eyes.

'You chased us!' Leo cried, bristling. She didn't think any of this was particularly funny, not one bit. 'You ran at us! You nearly blew over half the Dreadwald! And now you're . . . you're delivering a letter?' She took two handfuls of her own hair, staring at the envelope in disbelief. 'What *ghost* is writing to me?'

'YOU WON'T KNOW UNTIL— Oh, I'm sorry!' The ghost man wiped at his face, still grinning as he lowered his voice to a slightly quieter boom. 'Typically you need to OPEN the letter first! You won't know where it has come from until you open it, Leo the Vampire! You don't need a postman to tell you that, surely?'

Leo looked up at the ghost. He didn't seem hostile – in fact, he had a suspicious air of friendliness. It was certainly an improvement on the Orphanmaster, who had definitely tried to kill her the first time they had met. And the second time. And each time after that, now that she thought about it.

The newcomer was enormous and muscular and had eyes that darted around as though following invisible insects. He was probably some sort of pirate, Leo decided, judging by his clothes, which looked like they had been made from leather and animal pelts before they were turned to ghostly mist.

'Who sent you?' she demanded. Minna drifted to her side, glaring at the ghost man over the point of the poker.

'Erm. Well!' The question appeared to catch him off guard. 'Who do you think?'

'H-how should I know?'

'The POST OFFICE!' the ghost exclaimed, as though it was obvious. He lifted his beard and pointed proudly to a badge pinned to his vest, bearing the words

DREADWALD POSTAL SERVICE. 'Who *else* is in charge of letters? Now are you going to take yours or not?'

There was only one thing to do. Leo steeled herself, reaching for the envelope – but her grasping fingers went straight through it.

'Whoops! Ah yes, I didn't consider that.' The postman looked at Leo with something that might have been pity. 'Well, it would be against the rules for me to open this, as an employee . . .'

'Give me that,' Minna sighed, now thoroughly fed up and reaching for the letter. 'I'll open it for her. That's not against the rules.'

Inside the ghostly envelope was a piece of equally ghostly parchment, upon which a message was inscribed in flourishing ink:

On behalf of the Right Honourable
JUDGE HARKER,
Official Summons for
LEO THE VAMPIRE
of CASTLE MOTTEBERG.

The above is called to court to
stand trial for the following charge(s):

MURDER of
THE GHOSTLY CITIZEN
FORMERLY KNOWN AS THE ORPHANMASTER.

**The court will assemble in three nights' time.
Failure to attend will result in Consequences.**

'Called to court?' Leo squeaked, after a long moment of trying to find her voice. 'What does that even mean?'

'WAHAHA!' The postman put his hands on his hips. 'I'm impressed! I myself have slain a great many enemies in my time. Good for you! You might look puny, but I suppose appearances can be deceiving!' He solidified his ghostly hand to clap Leo heartily on the back, nearly sending her flying off the rooftop.

This was all wrong.

'I . . . I d-didn't murder anybody!' Leo stammered out, then caught Minna's flat stare. 'What? Well, okay, I know you think I murdered *you*, Minna – b-b-but I didn't murder the Orphanmaster!'

Except she sort of *had*. In the fire inadvertently started by Leo, the Orphanmaster had burned to death inside a fallen wardrobe. Minna and the Orphanmaster had both died in that blaze.

'That's not what the letter says,' Minna said, pointing. 'Look here. The ghostly citizen *formerly known* as the Orphanmaster. The summons is for the murder of the Orphanmaster's GHOST, Leo.'

Leo felt her face turn a paler grey. 'Is it even possible? I mean, I know we defeated him. K-killed him. But can you murder a ghost?'

Minna looked offended. The postman barked a laugh, amused by the unfolding scene.

'I should think you *could* murder a ghost!' Minna said curtly, shaking the letter. 'Given that we are actual people, too!'

'Oh, Minna, that's not what I meant.'

'Then what did you mean?'

'I, um . . . I mean he's . . . the Orphanmaster was ALREADY DEAD when we fought him, so . . .' Leo swallowed.

'If I pushed you off the tower now,' Minna said with a distinctly threatening aura, 'then that would definitely be murder. And you died a hundred years ago!'

'Are you two always like this?' the postman interjected, wiggling a finger in his own ear. He plucked out a nugget of ghostly earwax.

'No,' denied Minna crossly.

'Yes,' admitted Leo.

'Either way,' the postman said, gesturing to the letter with his waxy finger, 'a word of advice: you'd better be there, vampire. I wouldn't fall afoul of Judge Harker – now SHE'S a force to be reckoned with. The court meets tomorrow night in the Ghostly Realm. I'm sure it'll be quite the show! WAHAHA!'

Leo and Minna stared at each other.

'*Tomorrow night?*' Leo gasped. 'B-but the letter says three nights from now!'

'Yeah, about that . . .' The postman flicked the earwax away and began to count off the nights on his giant fingers. 'Well, there was a delay at the office, then I was on my break, and then YOU ran away from me in the forest, so . . .' He shrugged. 'If you want to lodge a complaint, you are welcome to do so.'

'Maybe I do!'

'Whoa now,' said the postman, alarmed. 'I mean. Come on. You don't really want to do that.' He looked suddenly serious. 'No, uh. Really. I need this job.'

Leo's green-clad bottom hit the roof tiles with a thud. She looked up at the moon – it was so far away, but not far enough for her to run to and escape. No matter where she went, the ghosts would find her. Even worse, MUM would find her.

Summoned to stand trial for the death of the Orphanmaster's ghost . . . on the same night as the Blood Moon Banquet. She couldn't believe it.

Hiding her face in her hands, Leo groaned.

'Okay, okay,' Minna said, touching Leo's shoulder.

'Nobody panic. This is all a misunderstanding.'

The postman bent down to peer at Leo. 'You mean, you *didn't* kill this Organmeister?'

'Orphanmaster,' corrected Minna. 'And, no, she definitely killed him. But there is a good reason why. I'm sure Judge Harker will understand when we explain—'

'When we *explain*?' Leo peeked out through her claws. 'Minna, I can't actually go to the Ghostly Realm! What about the banquet? It's tomorrow night! I've just had my Waxing Moon – everyone will expect me to be there, Marged and Dad and MUM and all the guests. If I go missing, Mum will . . . she'll . . .'

It would open up a whole new world of problems for Leo and Minna. A cascade of disastrous secrets would surely be revealed, starting with Leo's friendship with a ghost and ending with the failed Waxing Moon: the same Waxing Moon that Lady Sieglinde would be bragging about at the banquet . . .

'Young vampire,' the postman said, 'refusing Judge Harker's summons will mean TROUBLE. I don't know what kind of fancy-pants vampire party you're planning, but if you don't appear at the trial . . . it will be bad. VERY BAD. For you,' he added not unkindly. 'Just so you know.'

Worse than the wrath of Lady Sieglinde? Leo doubted it.

'What exactly do you mean by "VERY BAD"?' Minna asked.

'Well, I don't really understand the whole legal side of it – but I DO know that if you fail to show up, Judge Harker will bring the trial to your castle.' The postman straightened up again, smoothing his wild beard. 'Not everyone in town is so friendly with their fanged neighbours – in fact, I'm sure most of them would love a fight! I mean, even *I* would love a fight. Nothing against vampires! I just really like a good brawl.' He grinned. 'But if you don't want a bunch of ghosts crashing your party, vampire, I'd listen to your little friend here.'

Minna puffed up indignantly. 'Hey!'

'Of course,' the postman continued, 'there is the problem of how to *get* to the Ghostly Realm in the first place. Not so easy for a vampire.'

Leo barely heard him. Her head was awash with images of Castle Motteberg, decked out for the Blood Moon Banquet and besieged by furious ghosts who all knew exactly what she'd done.

There was no avoiding it, she realised, her stomach dropping. She couldn't allow the vampires and the ghosts to meet. Ruining the banquet – *Sieglinde's* Blood Moon Banquet – was not an option, whatever it might take to prevent it.

Leo would have to stand trial.

'Did you hear me?' the postman was asking. 'I said—'

'I'm sorry. I heard you.' Leo stood, the horrid green velvet creaking around her. 'Thank you for delivering the letter. Sorry as well about the, you know. The running-away thing. You are quite scary.'

Minna's mouth pressed into a thin worried line. 'Leo . . .'

Walking to the edge of the rooftop, Leo looked back at the two ghosts.

'I have some thinking to do.'

'If I sneak away to stand trial, Mum will DEFINITELY notice. She'll be after me for sure. She'll find out all about the ghosts – if she doesn't turn me to dust first,' Leo muttered aloud. 'But if I don't go, then this *Judge Harker* will storm the castle. Mum won't even need to look for the ghosts, because they'll be right there under her nose. At her party. With the rest of the vampire world there to see it all.'

Perched on the tip of Leo's knee, a firefly whirred sympathetically.

'I knew you'd understand,' Leo sighed. 'But what do I do?'

The firefly buzzed away, floating to join its friends on

the ceiling of the hollow. Their gentle glow illuminated the space, making the shadows bob comfortingly.

Here, hidden within the enormous trunk of the biggest and most magnificent tree in the Dreadwald, was Leo's favourite secret base.

Hollowhome.

Despite the howling winter, it was warm and dry inside. A hammock was strung up in one corner, and a hand-carved table sat in the centre of the space, surrounded by various nooks and crannies for storing treasures. Thick branches wound up into the sky, making a perfect lookout post that was accessible through a lockable trapdoor.

Letting her head tip back against the cool bark, Leo tried to clear her mind. Only a few months ago, she had been certain that her predicament with the Orphanmaster would end in deadly disaster. But she was still here. There must be a way through this, too.

She had left what remained of the hideous green dress on her bed, alongside a note of apology to Marged. She had also left Minna on the rooftop of the western tower, talking to the ghostly postman.

Ghost Post, Leo thought to herself with a snort. The Dreadwald Postal Service had missed a great rhyme with that one.

With a decisive swish of her cape, she rolled out of the

hammock. If she was going to face Judge Harker tomorrow, that would mean entering the Ghostly Realm first. Now was as good a time as any for a quick practice run.

In the wall of the tree trunk, beside the footholds leading up to the trapdoor, there was a long sliver of white ice. It was ghostly cold and glasslike, reflecting the Hollowhome interior back at Leo when she leaned in to look. Of course, without a reflection of her own, Leo herself was missing from the picture.

From the little she understood, *mirrors* were the key to how a ghost moved between the Ghostly Realm and the Realm of the Living and the Undead. Minna herself often travelled back and forth through these mirrors – or any reflective surface, given it was shiny enough. It was how she appeared in the dagger from time to time, giving Leo a rare glimpse into the world of the ghosts. Sometimes Minna arrived through the mirror over Leo's bathroom sink. Or through a polished candlestick. Or through a shiny spoon.

Not long after the defeat of the Orphanmaster, this icy portal had appeared in Hollowhome, despite the fact that the tree trunk was both watertight and impervious to deadly sunlight. It was another of the great tree's secrets, like how the fireflies lived here all year round, instead of going into hibernation like their Dreadwald cousins.

After Leo had asked Minna to share this special place with her, Hollowhome had accepted Minna, too – and made her a *gateway*.

Pressing a hand to the smooth, cold surface, Leo let herself calm. She stared straight ahead, focusing her mind.

She imagined her body melting through the polished surface, like stepping into a magical doorway . . .

There was a CLONK as Leo's forehead knocked against solid ice.

'Ow . . .' She rubbed at the sore spot, frowning. She touched her fingertips to the portal again. Her claws clicked.

'To the Ghostly Realm!' she shouted to no avail.

'Spirit portal, open!

'Ghost mode! Activate!'

Nothing. Maybe there was a secret knock? Leo tried tapping her knuckles on the mirrored ice, but still the portal didn't budge.

'You need to spin round three times first,' someone said drily, and Leo turned to see Minna poking her head through the wall of the trunk.

'Minna!' Leo flushed, leaping back. 'How long have you been there?'

'Long enough.' Emerging fully, Minna planted her hands on her hips. 'What were you planning to do? Sneak off without me?'

'No, I-I-I just . . . I wanted to take a look.' Leo swallowed guiltily. 'I wanted to see the Ghostly Realm for myself. If I'm being summoned there, I should at least know what I'm getting myself into.'

'Okay. But you won't get anywhere like that.'

'Well, how should I know?' Leo threw up her hands. She knew her cheeks must have been the same dark grey as her boots by now. 'You haven't told me *anything* about the Ghostly Realm!'

'Leo,' said Minna, with the air of someone being very, very patient, 'it's not what you were doing that was the problem, it's who you *are*.'

'Who I am?'

Minna shook her head solemnly. 'It's impossible for a vampire's body to enter the Ghostly Realm.'

This was it. This was how Leo's predicament would end: Castle Motteberg besieged by spirits, in the middle of the bustling Blood Moon Banquet.

'Impossible for a vampire?' she whispered. 'The postman . . . the postman said . . .'

She could vaguely hear Minna talking, saying something about *bodies* and *souls* and *the barrier between worlds*, but Leo's mind had gone somewhere far away, too far to properly—

'Listen!' Minna exclaimed. Leo jolted as a freezing

hand swiped at her shoulder. 'Hey. Look at me. I know what to do.'

'We're done, Minna,' Leo said hopelessly. 'If I can't go to the Ghostly Realm, I can't attend the trial. Judge Harker will come after me and it'll all be over – we'll both be done for!'

'No. We'll get you there.' Minna turned to the wall she had floated from. 'There's someone who can help.'

Around them, Hollowhome was silent for a long moment. A firefly buzzed.

Minna cleared her throat. 'I *said*, there's someone who can help!'

'Sorry, was that my cue?' a familiar voice said. The point of a hat emerged, perched on a shaven head. A ghostly beard bulged from the bark. 'It's hard to hear from outside!'

'Minna!' Leo gasped. 'You brought the *postman*? Here! To HH! Y-y-you can't go giving away our base to STRANGERS! Especially strange . . .'

Ghosts, she wanted to say, but stopped herself.

'ADULTS,' she finished. 'Hollowhome is kids-only! You know that!'

For a hundred years there hadn't been another soul here – only Leo and the fireflies. With *two* ghosts now the hollow tree was starting to feel cramped. The postman had to hunch down to fit inside the tight space, his big shoulders braced against the ceiling.

'*Given the circumstances*, I thought it best to bring him along,' Minna insisted. 'He has a plan, Leo. He can help us!' She turned to the postman. 'Tell her what you told me.'

The postman grinned. 'Right! Yes! No one with a body can cross over to the Ghostly Realm. It's impossible! No bodies allowed, you understand? Even dead ones, WAHAHA!' He swatted at the fireflies that flitted around to inspect his head. 'If you want to go to the Ghostly Realm, you have to leave your body behind, vampire!"

Minna turned to Leo. Her eyes were bright white pools. 'He knows a way to temporarily separate your body from your soul. He can get you to the Ghostly Realm safely! We can attend the trial, explain to Judge Harker that this is all a mistake, and then get you back in your body and to the banquet before anyone misses you. I wanted to go on my own, but . . . well . . .'

'The judge isn't seeing anyone,' the postman said with a shrug. 'Preparation for the trial.'

Leo lifted her gaze to Minna. 'And . . . you trust this man to help us?' she asked.

The girls looked round to where the postman was now distracted by the fireflies. He sucked one up through a giant nostril and then let it fly out of his mouth. It flapped away, disoriented but unhurt.

'Hm,' said Minna.

'We don't know him,' Leo pointed out. 'We don't even know his name, and you want him t-to remove my SOUL?'

'My name?' The postman's eyes lit up. 'Yes! My name! WAHAHA!' He pointed dramatically at Leo and Minna. 'You find yourself in the presence of PIRATE LORD ULFRIC ULFRICSSON THE SEVENTH!'

'Um . . .'

'RULER OF THE SCAPULA ISLES!' Pirate Lord Ulfric Ulfricsson the Seventh boomed. 'SCOURGE OF THE SEAS! CAPTAIN OF THE DREAD SHIP *MAGPIE*! SWINDLER AND SWASHBUCKLER! KING AMONGST ROGUES AND THIEVES!' Blinking, unclenching his fists, the postman seemed to remember where he was again. Hollowhome had taken on a peculiar salty scent, like seawater. 'You can call me Ulf if you like,' he added with a grin, 'considering that we're going to be crewmates on this voyage!'

'Wait a minute!' blurted Leo, pulling her cape tightly round herself. 'We didn't agree to anything yet! We haven't discussed any sort of plan! How do we know we can trust you?'

'Oh yeah, of course. About that . . .' Pirate-Lord-Postman Ulf folded his arms over his broad chest, suddenly serious. 'If you want me to risk my neck helping you, young vampire, then you have to do something for ME first. It's only fair – *never give yourself away for free*, there's a lesson for you. Wait, that was free advice. Forget I said that!'

Minna's mouth dropped open. 'You didn't say anything about this up on the rooftop! You promised you would help us!'

Ulf shrugged. 'It's a risky journey. And not only for the one being . . .' He made a slicing motion with one shovel-sized hand, as though miming a person being chopped in half. '*De-souled*. Judge Harker wants you there – but she won't like her people making it easy for you. I see you are fellow warriors who have heard the ROAR OF THE BATTLEFIELD! I respect that! But there is a price for my help.'

Wrapped inside her cape like a nervous sausage, Leo gulped. 'Um. What exactly do you want?'

Ulf grinned. 'A GREAT TREASURE of mine, vampire! A powerful and terrible treasure, sealed in a chest with a carving of a mighty kraken on its lid. It was stolen from me long ago by a marauding queen!'

He peered down at Leo, his eyes narrowing above his bristly beard.

'She really *did* look a lot like you . . .'

FIVE

INTO THE CRYPT

Far beneath Castle Motteberg, narrow stairways and claustrophobic corridors burrowed deep down into the frozen mountain. Leo's footsteps echoed as she crept onwards, leading Minna through the maze of tunnels.

'How much further?' Minna asked, her misty body wavering in a ghostly shiver. She kept looking over her shoulder, back up the dark passageway behind them. Her hand was glued to the poker.

'Not far now. Stay close, you don't want to get lost down here!'

In Leo's hand, a single candle cast her shadow up the walls around them. Her shape – long, menacing and spider-like – could easily have been Lady Sieglinde sneaking up on them. Mum's quarters were underground, almost as deep as the crypt. She liked the drip of the stalactites and the scampering of rats; the sounds lulled her to sleep when she retired to her coffin.

'Are you sure we're not *already* lost?' Minna hissed, following Leo so closely that Leo could feel the chill on her back. 'I'm certain we've already come through here. There'll be no treasure at all if we can't find our way!'

Leo pressed her claws to the wall, feeling the indentations carved into the rock. Truthfully she had lost count of the stairs around the eleventh flight – but the thirteen notches told her that they were on the thirteenth level down.

'Don't worry,' she said. 'We're on track!' Privately she allowed herself a small smile. There was definitely a part of Leo that loved to show off, especially to Minna.

As they turned the corner, they came to an abrupt dead end in the corridor. There was an open lift, made of an ornately carved but decidedly rickety box, attached to a system of pulleys and levers. Leo gestured to their ride with a flourish.

'After you!' she said brightly.

Minna gave her a *look*. 'You can't be serious.'

There was a dangerous gap between the lift and the vertical passage below. Peering down, she saw that the drop stretched away into the endless dark beneath them. The walls, slimy with moss, were thrown into illumination as Leo leaned in with her candle.

'This is the way to the crypt,' she said with a shrug, despite the twist of her belly when she said the word out loud. 'The only way in or out.'

She could probably count on one hand the number of times she had been down in the crypt – and that included not so long ago when she had *almost died* while fighting the Orphanmaster. Marged had brought her down here to recover, teetering on the brink between unlife and total, final, inescapable death.

Every Von Motteberg ended up here sooner or later. Leo leaned on the side of the lift in a way she hoped looked casual, wanting to appear brave. Next to her elbow, the snarling face of a vampire – a carving of what was probably an old Von Motteberg relative, long forgotten – glared at her.

'And it's . . . safe?' Minna eyed the frayed rope attached to the wheel above them.

'Of course it's safe!' Leo stepped into the lift, hoping the clench of her jaw wasn't too obvious. The wooden box groaned as it took her weight and held steady. She held a hand out to Minna. 'Come on. You can always *fly* out, remember!'

'I can! YOU can't!' Minna griped, but she floated in to hover next to Leo. 'Honestly, sometimes I think I'm the only one with any thought for self-preservation!'

'Says the girl who was determined to fight ANOTHER ghost earlier!'

'That's *different*.'

'Mmhmm.' Leo hid her smile in the collar of her cape. 'Going down!'

There was a rusty KER-CHUNK as she pulled the lever next to her head.

The lift rattled deep into the darkness, moved by grumbling gears down the bleak passage. Stony walls scraped past, slimy with mushrooms and moss. Every now and again, some small creature went scuttling for cover – perhaps a rat or a roach – spooked by the light of Leo's candle.

'So,' Minna said. Her voice cracked and she cleared her throat. 'Where do we start? Do you even know where this kraken treasure is?"

'Ulf's right – it's probably in the crypt.' Leo balled her free hand in her cape, picturing the small wooden chest Ulf had described, emblazoned with a mighty sea creature on its lid. 'I've never seen anything like it upstairs. We – m-my family, I mean – we keep a lot of our fortune down here. It's safe and, well, there's too much of it to display . . .'

Minna was staring at her. Leo averted her gaze, embarrassed, watching the moving gears. She knew Minna already thought she was rich and spoiled; she didn't want to make it any worse.

'Anyway, w-we could be looking for a while!' she continued. 'But if Ulf's treasure is as valuable as he says it is, it should be down here. This is where all the really good stuff goes.'

The lift finally thudded to a halt. Ropes slackened and the squeak of the gears echoed away into the empty shaft above them. This far into the mountain, all was deathly quiet. Stepping out into a crossroads of corridors, a tremor started up in Leo's knee. It travelled up her body and down her arm, jostling her candle until the flame began to sputter.

Now that she was actually here, there was a part of her that wasn't *quite* so brave. The thought of a crypt full of vampires – DEAD vampires, truly dead for all eternity – made her fangs feel funny. Some had turned to dust, some had turned to stone, some had left behind only their bones. The air was heavy with ancient magic and an undertone of something rotten . . .

'You okay?' Minna asked, making Leo jump.

'Y-y-yes!' Clutching her candle, Leo gestured with her free arm to the seven tunnels that spread out in every direction. 'Go ahead and decide which way. I promise they're all equally creepy.'

Minna considered this for a moment, revolving in place. Then she stretched out a hand and pointed the poker down a tunnel to their right.

'This is the one. This is where Ulf's chest is.'

'How do you know?'

'I'm feeling lucky, I suppose.'

Leo's belly did a queasy backflip. *Don't use up all your luck on this, Minna!* she thought, tentatively leading the way. They would need all their good fortune for the Ghostly Realm, Leo was sure. She couldn't imagine exactly how they were going to convince Judge Harker of her innocence. Nothing to do with ghosts was ever simple.

One thing at a time, Leo, she told herself firmly as they stepped into one of the chambers of the Castle Motteberg crypt.

'Oh,' said Minna, peering out from behind her. 'This isn't so bad. I was expecting more . . . coffins.'

Carved from mountain rock, the room was long and narrow. Its uneven flooring merged at the edges into equally uneven walls. The curved ceiling was so low Leo had to duck her head. There were indents underfoot and up the walls and ceiling: thin gaps between each stony slab.

At the end of the room a glittering mound of gold drew the eye. There were coins, gems, jewellery, an urn or two, a painting of a unicorn in a gilded frame – it all glimmered invitingly in the candlelight, DARING any greedy adventurer to draw closer.

Leo and Minna drew closer.

'Are you sure this is safe?' Minna asked warily. 'No vampire tricks? No *traps*?'

'No tricks and no traps,' Leo said, to reassure both Minna and her own fluttering heart. Approaching the precious hoard, piled so high it might spill at any moment into the world's most expensive avalanche, she bent down and plucked single golden coin. 'See? Von Mottebergs are welcome here.'

I'm a Von Motteberg. This is my castle. We're going to be okay.

'Hm.' Minna watched Leo's claws dance, rolling the coin deftly between them. 'Well, *I'm* not a Von Motteberg, am I?'

'Well . . . *no*, but . . . you're with me! Come on, we should look for the kraken chest.' Leo flicked the coin back on to the golden mountain and set her candle on the floor.

They searched through the pile of jewels and gold. Leo waded in and scooped handfuls of treasure while Minna floated warily round the edge, reluctant to touch anything. Every now and again, Leo popped up out of the heap, wearing a ruby earring or a bejewelled headpiece or, finally, a gold fang, shoved beneath her upper lip.

'Minna. Minna! Look!'

It was nice, Leo thought, to do something together that *wasn't* fighting for their unlives. She didn't care much about finery or jewels or riches, but swimming in the treasure like a golden pool, clowning around, Leo could almost forget why they were here.

'Yes, very good.' Minna sighed, determined not to laugh. Her mouth was curling in the corners before she fixed her serious face back on. 'But perhaps the chest isn't here at all. It could be in one of the other chambers.'

'You're right,' said Leo, shaking her head free. With a cough she blew a small diamond-encrusted brooch out of her mouth. It landed on the side of the pile with a metallic *clink*. 'Let's move to the next one.'

As she waded out, Leo's foot knocked against

something buried beneath her. It made a hollow wooden sound. Her eyes widened.

It couldn't be?

As fast as a fox down a burrow, she disappeared beneath the surface again.

Minna groaned. 'Please don't . . .' she began, at the same time as Leo emerged with a victorious 'TA-DAAA!' In her claws was indeed a small wooden chest – roughly the size of three Rodrigos, as was the standard measurement. It was padlocked shut and emblazoned with the image of a tentacled sea monster.

It was unmistakably the kraken chest.

'Wow,' said Minna, staring down at it. 'Maybe *you're* the lucky one?'

'Okay, so . . . Mission complete!' Leo exclaimed. 'Let's get this thing back to Ulf and figure out what—'

Something snagged round her ankle, pulling her foot down as she tried to take a step forward. Buried at the bottom of the treasure hoard was a necklace of pearls, which had probably belonged at one point to a mer princess, or perhaps even another vampire noble.

It was dainty. It was innocent and unassuming.

Toppling forward, Leo threw out her arms to steady herself. The kraken chest flew free of her loosened grip, airborne for a split second . . .

Before either of them could react, it sailed through Minna's body and crashed to the floor. The sound ricocheted through the chamber as it bounced once, twice and spun on its rounded lid before settling.

All around them, the room began to rumble.

'Leo?' Minna whirled round, pinning Leo with a look that was half terror and half rage. 'LEO?'

'I'm sorry! My . . . my foot . . .'

The floor started to quake. So did the walls, and the ceiling; the stone slabs shifted, lifting and sliding against and over each other. Dust rose and a horrible cacophony of scraping assaulted Leo's ears. She clamped both hands over them, looking helplessly at the roiling room between them and the door . . .

Minna was suddenly at her side, hefting the kraken chest beneath her solid ghostly arm. Miraculously it hadn't smashed to pieces – though whatever was inside had definitely been rattled about. Leo looked down at her hand, where Minna's cool grip was encircling her wrist.

'What is this?' Minna demanded. 'What's happening?'

From beneath the nearest stone slab, inches from Leo's feet, a skeletal hand emerged.

SIX

OLD BONES

All around Leo and Minna, the crypt burst into a flurry of clacking bones and gnashing teeth. From floor to ceiling the room was crawling with skeletons big and small, emerging stiffly from their sunken coffins.

'The chest! I TOLD you I shouldn't touch anything!' Minna cried. She pushed the kraken chest into Leo's arms, but it was too late – the skeletons kept coming, their empty eye sockets flashing red.

There must have been a time, once, when the crypt was much less crowded. But over the ages, as generations of Von Mottebergs came and went, more and more space was needed to house the dead. The end result was whole chambers packed full of skeletons: the bones of Von Motteberg ancestors, squeezed in so tightly, they were on top of each other.

The room Leo and Minna were standing in was entirely made of coffins. They had walked on their stony lids.

'I'm sorry!' Leo cried. 'I got caught on something!'

She waggled her foot. Hanging from her ankle was the necklace, its pearls gleaming yellow in the candlelight.

Minna's nostrils flared. '*Really?* Oh, well, this is JUST SO—'

They broke apart, dodging out of the way as the nearest skeleton lunged for them, hissing. Its movements were jerky, clumsy, like a puppet forced to dance. Its sharp teeth snapped, going for Leo's face.

'Grandma?' Leo sputtered.

'HWIIIIGH!' the skeleton shrieked.

Leo reeled back, using the kraken chest to bump her attacker away.

'Maybe not!' Leo backed up a step, looking desperately around them. Spotting her candle on the floor, she gestured to Minna. 'Grab that! We have to run!'

The bones were closing in. A reanimated army shuffled mindlessly towards the intruders, moved by ancient magic. Leo deflected another swipe and kicked away a reaching hand that tried to grab her leg. The necklace flew off and the precious pearls scattered. Above them, a smaller skeleton rotated its skull until it was sitting backwards on its neck, red sockets zeroing in on them.

Minna scooped up the candle. She held it out from her misty body. The nearest skeletons shied back, ducking away from its flame.

'Look!' she shouted, spinning in a circle, grinning as the bones scrambled away. 'The fire! They don't like the fire!'

'That's— Ugh!' Leo was busy wrestling another gaunt foe. Its spine rattled as she flipped it over her back.

She winced as its head came loose and rolled away. She knew they were only bones charmed to attack. But, all the same, Leo felt wrong inside as she swung the chest into what might have once been her aunt or uncle.

'Oh, come here!' Minna exclaimed, and Leo felt a frosty hand on her shoulder. 'Stick close to me!'

They spun, staring down the long chamber. The skeletons formed a huge mass of arms and legs and ribs and hissing skulls, writhing over each other like a bony tide. Some of them were slower moving, with a stony cast to their bones, chunks of crumbly stone flesh remaining here and there. Above them, a gritty cloud swelled and shrank angrily: the remains of more ancestors still, turned to dust. It was *every* Von Motteberg's fate to end up in the crypt.

'Uhhh—' Leo began, having second thoughts now about running head first into them, but then Minna was brandishing the candle and shouting in her ear—

'CHAAAAARGE!'

They plunged into the fray.

The crowd parted, fleeing from the light and crawling up the walls. The cloud of vampire dust dispersed. Running side by side, Leo and Minna cut a path through the swarming skeletons, making a dash for the door and for safety. Behind the frantic pounding of her heart, Leo was sure she heard a CRUNCH as she stepped on something brittle . . .

I'm sorry, I'm so sorry!

But there was no time to stop. The candle kept the bones at bay. Leo held the kraken chest like a shield. She wrapped her cape in tightly, feeling grasping hands reach greedily for her as they passed. The door was in sight, peeking above the thrashing limbs.

'Nearly there!' Leo gasped. Some of the skeletons were getting brave, crowding in on them. Noticing their brothers and sisters pushing closer, more piled in, until Minna had to hold the candle up over her head and it was a fight for Leo to move . . .

Then, with a puff of apologetic smoke, the candlelight was snuffed out.

The skeletons froze.

Leo froze.

At her side Minna's spectral body cast a blue glow over the wave of bones that rose up around them . . .

Screams of rage resounded. The skeletons swarmed,

crashing and crunching together in their haste to rip the intruders limb from limb. Their efforts to grab Minna's phantom form failed, but Leo was caught in the chaos, buffeted back and forth, still clutching the kraken chest tightly to her belly.

There was a hand on hers, trying to prise her claws away from their prize. She managed to shake it off and clambered up above the landslide of moving bones. Every step was a struggle, her feet slipping on the churning pile of bodies beneath her.

'Minna!' she cried, holding the chest up high. 'Take it!'

Floating above her, Minna's eyes widened.

'What?'

'The chest! Take the chest!'

'I can't LEAVE YOU HERE, you idiot!' Minna scolded her. Over Leo's shoulder, she skewered a snarling skull cleanly with her poker, right through the eye socket. 'Ugh! Skeletons! Remind me NEVER to visit the graveyard again!'

Leo was sinking. Bony hands climbed up her legs, clinging fast to her. 'I'll be fine!' she said desperately. 'This is the important thing – get it back to the lift!'

With an explosive sigh Minna sheathed the poker. Scowling furiously down at her own hands, her skin began to glow brighter.

Leo squeezed her eyes shut, now up to her shoulders

in skeletons. Her black blood was pounding, rushing in her ears. She held the chest desperately upwards, silently urging Minna to take it and . . .

Leo felt a cold grip on her wrists, wrenching her upwards.

The swarm seethed. As Leo's eyes popped open in shock, she could see Minna flying above her with gritted teeth.

'*Hnnngh!*'

Leo was heaved up, up away from the clutching hands and ferocious teeth, her feet pinwheeling as they lost their purchase and found only air. The ceiling loomed perilously close, but it was no problem for Minna – she sailed half through it, making a clumsy beeline for the chamber door, weighed down by the vampire dangling from her.

Still hanging tightly to the kraken chest, Leo kicked away the skeletons that tried to snag her legs.

'Minna!' she cried. 'Wh . . . you . . . you're *lifting* me!'

'You think I DON'T KNOW THAT?' Minna snapped furiously, giving it everything she had. Her face was as screwed up as Leo had ever seen it, so powerful was her focus. Her solid hands were beaming with white light. 'I'm DOING THE LIFTING!'

'Yes! You're amazing!'

'BE QUIET! Do you WANT me to drop you?'

Leo's fangs clicked shut and she stifled her grin. Her

heart was thumping hard enough to disturb the rest of her insides, but exhilaration shot through her as they swept across the room. The wave of bones – Leo's ancestors – rolled menacingly beneath them, swiping at Leo's feet.

Touching down, Leo and Minna fell through the doorway in a tangle of limbs and Leo lurched to her feet. She was running before she could properly stand, clutching the stolen chest.

'This way!' she cried, making a dash for the lift. At her heels, barely a heartbeat behind, the skeletons crashed into the crypt crossroads. The clacking of their bones followed Leo and Minna as they fled.

Skidding into the safety of the lift, Minna at her back, Leo yanked hard on the lever.

With a squeal of gears and a swoosh of rope the box began to rise. Hands scrabbled for them, some now with fingers missing, reaching blindly in the narrowing gap as the lift pulled away. Long fangs sank into the carved wood as a skeleton leapt up, chewing on the floor of the ascending box.

Minna's poker slashed, lightning fast, and the skull fell away. Left behind were its vampiric teeth, embedded deep.

The gap narrowed to a sliver and closed. The shriek of skeletons reverberated up the vertical passage. Leaving the crypt far below, Leo and Minna made their escape.

SEVEN

VON MOTTEBERG REPUTATION

Dark walls rolled past the lift. They were lit only by Minna's faint glow as the unlikely thieves made their way back towards the surface. Leo crumpled against the side of the box and her head knocked on the wooden panelling. The vibration from the moving rope made her fangs rattle, but she suddenly felt too exhausted to move.

She would never think of the crypt in the same way ever again. She had known it was scary down there, but this was something else.

'Pox and pustules . . .' she mumbled. She had disturbed the remains of the entire Von Motteberg lineage. What happened now? Would their bones be roaming around down there until Marged or Dad or MUM accidentally stumbled across them?

It was yet another thing to add to her list of woes. She looked down at the kraken chest in her hands. The tentacled carving stared blankly back at her.

This is good, Leo told herself firmly. *You got what you needed. You have Ulf's treasure! You can visit the Ghostly Realm!*

And, speaking of ghosts, Minna . . .

Leo hadn't known that Minna could pull off that sort of feat. Not too long ago, as a freshly made ghost, Minna hadn't been able to touch or move anything – much less lift a WHOLE VAMPIRE up off the floor while being dragged down by angry skeletons. All her ghostly training was paying off and thank goodness for that.

'What? What is it?' Minna said, and Leo realised she'd been staring.

'Nothing! Just . . .' Leo pointed sheepishly downwards, indicating the long drop below the lift and the frenzy of the crypt beyond. 'You saved me back there.'

Minna's eyebrows lifted. Then, as if realising exactly what Leo had said, she puffed out a breath and shook her head. 'I wouldn't go so far as to say SAVED, Leo.'

'I would. It was SO COOL! *You* were so cool! I was like *nooo, Minna, take the chest!* and you were like *swooshhh!*'

'I think it was a bit less graceful than that."

'I'm just saying – all your training, clearly it's working.'

For a long moment the only sound was the churning

gears above their heads. Leo's grin faltered. 'Minna? What's wrong?'

'Look, it was . . .' Minna sighed. 'It was nothing. Don't be impressed by a bit of flying. Remember when Ulf cornered us on the rooftop? I couldn't stop *him*. That would have been real power, if I'd . . . if . . .'

'If you'd what? Kicked him off the tower?'

'Maybe. Or I don't know – been able to do *anything at all*.' Minna balled her hands into bitter fists at her sides. The air around them froze.

Leo straightened from her slouch. She held the kraken chest tightly as she tentatively scooted a step closer.

'Did you see me, up there on the roof of the tower?' she asked quietly. 'I was terrified. There was nothing I could do either. I really thought Ulf was there to attack us – b-but he wasn't! He's . . .' Leo frowned. 'A weird friendly pirate guy. Who really wants whatever's in here.' She gave their prize the slightest shake, wiggling it as though it might cheer Minna up.

'Right. We were fortunate.' Minna's mouth twisted unhappily. 'But what if we *weren't*? What if Ulf had been there to hurt you? He could have been another Orphanmaster and I wouldn't have been strong enough to defeat him.'

'But—'

'Not every human is *friendly*, Leo. That means not every ghost we meet is going to be friendly, either. It's like I said earlier: nothing can overwhelm us when we're ready for it. *If* we are ready.' Minna scowled at the wooden floor of the lift. 'I don't want to chance another evil ghost attack.'

With a squeak of juddering gears and the twang of rope the lift came to a stop. They were back in the belly of Castle Motteberg, far above the chaotic crypt.

'What about the ghost-killing ingredients?' Leo reminded Minna gently, stepping out. She was privately glad to feel solid stone beneath her feet again. 'We didn't have what we needed to fight. That's not your fault.'

'I appreciate that, Leo, but I'm not talking about *killing* a ghost. I'm talking about *stopping* one. Being tough enough to stand our ground.' Floating up to match Leo's height, Minna looked her in the eye for a long moment. 'Look, if we really are . . . going to the Ghostly Realm, with Ulf . . . you should prepare yourself. If you think a crypt full of vampire skeletons is scary, you may need to think again!'

The little that Leo knew about the Ghostly Realm, she had learned from snatches of the world behind Minna's head during their chats in the dagger. There were a lot of trees, she had concluded. And, at this time of year, a lot of snow.

'You can tell me about it.' Leo tried not to fidget – Minna's intense face was making her uneasy. Whatever Minna wanted to say, it had clearly been on her mind for some time. Leo tried to appear as reassuring as possible. 'Whatever you need to tell me about the Ghostly Realm, you can. You're my best friend, Minna.'

Minna puffed out her cheeks. 'Oh gosh . . .' she mumbled, almost to herself. 'How are you ever going to survive?'

'I'm s-sorry?'

'Leo, the Ghostly Realm is SERIOUS BUSINESS! There are POWERFUL GHOSTS there – yes, they're normal people, mostly, but they're also strong.' Minna's brow pinched. 'They can do things that you can't even imagine. I mean, I couldn't have imagined it, before I moved there. And I'm a ghost, too!'

Leo suppressed a nervous chuckle. 'That's okay, we'll be—'

'I'm worried,' Minna gritted out, interrupting her, 'that I won't be able to protect us if something goes wrong. Maybe . . . maybe my training hasn't been enough. I need more time – time that we don't have!'

A shiver crept up Leo's back. She glanced behind herself, a reflex she had developed since their clash with the Orphanmaster. Of course there was no one there. Only

Minna, who was giving her that WORRIED look that set Leo's teeth on edge. Minna was meant to be the fierce one, the confident one. Of the two of them Leo was the worrywart.

'Whatever happened to, *come to the Ghostly Realm, Leo!*' she asked, dropping her voice to an urgent whisper. '*We'll explain everything to Judge Harker and it will all be okay, Leo!*'

Minna bobbed backwards. 'It will be! I'm certain it will be! But . . . what happens if it's not?'

'That's not what "certain" means!'

Before Minna could reply, a long, slow CREEEAAAK came from somewhere on the level above them. The cat-like pupils of Leo's eyes opened to inky circles, even as the rest of her body was frozen solid.

There was a pause, and then the reverberating clunk of a lock made Leo startle.

'Mum!' she hissed. 'Mum's quarters are nearby! You need to hide!'

Minna swivelled, looking very deliberately at the lift and then to Leo and back again.

'Yes, yes, I know!' Leo flapped her free hand, motioning for Minna to sneak away. 'Go! If she finds you here, she'll . . .'

It wasn't something Leo wanted to even consider.

When you had Lady Sieglinde's supremely evil vampiric power, you didn't *need* ghost-killing ingredients to cause total devastation. She had probably fought and triumphed over entire battlefields of ghostly enemies in her time.

'Leo—'

'Go!' Leo blurted, hefting the kraken chest. She cast one last pleading look back at Minna before making a run for it as the passageway was plunged into darkness.

Leo's eyes adjusted to the dark, her vampiric night vision kicking in as she scurried up the stone steps. Without Minna's light everything was cast in a greyish-purple hue. Leo couldn't let Mum find her down here. No matter what, she couldn't let Mum know she'd meddled in the crypt. ESPECIALLY NOT the night before the Blood Moon Banquet, when everything – right down to the finest detail – had to be totally, completely perfect.

Leo's heart was in her throat as she turned a murky corner, spotting an orange glow emerging from a passageway up ahead.

Dancing for a moment on the spot, she looked left and right – there was no place to stash the chest, only endless stony walls. She could risk retreating into the stairwell, but then it would be even more obvious where she had come from. A long shadow was cast down the passage, thin limbs stretching like black tendrils as it drew closer . . .

In one desperate move Leo dropped the kraken chest and slammed her bottom down on to it.

'Leo?' Mum frowned down at her youngest daughter. Leo didn't have to pretend to startle; her whole body jerked in horrible surprise, though she had *known* it was Lady Sieglinde. Who else moved like that? Who else could turn a heart to ice with their mere presence?

'Mum!' Leo squeaked. 'Hello!'

'What *are* you doing, child?' Mum's candlestick, three flames glimmering on their pillars of wax, made her face look even more nightmarish than usual. Pockets of shadow collected in the hollows of her eyes and in the corners of her downturned mouth.

'I-I-I—'

Mum reared back, her nostrils flaring impatiently. 'Well?'

Inching her cape more securely round the side of the kraken chest, Leo attempted a smile. It came out as more of a pained grimace. 'Uhhh, I was . . . exploring! And then I thought I'd have a little rest here because . . . the view . . . is so nice.' Her eyes widened. 'I've been here for a while. Enjoying the atmosphere. Probably an hour or more!'

Leo and Mum both turned to the wall in front of them.

 The gloomy stone somehow managed to look duller in the light of Mum's candles. A centipede poked its head out of a crack, its antennae wiggling curiously.

'Hm.' Mum tilted her head in the smallest of nods. 'It is rather pleasing down here.' She fixed Leo with a narrow glare. 'But YOU should be upstairs making preparations. The Blood Moon Banquet is in only a night's time.'

Shrinking down, Leo bit her lip.

A low hum rolled from Mum's throat, impossible to decipher. It could have been anger, or irritation, or perhaps she was simply lost in thought about tomorrow night's event. Leo wouldn't have dared to look at her, but she couldn't avert her eyes; Mum's stare was hypnotic. A painfully long moment passed while Leo sweated quietly, hyper-aware of the chest hidden behind her cape.

Finally, after what felt like forever, Mum leaned down. Her inky eyes, so much like Leo's own, felt like they could pull Leo in and drown her.

'The banquet is an *extremely important event*, Leo.'

'I know, Mum.'

'Everyone will be there. All the Council.' With a

piercing *skkkkkrrr* sound, Lady Sieglinde traced an idle claw along the stone behind Leo's head. 'All the main players will attend – these are the vampires who pull the strings that control the whole world. They'll all be watching you when we announce your successful Hunt and the continuation of the perfect Von Motteberg record.' Lady Sieglinde's mouth curled in a satisfied sneer. 'By the end of the night anything is possible. Including the realisation that I SHOULD BE HEAD.'

'Yes, Mum.' Leo let herself be earnest, even as the mention of the Waxing Moon made her shiver all over again. 'It will be perfect! I k-know you want to impress the Council – and they will be. Impressed, I mean. You're amazing. It will be the best banquet.'

Lady Sieglinde *was* amazing. She was the ideal fit for Head of the Council: cunning and deadly. There was no vampire better suited when you took raw EVILNESS into consideration. Achieving such an extreme level of malevolence was incredibly impressive. As much as Leo feared her mother, she admired her even more.

Mum might have her eternal quest to influence the Council and seize control, but Leo was only ever interested in winning her favour. Mum's good side was surely a wonderful place to be. It was something Leo could only dream of, even after a hundred years of trying.

Leaning back, Mum smoothed her grey robe. Her claws clicked on her opal brooch, shaped like a flitting moth. 'Leo.'

Leo sat up straighter. 'Yes?'

Mum's eyes flashed, striking through Leo right to her bones. 'You will be on your BEST BEHAVIOUR. It will be another century before the Blood Moon Banquet returns to Castle Motteberg. This is a rare opportunity and one that must not be squandered . . .'

With that Mum turned away. She had grown bored and she was done here. Gliding past, Mum retreated down the passage with graceful indifference.

'We are the greatest of the noble vampire families, Leo,' she called over her shoulder. 'The others are nothing

compared to us. They should be our playthings, grovelling at the foot of Mount Moth. Tomorrow night we need to make sure we ALL uphold the Von Motteberg reputation . . .'

Her parting words floated away and she was gone. The light of her candles went with her, melting silently away into the enveloping dark.

Heart knocking against her ribs, clammy hands clenched, Leo slumped on top of the chest. Her shrivelled vampire lungs swelled and deflated again as she blew out a long breath. It would be morning soon, she knew – her instincts could sense the sun's looming arrival even from deep underground. But that was nothing compared to the pressure and peril of being a Von Motteberg.

The tip of a ghostly nose emerged from the wall, followed by worried eyes and a downturned mouth. The handle of a poker jutted out from a pale shoulder. A cloud of white hair floated up.

'Split up for now?' Minna whispered.

Leo nodded. Her head felt so heavy. She let her arms drop to her sides, claws scratching the cold floor. She would sit for a few minutes. Just until her veins had stopped pulsing, and then she would make her move.

Minna looked her over. It seemed for a moment that she might have something she wanted to say – but she thought better of it, shaking her head to chase away the thought.

'I'll see you tomorrow, Leo,' she said instead, in her firm 'it will be okay' sort of voice. 'As soon as dusk falls, we'll go to find Ulf.'

Leo nodded. Then, with a grunt, she heaved herself to her feet.

Leo felt a little better as she crept up the western tower, the kraken chest in her hands. There was something about Mum that always drained the unlife out of her – that was nothing new to Leo. She would have to get used to it, especially once Mum inevitably conquered the Council. Leo was sure she would be joining Mum there as her apprentice, to learn all a truly powerful vampire had to know.

You're a Von Motteberg! she told herself sternly, opening the door to her bedroom. *We're the strongest of the vampire families. YOU are strong! You are brave!*

'Ugh!' Leo flumped face first onto her bed. The kraken chest bounced harmlessly on her pillow, its padlock rattling.

'You're back!' someone said, and Leo looked over to see Rodrigo poking his spidery head out of her sock drawer. His brown body bristled in a shiver. 'A-any more sign of ghostly activity?'

'Only Minna,' Leo replied. She wriggled on her belly to hang over the edge of her bed, lowering the kraken chest to the floor. It would be fine stashed beneath her bed, until the evening came and they could deliver it to Ulf.

'What is that?' Rodrigo asked, his sightless eyes swivelling as the chest scraped over the floorboards.

'The bed.' Leo didn't fancy another lecture. 'Just moving it back. Marged must have bumped it when she was cleaning.'

'Ah. Yes. The knight said she was leaving you a note?'

On Leo's bedside table was a large cup of blood. A quick sniff confirmed that it was deliciously fresh, as always – Leo slurped it greedily. Tucked next to the cup was indeed a scrap of paper:

Miss Leo,

Thank you for your note. I took the liberty of speaking with Madame Kinkatch after seeing (Leo imagined Marged's pause) *what was left of her handiwork.*

Have a look in the wardrobe. I think you will be pleasantly surprised!

Love, Marged

PS Make sure you wash your face and finish your blood before bed. I'm sorry I can't be there to tuck you in as usual. There are many preparations still to be made!

Leo stared at the note, wiping her mouth on her sleeve. She winced as she remembered the state of the green dress she had left for poor Marged to find. She was going to be in for it when Madame Kinkatch finally caught up with her . . .

'Have you got it?' Rodrigo asked as Leo crossed the room. 'Did you find the note?'

'I did,' Leo confirmed, already opening the wardrobe door curiously. She suppressed a nervous burp. What could Marged possibly have left for her?

Inside . . . was a dress.

The garment was as black as midnight and long-sleeved, like the shirt Leo currently wore. Apart from a frill at the collar and cuffs, there wasn't another ruffle in sight. Drawing it out, Leo looked at the skirt – knee-length and not too puffy, allowing for movement, and . . . Leo gasped, putting her hand inside.

Pockets. Deep pockets, too.

'What are you looking at, Leo?'

In spite of the blood she had guzzled, Leo's throat was dry. It clicked when she opened her mouth. 'It's . . . my dress for tomorrow's Banquet.'

Rodrigo snorted. 'Oh. Wow. How hideous is it?'

'No, no.' Leo couldn't believe her eyes. She rubbed the fabric between her fingers – it wasn't scratchy at all. 'It's actually quite nice.'

Thank you, Marged! she thought, closing her eyes in relief. At least she had something she could actually wear now. If she turned up to the party in her usual shorts and shirt and cape combo, it would be a catastrophe.

Something bristly rubbed round her legs, making her jump. A purr started and stopped and started again, like rusty cogs. From his drawer Rodrigo meeped and ducked down behind the socks.

'Button!' Leo scooped up the one-eyed wiry-haired creature, nuzzling her nose against his squashed one. 'You're here! Have you come to see my dress?'

The ancient cat, with his sparse black fur, spindly

limbs and jutting lower teeth, never failed to make Leo feel cheerier.

'Ugh . . .' Rodrigo gulped as Leo set Button on her shoulders. 'I'm not sure whether that weasel really has much fashion sense, Leo.'

Button meowed, dribbling as he always did when he was pleased to see her. His bent tail curled contentedly.

'He does,' Leo said, scratching Button's lopsided ear. 'He has *taste*. Don't you, Button?'

'Mmmrrr,' said Button.

'Hmph!' Rodrigo clicked his spidery fangs. 'W-well, I'm glad you're sorted for tomorrow's shindig, at least. Your Blood Banquet.'

'Blood *Moon* Banquet,' Leo corrected, then buried her face in Button's knobbly back as an unwelcome thought flitted across her mind:

Gosh, it really IS tomorrow . . .

There was only one slumber between Leo and the Blood Moon Banquet – and her expedition to the Ghostly Realm, whatever that would bring. She had no idea what to expect. Unease crept like cold fingertips walking up her back, and then gripped her tightly.

Would it hurt, she wondered faintly, when her body and soul were split?

EIGHT

THE POOL OF SOULS

The moon rose, red as blood, on the most important night of the century: the night the Blood Moon Banquet would come to Castle Motteberg. Across the Dreadwald, lavish carriages were already swaying steadily through the pines, their shutters tightly closed against any lingering shred of lethal daylight.

In the western tower the youngest lady of the castle had risen early. Leo had scrubbed her body twice in the tub, brushed her fangs and even attempted to comb her nest of hair. Dressing in her usual outfit, complete with trusty cape, felt like putting on armour.

On her bed two items were waiting for her. Ulf's kraken chest, still locked and mysterious, sat beside the black dress Marged had requested on her behalf.

Leo stood for a long moment, looking back and forth between the two. She could hardly believe she was running away to the Ghostly Realm – on THIS NIGHT of all nights – but it was the only way to avoid calamity. Tucking the chest beneath her arm, Leo touched the skirt of the dress as though she could magically weave an apology into the fabric.

I'm sorry, Marged. I'll be back as soon as I can!

As she wound her way towards Hollowhome, Leo was a jumble of nerves.

She tripped twice on her journey through the Dreadwald – most unlike her, since she had been running these forest pathways ever since she was a newborn vampire. Leo clutched the kraken chest and blew out a breath to steady herself.

A rattling sound caught her ear as she reached the River Mothling. Ducking behind a tree trunk, Leo peeked out to see a carriage drawn by red-eyed horses. Wooden wheels creaked, unsuited to the uneven terrain of the forest floor. The vehicle rocked dangerously, making the decorative beads hanging from its roof clack together.

Vampires, Leo thought, clinging hard to the tree. The carriage was distinctive, built from cherrywood and painted with preening peacocks, their showy blue and green feathers fanning round the door.

As it passed by Leo's hiding spot, a pale grey nose poked out from round the curtain that concealed the window. It sniffed and then promptly turned up in disgust.

'Aren't we THERE yet?' someone complained, a clawed hand curling round the edge of the window. 'Ugh! We've been travelling for NIGHTS – I don't remember it being *this* far to Castle Moth-berg!'

'Not long now, my dear,' another voice, an older voice, said soothingly. There was the click of claws on hollow wood. Paper rustled. 'Why don't you have another blood truffle?'

'Why do they have to live in the MIDDLE OF NOWHERE? Are they *country bumpkins*?' the first voice whined, quieter now and muffled by the horses' hooves as the carriage drew away. Piled high on the back were multiple trunks, adding to the top-heavy sway of the vehicle as it trundled into the night.

Leo bared her teeth at its retreating back. Country bumpkins! The nerve!

From the top of the chest the kraken stared at her.

Don't get distracted, she imagined it saying, wiggling a tentacle in admonishment. *Remember the plan!*

Hissing, Leo turned and darted down the bank, letting her cape swoosh dramatically behind her. She would be back to defend her family's honour soon, but for now . . . she had a trial to attend.

Hollowhome was silent and stoic in her clearing, tinged red in the light of the moon. Dripping icicles glistened on her vast branches. The spread of them was enormous enough to nudge her nearest neighbours at the edge of the clearing; the Dreadwald pines bowed out of the way like peasants before their queen.

A thick layer of snow had fallen, glistening orange now as Leo crept up to the trunk. She placed a reverent hand on the knotted bark – it was chilled by the winter night, but still thrummed with magical energy.

Slipping through the narrow gap to enter the base, Leo jolted as two ghosts turned to look at her.

'Leo!' Minna exclaimed.

'H-hello,' Leo said, taken aback. She had known they would be here – this was where Leo and Minna always met, it was their *secret base*. But there was something startling about the sight of the ghostly man lounging in the hammock. Ulf was idly biting his fingernails and spitting out the little crescents, which floated away and evaporated on the air.

'Oh! Vampire!' He floated upright as he noticed her arrival. 'HAH! And LOOKIE HERE, you have my chest!'

'I *told* you!' Minna grumped. 'We had to fight a crypt

full of vampire bones to fetch it for you – the least you can do is BELIEVE me!'

'Huh.' Ulf looked down at Leo and Minna, nodding his head in a way that appeared grudgingly impressed. 'I suppose you really are the warriors you said you were!'

'We said we were warriors?' Leo murmured to Minna, but before she could reply, Ulf was holding out his hands. The misty translucence of his skin swirled and spun, becoming more solid.

'May I?'

Leo offered the kraken chest for inspection. After a beat of concentration, Ulf held it gently in his giant hands – it suddenly looked a lot smaller enveloped in his ghostly grasp.

'My treasure,' he said on a sigh. 'Lost to me, long ago. An item so valuable I would have given my life for it – if I had any more life to give!' He turned to Leo and Minna. 'You've returned it to me, vampire. Small ghost warrior. I appreciate it more than you know.'

'Um . . .' Leo said somewhat awkwardly. She felt as though she was interrupting a family reunion between Ulf and the treasure. 'Only thing is, there's this lock here . . .'

Ulf tilted the chest. 'Oh!' he said cheerfully, and promptly smashed the padlock clean off the box with one thump of his massive fist.

'Ack!' Leo leapt aside to avoid taking a chunk of metal to the shin. The Hollowhome fireflies buzzed in alarm.

'WAHAHA! Come here, my pretty!' The chest clattered to the floor, forgotten as Ulf lifted out its precious contents. There, sitting neatly in the palm of his hand was . . .

Leo and Minna both drew closer, curious.

It was a tiara, delicate and made for a dainty head. Its metal swirls looked fragile, at odds with the enormous ruby that winked at its centre, the size of Rodrigo.

'What does it do?' Minna asked, backing away oh-so-slightly. 'Is it magical?'

'Hmmm? Magical? Nah!' The tiara floated up through Ulf's misty body, coming to

rest above his three-cornered hat. It bobbed there, slightly askew. 'What do you think? Doesn't it look good on me?'

Well, yes, Leo thought, shrugging helplessly. *It does look good on him.*

Minna, on the other claw, looked like she was about to explode.

'You're telling me . . .' she began, with the kind of calm that Leo knew was pretend, 'that we were almost *torn apart* by skeletons . . . for THIS? THIS is the REALLY IMPORTANT THING we needed to find? You said it was powerful! Terribly powerful!'

Leo shuffled aside a step, putting some distance between them.

'Well, yeah. Don't you think this is a powerful look?' Ulf blinked down at her. The ruby blinked, too, reflecting the lights of the fireflies. 'This is the treasure! This is what the marauding vampire stole from me and stashed away in her castle on the mountain. It's been on my mind ever since. I couldn't let it go – I'm sure it's worth a fortune!'

Leo cleared her throat awkwardly. She could make an educated guess as to *exactly* who this vampiric thief might have been – but before she could apologise on behalf of Lady Sieglinde and all the Von Mottebergs, she caught sight of Minna out of the corner of her eye.

Twin trails of black smoke blew from Minna's nose: a

leftover power from her death in the burning orphanage. Leo understood her frustration. Ulf really *had* made it sound like the kraken chest was of grave importance. The treasure had felt like the difference between unlife and death while it was still sealed in the chest.

But . . .

'Minna.' Leo hovered a calming hand over Minna's chilly shoulder. 'This was the deal.' She looked to Ulf. 'You have your lost treasure. Now it's time for your end of the bargain. It's time to go to the Ghostly Realm.'

Letting Ulf lead them through the red-tinged trees, Leo kept close to Minna. Looking up at the canopy behind her, she realised with a sinking feeling that they could no longer see Mount Moth.

It felt like a long time since they had left Hollowhome. Leo was certain she had heard the frosty tree groan as they left – a mournful goodbye. She wrapped her arms round her body, enveloping herself in her cape. It smelled comforting; Marged must have washed it and aired it out for her recently.

Oh, Marged, Leo thought to herself, her shoulders around her ears. *What am I doing?*

She wondered whether the guests were arriving at Castle Motteberg. The carriages might be pulling in along the bridge. Perhaps there were a few families already milling around in the foyer, exchanging pleasantries and sipping blood wine while awaiting Lady Sieglinde. Mum would want to be fashionably late to create the grandest of impressions when she finally made an appearance . . .

'Good news!' Ulf boomed, making Leo and Minna both jump. Pine needles scattered, swirling through his broad body as he turned to them, half sticking out of a bowed tree. 'We're here!'

They emerged into a quiet glade, sunk down into the earth and surrounded by tall trees. At its centre, a pond of still water was silvery in the moonlight – peculiar, Leo thought, given the red face of the blood moon and the fiery glow it had given the surrounding Dreadwald. Rushes grew round the pond's edge, full and leafy despite the winter. They too were cast in a whitish light that felt . . .

Otherworldly.

'Where . . . are we?' Leo asked, staring around them. All the trees looked the same. Every path was thick with unwelcoming thorns. Mount Moth was nowhere to be seen.

She thought she knew every route through the forest – and yet now Leo didn't have a clue how to get back to Hollowhome. She had no idea how far they were from

Castle Motteberg, or the town of Otto's End and the humans who lived there.

She was entirely unused to this feeling of disorientation. No matter what, Leo had always known where she was in the Dreadwald – until now.

'This is it!' Ulf said, puffing up his chest proudly. 'This is our door to the Ghostly Realm! Come on, then!'

Leo crept hesitantly down the bank, hanging back. She let Minna go first as they approached the water's edge.

'It's . . . a pond,' Minna said, peering down into it. 'I don't know quite what I expected, but . . . ah . . .'

'This wasn't it,' Leo agreed, staring at its surface. The water was perfectly tranquil, reflecting a pale version of the night sky above them. It was like staring down into another world.

'What is this place, Ulf?' Minna asked.

'It's a POOL OF SOULS! One of only a few in the whole world. It's the only way for a visitor to detach body from soul and enter the Ghostly Realm. And right on your doorstep! Very handy and perfectly safe!' Ulf cleared his throat. 'Er, I think.'

A strange and sudden feeling came over Leo, something between fear and loneliness. She knew logically that Minna and Ulf were beside her, but her vision tunnelled until she could see nothing but the pond. The Dreadwald trees melted away, as did the ground beneath her feet. Then . . .

'What's wrong? Leo? Are you all right?'

'I . . .' Leo stepped back, feeling herself go pale. 'I . . . I just . . .'

A bright hand appeared in front of her, palm outstretched. Reaching out, Leo felt a moment's chill, and then Minna's hand was comfortingly solid in her own. Together, they looked down into the Pool of Souls.

There was Ulf, grinning proudly in his tiara. There was Minna, with her round cheeks and sharp poker.

In between them was a monster.

It was rake-thin and black-eyed, with a wickedly fanged mouth and grey skin. Its face, though young-looking, was pinched in worry. It was hanging on to Minna's ghostly hand for dear unlife.

Leo jerked back. She felt her blood move, startled by the squeeze of her heart. She hadn't seen her reflection – her ACTUAL reflection, not only a portrait – for more than a century.

'Oh wow,' Minna breathed, blinking down at the water. 'That's . . .'

'Terrifying,' Leo whispered back.

NINE

THE GHOSTLY REALM

A giant, solid ghostly hand clapped Leo on the back; Minna grabbed her before she could topple head first into the pond.

'Hah!' Ulf cheered. 'Well, there's some good news for you, young vampire! It can SEE YOUR SOUL!'

Leo choked. In the water her reflection's eyes bulged, eyebrows knitted and lips pulled back in a grimace. The sight of it in motion was unnerving. Had she always looked so . . . strange?

'It had crossed my mind that maybe you'd lost your soul,' Ulf said, his booted feet clomping away on the air. He held up a thumb, closing one eye to judge the distance between him and the bent tree. 'Vampires, you know? I think after a while the soul sort of . . . shrivels up. Like maggoty fruit.' He turned to shrug at her. 'No offence!'

Blinking hard, Leo let the image settle in her mind.

'None taken,' she mumbled, watching Ulf spin in circles. The floating tiara wobbled above his hat but didn't fall. He was looking for something in the mulchy soil that surrounded the pool.

'So what do we do now?' Minna asked. 'Does Leo . . . need to drink the water? Does she have to wade in? *Swim* to the Ghostly Realm?' She huffed as Ulf dropped to his knees, occupied with digging in the soft earth and clearly not listening. 'Honestly, Leo, this guy – he's even more barmy than you! Ulf! Did you hear me?'

'Yes, yeah, that's right . . .' Ulf mumbled, then sat back on his ghostly heels. There was a POOF and soil rained down, splattering around where he was kneeling. 'Ah! THERE you are, you sneaky scallion!'

Scallion? Leo mouthed at Minna, then startled to attention as Ulf whirled round, his hand outstretched. He was waving what looked like a smooth dark pebble, brushing it clear of dirt. Its surface was swirled through with different greys and browns, as though cut from marble.

'I knew I still had one buried here!' Ulf said smugly. He waited for a moment, his eyes swivelling from Leo to the weird pebble and back again.

'O-oh. It's . . . great?'

'ISN'T IT!' Ulf's beard bristled with the force of his

shout. 'It's a *splitting stone*! This thing contains POWERFUL MAGIC – it's how we'll get you to the Ghostly Realm!'

'And, um . . .' Leo eyed the weird stone warily. 'What exactly do we need to *do* with it?'

'Hah! What do *you* think?' Ulf didn't wait for her to answer before he continued. 'You swallow it, of course!'

Leo's throat seized and she suppressed the urge to gag. For a long moment she couldn't speak – but Ulf was happy to do the talking for her.

'You float on your back and swallow this thing. The pool does the rest! It's . . . I don't know. It's some kind of ghostly magic at work; you'll see what I mean!'

'How do you even know about this?' Minna asked, raising an eyebrow. 'No other ghost has ever mentioned this place. And where did you find this stone thing?'

Ulf touched the back of his head with one huge hand. 'Well, er . . . I buried a bunch of these here, back in the day. I had a THING going. I was . . . in logistics! You know, moving stuff around!' His gaze flickered guiltily off to one side. 'I needed lots of stones for my . . . transport business.'

Oh dear, Leo thought, unlacing her boots. Her hands shook as she placed them carefully at the water's edge. She thought about taking off her cape – but she couldn't bear to part with it, somehow.

'You were pushing people into the pool,' Minna concluded bluntly, unimpressed. 'Stealing their souls and turning them into ghosts. Why?'

'Whoa, whoa, whoa! That's quite the accusation!' Ulf deflated, his broad shoulders slumping. 'But, ah . . . okay, it's an accurate one. I *am* a pirate lord, after all. Ships are expensive! I had a patron in the Ghostly Realm, someone with a lot of REAL gold sitting around, like.'

'So someone *paid* you to turn people into ghosts? Whatever did they want them for?'

'I – you know, I can't remember? I don't know if they ever told me? B-but it was a LONG TIME AGO! I turned over a new leaf when I died – I've been a servant of the people ever since!' Ulf flashed his *DREADWALD POSTAL SERVICE* badge, looking between Leo and Minna as though he was a small boy expecting a telling-off.

Leo sighed, reaching for the splitting stone. It was smooth and heavy when she picked it up. 'Let's get this over and done with.'

Opening wide, her black tongue unfurling, Leo paused as she caught Minna's eye. Minna's nose crinkled and her mouth twisted. Leo turned away, hunching her shoulders.

'Don't watch me!' she protested.

'Fine, fine! Just . . .' Minna hovered curiously closer. 'Does it taste really bad?'

'Ugh . . .' Leo said by way of a reply as the stone touched her tongue. It was enormous – too big to swallow, she thought with a flash of panic – but Ulf was already steering her merrily towards the water and it was too late to think about it.

'That's it!' he said over the sound of splashing water as Leo stumbled in, up to her knees in the freezing pond. 'You hold the splitting stone in your mouth and float on your back. The Pool of Souls will do the rest.' He smiled in what he probably thought was an encouraging way as Leo tipped backwards. Her clothes and her cape were instantly sodden, weighing her heavily down. Her wild hair floated around her face.

Above her, the two ghosts loomed. Ulf looked as happy as ever. Minna didn't seem so sure about all of this.

This is supposed to be YOUR plan, Minna! Leo thought, grunting out a grumpy sound around the splitting stone. It tasted foul – like earth and dust. Now that it was on her tongue, it had a slightly grainy texture that felt suspiciously like compressed hair. Saliva filled what little space was left in her mouth, and the hairy feeling was replaced by an unpleasant sliminess.

'It will be okay!' Minna
was saying frantically.
'We'll see you on the other
side, it will be fine, it's
glub blub blub!'

'Whhh?' Leo tried
to ask, but her tongue
was pinned by the stone
and her ears were full
of rushing water.
She tried to cough as
she felt the splitting
stone SLIDE,
a sickening lurch
overtaking her.

By some terrible
miracle, Leo swallowed
the disgusting thing.
Her body tried to
reject it. Her chest
tightened and her
arms and legs kicked
reflexively, bubbles
rising to the surface
of the pool . . .

She was SINKING, she realised.

Minna and Ulf were gone. So were the Dreadwald trees and the red face of the moon. All were replaced by miles of silvery water, stretching out in every direction. Down and down, Leo was dragged by ghostly hands, her cape streaming behind her.

The splitting stone finally settled into her belly, like a rock weighing her down. No matter how hard she kicked, she couldn't swim to the surface. This was the power of the Pool of Souls.

A peculiar calm washed over Leo and she let herself drift. She squeezed her eyes shut, feeling her body pushed by an invisible current, tipping her over in a lazy somersault. Her cape swirled over her head, the material gliding over her face for a moment, and then the sensation was gone.

When Leo opened her eyes again, she was looking down at herself.

Leo's body, gangly limbs floating and expression peaceful, drifted at the bottom of the Pool of Souls, surrounded by the sunken half-buried bones of other stolen souls.

There was a swooshing sound. Shards of flashing light blinking in and out of view. A rattling gasp.

Wobbling unsteadily, Leo emerged from the pond upside down. Her kicking feet floated up first, followed by her squirming legs and thrashing arms. Her cape flowed up to tangle around her face – or, it would have done, had it not floated right through Leo's suddenly misty body.

'Wauuugh!' she blurted. The sound of her voice reverberated through her in a weird way, like she was standing in the echoey castle foyer. This was definitely not Castle Motteberg, though – in fact, she was back in the glade, surrounded by upside-down pines that were all . . .

Ghost . . . trees? she thought disbelievingly. All around her, everything was a washed-out grey, as though the world had been dipped in paint. When Leo looked up, past her crooked legs, even the blood moon was now as pale as parchment.

'LEO! You made it!' someone cried, and Leo spun to see Minna's ankles inches from her nose. Minna's toes wriggled.

'I . . . did?'

Hands grabbed her and the Dreadwald spun, whirling in a queasy cartwheel until it was the right way up again. Minna's round face lurched into view.

'I can't believe it. We followed you through, but I didn't

actually *see* it happen – it's so weird! You're a GHOST, Leo!'

Leo looked down at herself. Her body had become startlingly translucent, all the way from the top of her head to the tips of her clawed toes. She floated, swimming in the air, held aloft by some unknowable ghost power. Next to her, her right leg – her prosthetic leg – hovered, equally as ghostly as the rest of her. It must have come unstuck during her flip.

'S-so I am!' Leo tried to keep her cool. A little stab of panic was fluttering somewhere behind her see-through ribs. She focused on trying to reattach her leg to distract herself while Minna swept around her.

'It's amazing!' Minna breathed, taking two handfuls of Leo's cape and stretching it between her hands. 'We've really done it. You're here, in the Ghostly Realm! You've passed through! And you didn't even have to wait for seven moons to sink. Figures.'

Leo struggled resolutely with the strap. Though her leg was made of the same ghostly fog as the rest of her, getting a good grip was awkward. It was made even more difficult as Minna grabbed her arm with a glassy *clink*, forcing it up to have a look at her ghostly armpit . . .

And they both froze.

Over the other side of the pool, an already heated

argument was becoming fierier.

'We have AUTHORISATION from JUDGE HARKER; it says so right here!' Ulf was shouting, waving the summons letter back and forth as though swatting a ghost fly. 'So you can stick THAT up your bugle and toot it!'

'Well, I never!' blustered a second ghost – a pudgy man with boyish features and curly hair gathered at the back of his head. He was dressed smartly in a tailcoat, and shiny shoes, with a brass horn hanging at his waist. He was also holding a clipboard and tapping his foot to an agitated rhythm. 'You're COMPLETELY out of line, Ulfricsson! A VAMPIRE!' He looked furtively around them, dropping his nasally voice to a hiss. 'Judge Harker would *never* bring a vampire to the Ghostly Realm! That's an ENEMY of ghostkind! What were you thinking? Oh wait, I know – you *weren't thinking at all*! As usual! What if you'd BROKEN the Pool of Souls!'

'Judge's orders. No mistake about it.' Ulf folded his massive arms across his chest. The tiara glistened dramatically in the moonlight. 'These young warriors have weathered a great journey to get here, Clemens! The pool is fine and the vampire has been summoned; the letter says so. And it's YOUR job –' Ulf poked a thick finger into the other ghost's chest – 'to check in this newbie! Or do you want to tell Judge Harker why you ignored her orders?'

'Hmph!' The ghost called Clemens straightened his coat, looking from his clipboard to Leo and back again. He shrank down even shorter next to Ulf, but his haughty expression remained.

Leo raised a hand. 'Hello.'

'Ack!' Clemens leapt backwards. 'It can talk!'

'Um, well, yes.' Leo tried to straighten up as Clemens approached warily. The movement upset her balance and she almost did a flip before Minna grabbed her shoulder.

'Clemens, this is Leo,' Minna began, but then Clemens raised his feathered quill rudely.

'Yes, yes, I know EXACTLY who this is, Wilhelmina,' he puffed. 'Or I know WHAT this is, which is enough. Soul number one-two-six-zero.' He scribbled furiously with the quill. 'Sign here.'

Leo reared back, startled by the clipboard shoved in her face. All the words jumbled into one.

'Sign here! Quickly!' Clemens snapped.

Leo hastily took the quill – or, she tried to, but her hand phased right through it. She frowned: touching things as a ghost was a LOT harder than Minna made it seem. Clemens, meanwhile, looked like he might explode.

'Here!' Minna grabbed the quill, inking a squiggle at the bottom of the page. 'There! She's in; she's done.'

Shuffling papers, Clemens still looked unimpressed. Finally he thrust out a piece of parchment, leaving it to float in the air in front of Leo.

'Fine. Welcome to the Ghostly Realm,' he said dully, as though reading from a script. 'I'm sure you will have many questions; the answers will come in time. Please familiarise yourself with the Ghostly Guidelines in order to make your stay here as pleasant as possible.' Clemens cast a sour look back at Ulf before continuing, 'I might not know the precise nature of your visit, vampire, but, rest assured, I am a BIG DEAL around here. And I am *watching* you!'

Leo blinked down at him, a good head and shoulders taller. She could probably fend him off with one hand once she got the hang of this ghostly-form business.

But because she was a polite girl, and a true lady of Castle Motteberg, she said, 'Yes, sir.'

Clemens lifted his chubby chin. 'Hmph! Well. At least you have manners.' He flapped a hand at the floating parchment. 'Come on, then. Get them read so we can get you to the judge. I don't have all night!'

In cheerful lettering, inches from her nose, the parchment read:

THE GHOSTLY GUIDELINES

MAKING THE AFTERLIFE
SAFE AND FUN – FOR EVERYSOUL!

1. **Spectral is safe!** Enjoy your new afterlife here in the Ghostly Realm – there is a whole eternity to keep you busy!

2. **First-class travel!** Want to quietly check in on the grandkids? Why not pop in through the mirror to see them from afar?

3. **Human hazards!** For your safety do not interact or interfere with the Living (or the Undead enemies of the Ghostly Realm – see rule six!)

4. **YOU are special!** Every ghostly citizen is protected by law. We protect YOUR RIGHT to a happy, healthy hereafter!

5. **Death is a gift!** Test your unique GHOSTLY POWERS today! Do you want to touch and move things? Do you want to fly through walls? Feel free to speak to one of our friendly Death Advisers for more information.

6. **Nasty neighbours!** BEWARE the creature known as VAMPIRE, for they are the enemy of ghostkind . . .

7. **No bodies allowed!** Only disconnected souls are permitted entrance into the Ghostly Realm – please check in your body before entry.

'Huh,' said Leo weakly. 'Right, yes. That's great. Got it.'

Clemens sighed through his nose. 'Whatever am I going to do now . . . ?' he muttered to himself.

'Take me to Judge Harker?' Leo suggested gently.

'I know that! Of COURSE I'm going to take you to Judge Harker, I've already said that!' Clemens threw up his hands, clipboard and quill flying. 'I meant, what am I going to do IN GENERAL? About all of this!'

'Wow,' Leo whispered to Minna.

'Indeed,' Minna replied, though unsurprised by the outburst.

Shaking his head, Clemens snagged his clipboard and tucked it under his arm in a business-like manner. He stashed his feathered quill behind one ear. 'Oh, stop it. I can hear you. You don't know how hard it is being the town record keeper! It's been a rotten night already: we had a mad poltergeist come wandering through and . . . Never mind. I have a job to do. I will show you, Miss Vampire, why ghostly decorum is famous! We do things BETTER in the Ghostly Realm! Follow me.'

With that he turned on his heel and began to float-stomp towards the trees.

'Look at you.' Ulf chuckled as Clemens passed him with his nose in the air. 'So *professional*!'

'Well, one of us has to be! And it's not HER fault, is it, that she was made into a hideous vampire? Someone has to help the girl!'

Ulf blinked at the back of Clemens's curly head, darting after him. 'Erm, Clem, exactly what do you think Judge Harker wants with these kids?'

'Let's go, Leo,' Minna said, hushed. 'The sooner we talk to Judge Harker, the sooner we can get you back to the castle. We should be quick about it.'

Of course. The castle. Leo couldn't help but fret. Would the banquet be starting now? Would Marged notice she was missing? Would *Lady Sieglinde* notice? The longer Leo spent here in the Ghostly Realm, the greater the risk of discovery.

Her first attempt at flying nearly sent her pitching forward into the water again, so Leo let Minna lead her by the hand. Passing over the Pool of Souls, she looked down into its shiny, mysterious depths. An unpleasant thought occurred to her.

'What happens to my body? Will it wait for me here?'

'All under control, my vampire friend!' Ulf shouted back to them. 'Nothing to worry about. Your body will be here safe and sound for you when we get back.'

Will it really? Leo wondered, imagining her empty shell sleeping silently at the bottom of the pool, weighed down by the splitting stone in her belly. It felt so strange being cut in half like this. Of course, for the ghosts – the REAL ghosts – it was nothing; they had no bodies to lose. But it was a vulnerable feeling for Leo leaving herself behind. Her vampiric body was defenceless.

But she had known it would be a dangerous mission.

She was a Von Motteberg, and Von Mottebergs were made for danger.

Summoning her bravery, and with an unusually quiet Minna at her side, Leo left her body behind. Together, the girls followed the postman and the record keeper through the phantom Dreadwald.

TEN

RETURN TO OTTO'S END

Floating along after Ulf and Clemens, unsteady but stabilised by Minna's hold on her wrist, Leo tried to tame her racing thoughts. Being here, on a *whole new plane of existence*, was sending her into a spin. All around them, the Dreadwald looked so strange in the otherworldly half-light, enveloped in a fog that Leo was somehow magically attuned to.

She felt an odd affinity with this place, as though she and the Ghostly Realm were now made of the same spooky stuff. Leo held her hand up to her face, still amazed that she could see right through it.

'Hey,' Minna said, glancing sideways at her. 'You'll definitely stick out like a boil on the bottom if you fly around doing that.'

Leo hastily lowered her hand. She pushed it into the pocket of her shorts – or, into the side of her leg, just below the hip. 'Sorry. It's . . . It feels so weird. Being a ghost, I mean. It's a l-lot to take in.'

'Please, tell me all about it,' Minna said wryly – but she didn't look any more annoyed than normal. 'Look, Leo . . . you remember what I told you, down in the tunnels below Castle Motteberg? About the Ghostly Realm being dangerous?'

Leo remembered Minna's frowny face after the attack in the crypt. It took her a moment to connect that particular grimace to Minna's warning . . .

'There are powerful ghosts here,' Leo said, looking at Ulf. He was swinging his big arms as he flew alongside Clemens, the two of them busy bickering again. 'I remember. I'll be careful.'

'*Careful* might not be good enough . . .'

'What else do we have?' Leo asked, and then immediately felt bad. She squeezed Minna's hand in apology – or she tried to. 'Minna, I appreciate the reminder but . . . remember who's back at home! It's either talk to Judge Harker now, here in the Ghostly Realm, OR upset the ghosts and REALLY get on Mum's bad side.' There was a flutter in her chest at the thought – perhaps her soul was remembering how her body would instinctively react.

She tried not to wince as they flew straight through a tree, still expecting a faceful of pine needles.

'Right. Evil vampire mum – how could I forget?' Minna sighed when they emerged.

'A-and besides,' Leo added, trying to cheer her up, 'how bad can these ghosts really be? As evil as the Orphanmaster?'

'I never said they were evil.'

'No, but you saw those GHOSTLY GUIDELINES. They're all, *have a great afterlife! Enjoy your spookily ever after!* I'm just saying, maybe this . . . won't be as difficult as you think?'

Minna's eyes were round. 'I knew it! You *aren't* taking this seriously!' she accused. 'This is what I've been trying to tell you – you need to keep your guard up! You're a vampire in the Ghostly Realm, Leo. This is unheard of. I don't know how any of them will react to you!'

'No, no, I am serious! I am!' Leo cleared her throat. 'But the ghosts seem . . . nice? Ulf is nice. Your parents are nice. *Him* and his clipboard maybe not . . .' She pointed to Clemens, who was now imitating Ulf in a mocking voice. 'But even he seems harmless, though? Like a little dog who barks at nothing.'

Get to Judge Harker, explain the situation, go home. Now that she was actually here – now that she had overcome her fear and managed to swallow down the disgusting stone – Leo felt . . . cautiously optimistic.

One look at Minna's face, however, told Leo exactly how Minna felt about *that*.

'Leo von Motteberg,' Minna snarled, 'you *absolute—*'

'Here we are!' Clemens cut in. 'First stop and the last! Take a look, vampire.' The quill behind his ear bobbed as he nodded to something up ahead.

Minna snapped her mouth shut, pinning Leo with a fierce glower. 'Well?' she growled. 'Come on, then. Come and see the FRIENDLY GHOST TOWN!'

'Minna, I'm . . .' The words died on her tongue, as Minna pulled her along to join Ulf and Clemens at the forest's edge. They were on top of a long verge covered in brittle winter grass and down in the valley was a familiar sight.

Otto's End? Leo felt a pang of something that might have been fear, or regret, or some mix of the two. It was the human town where Minna had once lived. Leo hadn't been back since her final battle with the Orphanmaster – this was where the trouble had begun *and* where it had reached its explosive conclusion.

There was no mistaking it. The Otto's End houses with their crooked rooftops and wooden beams were clustered tightly together, cut through by winding cobbled streets. A few chimneys were gently smoking, but all the shutters were closed. There was the clocktower, and St Maja's Church, and the butcher's yard. On the edge of town, visible from their vantage point, the ruin of a once-formidable building stared damningly at Leo: St Frieda's Home for Unfortunate Children, as it had been known, now a burnt-out husk.

Of course, there was one difference. Every peaked rooftop, every shadowy alleyway, every secretive nook – they all had the unearthly glow of the Ghostly Realm, as though stained glass had been laid over an image of Otto's End to transform it into . . .

Something else. A town that was both new and old. Leo gasped as she spotted spectral figures, indistinct from this far away, but, sure enough, there were GHOSTS in Otto's End.

'Ohhh yes!' Ulf guffawed with his usual enthusiasm. 'Isn't she a beauty? Welcome, vampire, to the REAL Otto's End!'

The ghostly town of Otto's End was a flurry of activity after dark. Its citizens preferred to go about their business at night to avoid the constant interruption of their Living counterparts. It was an important balance, when you were sharing your house with noisy, messy humans who didn't even know you were there.

Leo stuck close to Minna as the group floated into town. She could just about manage to fly on her own as long as she kept to a straight line – which was good, as Minna was giving off a distinctly cross sort of aura. On the road, they passed a ghostly stable boy tending to ghost horses. They passed a ghostly beekeeper in a netted hat, surrounded by a swarm of ghost bees. They passed a ghostly sign:

WELCOME TO CHARMING
OTTO'S END
WHERE DEATH IS ONLY THE BEGINNING!
POPULATION: -52

'Minus fifty-two?' Leo mumbled to Minna as they passed. 'That can't be right?'

'It's right,' Minna said tightly.

'Are you . . . angry with me?'

Minna didn't reply, staring sternly at the silvery cobblestones beneath their dangling feet.

'Minna, I'm sorry. I know we have to . . . to *proceed with caution* and all that.' Leo cleared her throat. Or she made the right sound, but there was no feeling at all in her neck. 'I didn't mean that this place isn't as dangerous as Castle Motteberg.'

Did I? Now that Leo thought about it, perhaps she *had* downplayed the dangers of the Ghostly Realm. It was hard to be TOO scared of anything when you lived under the same roof as the world's most evil vampire. Or when you had already fought the world's most evil ghost. Leo slumped.

'Otto's End is a very SAFE place,' Clemens piped up snootily. 'In fact, we've been named Most Lovely Town by the *Dreadwald Dirge* for two years running now!'

'Local newspaper,' Ulf supplied. 'By ghosts, for ghosts. Clem loves it; they ran a story about his petunias dying SO PERFECTLY last summer and he hasn't shut up about it since.'

All around them, ghostly townsfolk were . . . staring, Leo realised. Curious eyes followed their every move. A portly man watched them as he hung laundry on a washing line. A group of young boys playing with a wooden hoop stopped mid-game. A woman leaned through a shuttered window, a book dangling from her grasp; she dropped it when she noticed Leo.

Leo remembered Ghostly Guideline number six:

BEWARE the creature known as VAMPIRE, for they are the enemy of ghostkind . . .

The Otto's End residents had definitely noticed the vampire floating into town. Despite Leo's ghostification, there was no mistaking her gangly limbs or her slitted pupils or her sharp teeth and claws. Leo had anticipated that her arrival might come as a surprise – but she hadn't expected the townsfolk to glare at *Minna*, too.

Why? Leo wondered. *Do I make her look bad by association?*

Minna ignored the whispers and said nothing.

The group made their way towards the clocktower, passing the school where some elderly ghosts were doing stretches along with an enthusiastic instructor. They all turned to look as Leo passed, her head ducked low. She longed to wrap her cape round herself, but getting a grip on it was still impossible. Her prosthetic leg floated along after her, bobbing gently.

'Well!' Ulf came to an abrupt halt and Leo crashed into his back, seeing his ghostly insides for a moment before she could catch herself. 'WAHAHA! The town hall! Most important stop on the tour!'

It made sense that ghostly Otto's End would hold its council here, Leo supposed queasily. Her gaze followed the long neck of the tower to its numbered face at the top. Each faraway tick of its hands sent a jolt of nerves through her.

Around the base of the clocktower, window boxes were bursting with silvery plants. Long banners wafted in the breeze, proudly declaring Otto's End to be the *Dreadwald Dirge*'s most lovely town – twice running!

'Is Judge Harker in there?' Leo asked, wincing as her voice cracked. When she turned to Minna, she noticed that a congregation had gathered around the clocktower steps. Curiosity had curdled into suspicion. Word had gone around about the killer vampire coming to town with her traitor ghost friend. Leo took a step back, scooting behind Ulf's broad body.

A murmur went up amongst the crowd.

'Now, now, everyone!' Clemens waved a hand, clearly enjoying himself. 'Yes, we are here to see Judge Harker about the . . .' He held his forefinger and little finger up to his mouth to mimic sharp vampire teeth. 'But I assure you, this is all VERY OFFICIAL and UNDER CONTROL!'

There was a pause. Then—

'KILL THE VAMPIRE!' someone shouted to cheers of agreement.

'Burn her!'

'Stake her!'

'BAKE HER IN A PIE!' added a sweet-looking old lady menacingly, waving a rolling pin in one hand and a newspaper in the other. On the front page, the headline screamed out:

LEO VON MOTTEBERG: VAMPIRE MOST WANTED

Mount Moth vampire's rampage of revenge kills ghostly citizen!

'I've changed my mind, Minna!' Leo squeaked hastily, wondering whether Ulf could hide her in his beard. Something went flying – a phantom book – and she ducked to narrowly avoid it. 'I get it. I understand what you meant. Oh, pox! I'm so sorry!'

A ghostly pitchfork jabbed at the air from the back of the crowd.

'Vampires are *not welcome* here!'

'She's killed before – she'll kill again!'

'Wilhelmina, do your PARENTS know you're running around with—'

There was a BANG as the doors behind them slammed open, blown on a spectral wind. An elegant figure was silhouetted in the entranceway.

A hush fell over the crowd. Clemens leapt to attention and Ulf nearly dropped his tiara. Minna took Leo's arm, grabbing for the handle of the poker as the figure emerged into the ghostly light . . .

And raised an eyebrow.

'Leo the Vampire of Castle Motteberg . . .'

ELEVEN

THE BLOOD MOON BANQUET I

Meanwhile, on top of Mount Moth, Castle Motteberg was resplendent in its Blood Moon elegance as the guests filed across the grand bridge. Flags bearing the family emblem fluttered from every alcove. The brass had been shined, the portraits dusted and fresh cobwebs added around the high ceilings. Marged had worked night and day to ready the castle for a party befitting the future Head of the Vampiric Council.

Mercifully unseen by the gathering vampire nobility, a long, thin and shadowy creature crept nimbly round the edge of the mountain lake. Its footsteps – wet and squelchy, every other one a wooden CLUNK – were lost in the sounds of laughter and off-key music from the foyer. When the creature looked up, its black eyes glimmered in the light from the great braziers. Its cloak, heavy with pondwater and half frozen, flapped sluggishly in the wind.

The creature turned away from the entrance, scurrying instead along the castle ramparts. High above it, the western tower soared up into the night sky. Pausing, the creature tilted its head in consideration.

Leo's empty body, no longer piloted by her soul, zeroed in on her bedroom window. Yes. This was where she needed to go. She always returned to her room after playing in the forest.

She bounded up on to the side of the tower, running horizontally up the crumbling brick. Far below, the snow-tipped trees of the Dreadwald shrank back. If Leo's stomach swooped, she didn't feel it – or, rather, her brain didn't register the feeling. Her vampiric instinct was so strong, there was nothing but the urge to run.

Of course, had she been able to feel any sort of shock, this would certainly be cause for alarm. Ulf had assured Leo that her body would be safe. He hadn't said anything about it WALKING OFF WITHOUT HER.

Leo's claws scraped on the window frame as she landed, the momentum carrying her body into her bedroom. The curtains fluttered on the rush of air. Her feet clunked down on to the floorboards and her empty shell came to a halt.

'Leo!' someone shouted, and Leo turned to see Rodrigo sitting on her desk, clicking his fangs impatiently in her direction. 'There you are! You're going to be late!'

Staring at her spidery roommate, there was no urgency or panic in Leo's mind. Only a calm mist remained, drifting vaguely by.

'Yes,' she replied dully.

'Come on, then!' Rodrigo did a frantic side-to-side shuffle that made him look like a furry crab. 'The dress! Let's get you ready – your mum will go mad if you miss this party!'

'Yes.' Leo's eyes, large and blank, swivelled. On her bed, the black dress from Madame Kinkatch was waiting. Next to it were a pair of simple silk slippers to cover her knobbly feet, and something else she hadn't noticed when she left earlier that evening: a moth-shaped brooch made of recently polished brass. Marged must have unearthed it while she was cleaning.

Mum had a brooch like this – though larger and fancier and adorned with opals. If the sight triggered any thought, it was immediately lost in the empty chasm of Leo's brain.

'Come on, come on!' Rodrigo said impatiently when he heard no movement, clicking his spidery fangs in agitation. He was fumbling around on her desk, feeling for something. 'Hurry up! If Lady Sieglinde realises you're missing . . . I . . . I don't want to think about it!'

'Hm.' Leo's claws moved without her thinking, pulling the knot of her cape. Fabric rustled as she removed her clothing, still wet and smelling of pondwater. The dress went on easily over the extra vest that Marged always insisted she wear in the winter. From beneath the bed a single yellow eye watched her suspiciously. There was a feline rumble and the hint of a crooked tail lashing back and forth, but Leo ignored it, busy pulling on the slippers. She picked up the moth brooch.

Pinning it to her front, Leo didn't react when she accidentally pricked her thumb. The small smear of her vampire blood – inky black – blended with the dark fabric as the wound began to heal. There were many perks to having a vampire body and this was one of them.

'Well?' Rodrigo asked.

Leo lifted her head. Words and phrases shuffled around in her brain, trying to connect to her mouth.

'The weather is pleasant tonight,' she said.

'Right. Yes, I suppose it is. But the dress! How is the dress!'

'Yes.'

'Oh, good!' Rodrigo tapped a limb against the desk. In his two front legs he waved the comb. 'That's great. Come here now – hurry, hurry!'

Five minutes later, balanced on top of Leo's head, Rodrigo was still struggling with her hair. Some of the tangles were impossible (*where had the girl BEEN?*) but he had removed the worst of the leaves and twigs. Leo held perfectly still, staring at the wall with unblinking eyes. She didn't flinch even with the harsh treatment of her scalp.

'I think,' Rodrigo panted, 'this is as good as it's going to get.' Optimism was important when you were a blind spider and your young roommate was a vampire with no reflection. Rodrigo nodded, satisfied with his handiwork. 'You, er . . . you smell a bit funny, but I'm sure no one will notice.'

'Hm.'

'Better *I* be the one to tell you, rather than your vampire friends. Ahhh!' Rodrigo buried his face in her hair, suddenly emotional. 'I'm proud of you! Off to attend your grown-up party! It sounds like a good time downstairs.'

'Yes.'

'Old Rodrigo, getting you ready.' Rodrigo sniffed. He wiped away a little tear with the tip of a leg. 'I promised the knight I would look after you, you know. That I would make sure you were okay and on time.'

Leo paused for a moment. 'Oh, how nice,' she said.

Rodrigo beamed. 'It IS nice! I feel like we've reached a real understanding today, you and me. What a pair we are!' He stopped to mull over a thought. 'It's . . . almost a shame I can't *come with you*. To the shindig, I mean.'

'Yes.'

'It would be COMPLETELY LUDICROUS,' Rodrigo scoffed. 'Me, hiding out in your hair. Mingling with high society. The music and the dancing, the FOOD . . .'

'Yes.'

Perching on Leo's shoulder, Rodrigo's eight eyes fixed her with a long blind look.

'Hmmm . . . I suppose it *could* work. If you really needed me there. As moral support, to help you through it. A friendly chaperone.'

'Hm,' Leo said.

Rodrigo perked up. 'Oh!' he said, pleased. 'If you're insisting . . . Well, okay, then! I SUPPOSE I'll come along! But only because you asked me. A favour to a friend!'

Leo said nothing while Rodrigo scurried down her arm. On the desk he fussed with a frayed scrap of green ribbon that had fallen off the monstrosity of a dress from before. His pointed feet worked deftly to loop it round his neck, tying it off in an approximation of a bow tie.

'What?' he said, sensing Leo's stare. 'Just because I'm in hiding, doesn't mean I shouldn't dress up!' His spidery eyebrows waggled. 'Let's get going!'

Down in the foyer, the Blood Moon Banquet was gathering

momentum. The castle was abuzz with conversation as vampires of all shapes and sizes mingled, sipping blood wine. Everyone was dressed to impress in elegant gowns and tailored suits, glittering with priceless jewellery.

The finger of fashion tonight was pointed firmly at the collar. The rufflier, the better. Leo's empty shell of a body had enough instinct to duck as she emerged from the western tower – she would have been sent flying by the enormous ruff of a vampire guest, which spread out around his head like the tail of a peacock.

'What was *that*?' Rodrigo hissed in her ear as she slipped round the edge of the crowd.

Leo didn't reply, instead staring vacantly at their visitors.

Another of the nobles wore a towering number that would be impossible to fit through the castle doors without careful manoeuvring. Others looked less like vampires and more like poisonous lizards with vibrant frills. All around her, snippets of fancy conversation filled the air:

'I TOLD Rupert the coffin was too small for him, but would he listen? Anyway, we had to send a bat for the emergency services; it took them three hours to cut him out . . .'

'So then I said, "I ordered *twelve* candelabras! Twelve! What am I supposed to do with eleven? The feng shui of the room will be all wrong!" Anyway, we had to have the entire eastern wing ripped out . . .'

'I see *Marcel* is wearing the blue tailcoat with the pearl detailing. He said he wasn't going to wear the blue tailcoat with the pearl detailing. I'M WEARING THE BLUE TAILCOAT WITH THE PEARL DETAILING!'

On a raised stage, a string quartet of zombie musicians sawed away slowly at their instruments – apart from one, who was chewing on the neck of his cello. The great doors had been thrown wide, giving an arresting view of the mountain lake, which reflected the scarlet orb of the moon. To welcome the carriages of their guests, the

drawbridge had been lowered, and the rattling of wheels
signalled the arrival of even more vampire nobility.

Leo passed Marged, who was holding a platter of what
was probably meant to be hors d'oeuvres but looked to
Leo like a perfectly ordinary selection of eyeballs. Marged
didn't notice her right away; she was too busy having an
aggressively polite conversation with someone next to her.
She was also shaking so hard her armour was clattering.

'I'm JUST SAYING, *Marged*, the Blood Moon Banquet
doesn't come around every night!' her companion said in
a smug tone. She raised a bandage-wrapped hand, which
was connected to her bandage-wrapped arm, which – in
turn – was connected to the rest of her, also wrapped in
bandages beneath her dapper suit. Through the sliver of a
gap across her face, her eyes were orange lights. 'When it

was Lord Ayman's turn to host as the CURRENT Head of the Council. *I* pulled out all the stops to ensure that—'

'Nesh, I *know*,' Marged cut in. If she had teeth, they would have been gritted. 'It was a LOVELY night. You did a SPLENDID job.'

'As have you!' the bandaged woman called Nesh said sweetly, draping an arm round Marged's pauldrons. 'But I know what an enormous undertaking it is, preparing for this sort of event! We wouldn't want to disgrace our employers by being –' she dropped her voice to a low murmur – '*underprepared*, would we?'

Marged's plume pinged in a way that meant she was EXTREMELY OFFENDED, but wasn't about to say so.

'Lady Sieglinde has the highest of standards,' she said tightly, taking a step sideways. The joints in her armour creaked. 'Of course we have made every special effort for the celebrations tonight – but *every night* is an event at Castle Motteberg.' She looked anxiously out over the crowd. The platter in her hands trembled dangerously, making the eyeballs roll around.
'There really was no need for . . . for all of this . . .'

Leo turned her face back to the crowd. Rodrigo peeked out of her nest of hair. Amongst the swarm of partygoers, skeletal waitstaff in matching bow ties were serving drinks, their skulls shined to perfection. If Leo's soul was with her, the sight of them might have struck fear into her, particularly after yesternight's encounter with her bony ancestors in the crypt . . . but she felt nothing.

Nesh, butler to Lord Ayman – the Head of the Vampiric Council – hummed. 'No, no, Marged. I won't hear of it.' She clapped Marged on the back and the clang echoed through her. 'You are VERY WELCOME! Honestly, I couldn't expect Lord Ayman to come all this way without proper staff! It's been . . . Hey!' Nesh clicked her fingers, calling over a skeleton who wandered past. 'You! Stop right there!'

Marged made a strangled noise, watching as Nesh fixed the skeleton's tie where it had been slightly askew. She yanked it so roughly that the servant's skull wobbled on its thin neck.

'Don't come out looking like a scruff again,' she warned, her eyes flashing a dangerous red. The skeleton nodded and hastily clacked away into the crowd. Nesh bounced her shoulders cheerfully as she turned back to Marged, the picture of positivity again. 'Really, now. Can't get the staff! But of course you know *all* about that here at Castle Motteberg!'

'I'm s-sure Lord Ayman would have found the service here to be more than sufficient!' Marged insisted.

Nesh snorted. 'Lord Ayman is HEAD OF THE COUNCIL, Marged. You expect MORE when you have that kind of power.' She straightened her jacket primly, smoothing down the tasselled trim. 'And ever since . . . Well. You know.' They looked across the floor, where a skeleton was carrying a velvet pillow, surrounded by fawning guests.

On the pillow the severed head of a man was smiling brightly. He was handsome, with dark grey skin and a neatly trimmed beard. He wore a silk scarf tucked round the base of his neck. Whatever he was saying, it was enough to charm the crowd around him; they all laughed heartily in unison as Lord Ayman concluded whatever story he was telling.

When you were Head – and no matter if you were *only* a head – everything you said was golden. Other vampires hung off your every word.

'Ever since Lord Ayman's accident, his staff has worked tirelessly to give him the best of care,' Nesh said with a hint of a well-timed wobble in her voice. Somehow the violins took a sudden sombre turn. 'It has been very hard for him, but he is a brave man. He has a job to do, after all.'

Everyone knew about Lord Ayman's recent misfortune. He had been torn apart by vicious wolves – wolves that, conveniently, no one had seen or found any trace of in the subsequent investigation. Only his head had been recovered so far; it had been mysteriously sealed in a chest and sunk to the bottom of a lake.

Lord Ayman had not seen his attacker. Nor could he recall what had happened to him, except for the sensation of being torn apart by beasts. Or, as Leo rather suspected . . . one GREAT AND TERRIBLE beast. But there was no solid evidence of that.

Nesh stared at Marged and Marged stared back at Nesh.

Unnoticed, Leo stared at the back of Marged's helmet, at the reflection of the foyer. The mirror image of the room looked strangely deserted, except for skeleton servants, zombie musicians and floating glasses of blood wine. Where Leo herself stood, Rodrigo was hovering in mid-air, his beady eyes darting nervously back and forth. He didn't seem to know what to make of this sudden stand-off. Who would emerge as the ultimate butler?

'Yes,' Marged said carefully, after a long moment. 'He truly deserves the best of the best.' Then, with VON MOTTEBERG slyness Leo rarely saw from her, she added, 'I'm surprised *you're* not escorting him tonight, Nesh. I thought that carrying Lord Ayman was an honour only given to the head butler . . .'

Nesh leapt where she stood. Her elbow knocked into Marged's

gauntlet and almost scattered eyeballs all over the floor.

'Ah! My goodness, doesn't time fly?' she blustered. She was already walking away as she pretended to look at a non-existent pocket watch. 'I really must keep circulating, lots to do. It's been VERY NICE talking with you, Marged! Keep an eye out for me tonight, won't you? Always good to see a friendly face!'

From behind her slitted visor Marged watched Nesh worm her way into the crowd, slipping delicately past vampire nobles and barging rudely through skeleton servants. Marged's metal shoulders lifted and fell with a tinny sigh. She straightened the eyeballs on the platter she was holding . . .

And nearly threw them all in the air when she turned and saw—

'Miss Leo! Ohhh, *look* at you!' Marged balanced the platter on one gauntlet, using the other to fuss with Leo's skirt. 'Oh, you always cheer me up, little one. You look simply wonderful; every inch a Von Motteberg!'

'Hm,' said Leo.

'Your parents will be so proud.' Marged's giant metal fingers pinched the moth brooch delicately between them, straightening it carefully. 'I knew this would look splendid on you. I believe it belonged to your great-great grandmother.'

Leo said nothing.

'And what do you think of the *party*?' Marged asked, undeterred, spinning Leo round. 'Do you like the music? The décor?'

An invisible wheel turned inside Leo's mind, picking between whatever she might say next.

'Eyeballs are my favourite food,' she said.

'You noticed!' Marged exclaimed, delighted. 'Here you are. They're the popping kind – exactly how you like them!' She offered the platter. Leo looked down at the selection, her mouth starting to water instinctively.

She reached out with all ten claws and skewered an eyeball on each. Marged hadn't lied about the popping; they all oozed deliciously.

'Wow,' Marged said as the platter was plundered, 'you really ARE a hungry bug! Well, you go ahead and enjoy them. But remember that there is still the actual BANQUET to come!'

On the very edge of Leo's comfortingly empty mind, she vaguely registered the way the foyer felt suddenly colder. Out of the corner of her eye, she spied the long gaunt shape that had suddenly appeared in the doorway behind them, rising from the shadows . . .

She had grown tired of waiting for her moment and was ready to make her grand entrance.

There was a booming clap of thunder and a zigzag of lightning lit up the room. The crowd gasped. The candles spluttered, making the shadows leap. The zombie band stopped with an abrupt squeak of their instruments as everybody turned to look.

'Ah!' Marged jumped. She pressed the platter hurriedly into Leo's eyeball-covered claws. 'Hold this for me, little one!' she whispered, already moving forward to stand to attention.

Except for Marged, no one moved. No one dared. The rattling of Marged's armour was the only sound as she bustled forward.

'Ahem! Ladies and gentlemen! May I present your esteemed host: *Lady Sieglinde von Motteberg*!' Marged announced. She made a sweeping bow that folded her in half, her plume bristling dramatically.

Stepping forward in a glittering floor-length gown, Lady Sieglinde von Motteberg glared at the crowd. Her lip curled in a pleased sneer as everyone stared. She was the picture of opulence, wearing her best opals and a voluminous feather boa wrapped round her knobbly shoulders. Her claws glinted, as long and sharp as needles.

The crowd shied back as she burst into a storm of

enormous flapping moths, her GRIMWALK, a rare and arresting sight that sent goosebumps crawling up the back of all who witnessed it. The swarm soared in a triumphant lap of the room before plummeting with a sharp CRACK, leaving Lady Sieglinde standing in the middle of the room, all eyes fixed on her in amazement.

She straightened her boa and smiled nastily as applause erupted. 'Yes, yes,' she rumbled. 'Welcome, everyone, to Castle Motteberg – and to the Blood Moon Banquet!'

Unnoticed in the adoring crowd, Lady Eleonore von Motteberg – youngest daughter of Lady Sieglinde – opened her jaws wide in a most unladylike manner. Into her mouth she crammed the five claws of her left hand, covered in eyeballs.

TWELVE

JUDGE HARKER

Ghostly twilight filtered in through the stained-glass windows, still spookily colourless as it touched on the rows of cramped pews. The benches faced a raised desk with an official-looking gavel and block – the kind a judge would bang to sentence a MURDERER to her fate. One by one the townsfolk filed in. The air was abuzz with voices and the clinking of spectral bodies. Ulf and Clemens elbowed each other as they squished into the front row.

It looked like the whole town was here. Amidst the crowd was the old woman who had called for Leo to be baked into a pie. There was the lady with the book, which was now sticking up out of the back of her head. The heavy-set man doing the laundry had his ghostly washing line strung across the back of the room, doomed to be hanging socks into eternity. Now that Leo looked closer, the middle of the line was looped round his neck.

The heads of the ghost horses poked in through the walls, nostrils flaring curiously. The ghost bees hung in an ominous, humming swarm above their keeper. There were ghosts young and old, clad in various kinds of uniform or nightclothes or, in one unfortunate case, a spotty pair of underpants and fluffy slippers. Several of them bore the evidence of their deaths, forever followed by the weapons of their own murders.

A metal staircase spiralled above the heads of the congregation, reaching up into the cogs and pulleys of the clock. Every little sound bounced away up the tower, as though they might escape out into the night.

The doors closed with a heavy CLUNK, powerful enough to rattle the windows, and Leo couldn't help but feel that her escape was looking increasingly unlikely.

'What's going on?' she whispered to Minna, her eyes swivelling to watch the townsfolk nervously. 'Since when do ghosts use doors?'

Minna was stood to attention, her back straight. She looked up at Leo with an equally anxious expression. 'Since they want to make an impression,' she replied tightly.

They floated awkwardly in the middle of the room, out of place and unable to do anything but watch as someone stepped up to the judge's seat.

There was an aura of power about the mystery ghost,

Leo thought, in the same way that Lady Sieglinde could turn someone to stone with a glare. She was clad in a long, flowing gown and robe, bare toes peeking out of the bottom of the skirt. Her hair was swept back from her brow, forming a soft cloud around her head. Her face was that of a young woman and her features might have been gentle, if not for the steely set of her eyes when she glanced Leo's way. Her gaze glinted like a sharp blade.

'Leo the Vampire!' the newcomer announced, holding up a slim hand as she flew behind the desk. The sound of the rabble instantly died down. 'You're . . . here. *How*, may I ask, did you make it to the Ghostly Realm?'

It took a moment for Leo to find her voice. 'I . . . I . . .' She looked helplessly at Ulf, who whistled and turned away. 'Judge Harker summoned me? She asked me to come here?'

A weary sigh. The newcomer leaned over the desk to peer down at her, her brow furrowing in scrutiny. 'Indeed she did. I'll ask again, since you didn't answer my question: precisely *how* does a vampire enter our world? You must have had help, no?'

If Leo had been standing on solid ground, she would have shuffled her foot guiltily. The ghosts had called her here – why was her arrival a shock? Had they expected her not to show up?

'It was Wilhelmina!' someone shouted from the crowd, pointing at Minna. 'Wilhelm and Willa's girl! She's been helping the vampire!'

'It's right here in the *Dirge*!' someone else added, waving the newspaper.

Minna looked very much like she would enjoy setting the *Dreadwald Dirge* on fire.

'Um!' Leo cut in hastily, before Minna could draw her poker. 'Well! You see, I knew the summons was important and I didn't want to be d-disrespectful, so I made sure to be here. To sort all this out. It's not Minna's fault, or anyone else's!'

Clemens shot a sideways glare at Ulf, whose beard was bristling enough to half obscure him from view. Neither of them said anything.

The ghostly woman at the judge's desk leaned on one elbow, pinching the space between her brows. She looked grimly from Leo to Minna and back again.

'The circumstances of your arrival aside, there's no denying that you *have* made it.' Her mouth thinned as she glanced down at something on the desk: paper, Leo realised, watching the newcomer scan some ghostly document. 'I have to say I'm . . . surprised. But it's in keeping with our laws; you are here and therefore the trial can commence.'

'Yes, about that, I—'

The ghostly woman cut her off. 'Leo the Vampire, you stand accused of the murder of the ghostly citizen formerly known as the Orphanmaster. *I* am Judge Harker, and I will be conducting this trial tonight.'

So YOU summoned me, Leo thought, her fangs snapping shut. *You're the judge . . .*

'Judge Harker, please!' Minna cried. 'There's been a HUGE mistake! The Orphanmaster, he—'

Leo shrank back behind Minna, expecting a shout . . .

But instead, there was another sigh.

'The Orphanmaster, young Minna, was a *citizen* of this town.'

'For barely more than a minute!' Minna argued. She was so small as she looked up at Judge Harker, but no less fierce than usual. 'The Orphanmaster had *only just* entered the Ghostly Realm when he was finally defeated! The seventh moon had hardly sunk!'

Leo peered over the top of Minna's head, remembering how the seventh sinking moon had disappeared down behind the Dreadwald trees.

After a Living person was turned into a ghost, they wandered in limbo for seven moons before entering the Ghostly Realm. Even for a short time it was undeniable: the Orphanmaster had come into his true power, as all ghosts did. As it happened, the Orphanmaster's power was EVIL.

'It may be that his time here was short, but he *was* in the Ghostly Realm, nonetheless. There are rules that must be followed.' Judge Harker tapped the paper on her desk. 'We can't all go around KILLING EACH OTHER willy-nilly. Ghosts are people, too.'

'Ghosts are people, too,' repeated the congregation solemnly.

'—people, too,' finished Ulf, a beat behind everyone else. He straightened his tiara conspicuously and shot Leo and Minna a reassuring grin.

'And so,' Judge Harker said, as though she would very much prefer to be somewhere else, 'this is what must be done. A trial, *vampire*.' Her gaze pierced Leo's, making Leo gulp. 'You are only a child, but it doesn't change the fact that the second death of the Orphanmaster was a breach of his ghostly rights. You *killed* him.'

Leo tucked her chin into her cape. 'I did,' she admitted. 'But I . . . I . . .'

'Then the court demands a full assessment of your character to determine your exact fault in this . . . nasty situation. You will undertake three ghostly tests, designed to discover how much you understand about our world.'

Tests? GHOST tests? Leo's heart sank. She looked helplessly to Minna, who was lost for words. This hadn't gone AT ALL how Leo had hoped.

'Pass these tests,' Judge Harker continued, 'and we will let you go. Fail . . . and I'm afraid the price is EXEC—'

There was clamouring from the back of the room. Judge Harker's speech was interrupted as two familiar figures flew in – one was tall with a gap between his two front teeth, and the other short and plump with distinctively coiled hair.

'Oh crumbs!' gasped Minna's dad. 'Willa, I *knew* we were late!'

'Don't mind us!' Minna's mum piped up, already muscling her way through the crowd. Noticing Leo and Minna, she waved a pudgy hand. 'Oh! Look, Wilhelm! That must be Leo!'

'So it is! Hello, Leo!' Minna's dad called out cheerily.

Bewildered, Leo raised a hand in return. Minna's hand, meanwhile, was planted on her own forehead.

'Minna has told us ALL about you! Or, well . . . she really *hasn't*, but we are VERY GLAD TO FINALLY MEET YOU!' Minna's mum had the kind of booming voice that could cut through walls. When she laughed, it made the ghostly bodies of the townsfolk around her waver as though caught in a strong wind.

Minna's parents squashed into their seats. The townsfolk muttered disapprovingly amongst themselves.

Judge Harker wrinkled her nose thoughtfully. 'Where was I again?' she asked Leo. 'Don't grow up and become a judge, young vampire. It's a lot of hassle.'

'Y-you were saying if I fail your tests . . .'

'Ah! Thank you.' Judge Harker nodded. 'Yes – EXECUTION.'

A ripple swept through the room. Leo knew that everyone was talking at once – she could hear voices around her, but her brain was busy shutting down. She looked behind her, to where all but a few faces were satisfied with this conclusion. Minna's parents were open-mouthed at the back of the crowd. At the front Ulf was staring at Judge Harker with round eyes. Even Clemens, his body half sticking out of the wall where Ulf had squashed him into the corner, seemed . . .

Shocked? Leo's thoughts scrambled to catch up. Clemens had been so sure of the superior ways of the Ghostly Realm. Had he changed his mind?

'Judge Harker,' Clemens piped up with a disbelieving little laugh, 'we haven't had an actual, formal execution in town for . . . for . . .'

'For more than two centuries,' Judge Harker finished for him, tapping the papers on her desk to straighten them again. 'I know. It's all here in our records. We have our law; all we need to do is follow it.'

Ulf raised a massive hand sheepishly. 'Execution seems a bit . . . harsh, Your Judgliness? These young warriors tell me the Organmeister was a WRONG'UN. Wasn't he?'

Minna's mum leapt to her feet before her husband could grab her. 'We CAN'T execute Leo! These girls are HEROES!' she cried. 'We all saw the Orphanmaster in life – he lived in THIS VERY TOWN! He was mistreating the children under our noses! Ghostly Guidelines, interfering with the Living, blah blah blah – Minna and Leo did what we couldn't!'

There was a pause.

'EXECUTE THE VAMPIRE!' someone else shouted back.

'She *conspired* with Wilhelmina and broke our laws!' another townsperson added. 'Who will she kill next?'

The ghost bees buzzed in agreement. The ghost horses snorted and stamped.

Someone brandished a rolling pin. 'GRIND HER UP AND MAKE HER INTO A CAKE!'

Three bangs echoed up the long neck of the clocktower, startling everyone into silence.

'EVERYONE!' Judge Harker boomed, gavel in hand. 'LISTEN TO ME!' She slumped in her seat as though the effort of shouting had drained her. Her body was wracked by a short coughing fit while the crowd shrank silently back.

They're going to execute me, Leo thought, feeling faint. Somehow she couldn't move – though every inch of her wanted to flee. *If I can't pass their tests, they will execute me.*

A flash of a memory came to her. She pictured the Orphanmaster's screaming face as he was dragged away into a void of nothingness. Leo knew all too well how to kill a ghost, and it wasn't pretty.

'These are *our laws*,' Judge Harker finally rasped out, leaning forward on her elbows. She dabbed at her mouth with a translucent handkerchief. It came away black – as black as Leo's vampiric blood – before she stashed it in the pocket of her robe. 'Hngh. Hm. The rules have kept our kind safe from those who would do us harm.' She looked down at Leo. 'I know you probably won't understand this, but vampires have been a threat to all things, Living and Undead, since the beginning of time. You are an ancient menace on both worlds.'

'The Orphanmaster was more of a threat than Leo could ever be!' Minna insisted. 'I promise, Judge Harker, she's . . . she's a bit rubbish at the whole VAMPIRE THING, actually. She couldn't even bite ME before I died in a fire!'

'That wasn't my fault,' Leo whispered in Minna's ear, offended. 'If the Orphanmaster hadn't woken up, I'd have had you for breakfast, no problem!'

'I'm trying to save you, you idiot!'

'A vampire is a vampire,' Judge Harker declared solemnly, ignoring their bickering. 'A cold and calculating creature with only murder on its mind. I am sure you have not yet caused as much tragedy as your parents. As your . . .' She trailed off. A dark look flashed across her face, and then was gone. 'But you will. If I let you go, you will certainly kill many times again, as you killed the Orphanmaster. Clemens! Take note!'

Clemens startled, fumbling for his clipboard.

Judge Harker stood, the ghostly half-light silhouetting her against the ornate windows. 'Vampire. As it was written by those who sought to protect us, I officially sentence you to undergo our three tests. It is a fact that you brought about the death of the Orphanmaster. By the end of this trial we will have our assessment. Would you *knowingly* and *deliberately* murder a ghostly citizen? We will find out.'

'You s-said if I passed, you would let me go?' Leo pointed out, reaching for Minna's arm. Her misty hand phased right through and she was left clutching the air instead.

'Yes,' Judge Harker agreed. 'That is what our law states. Though we have never had an ACTUAL VAMPIRE put to trial before. These are uncharted waters. Do you wish to proceed?'

Leo wavered. She could feel everyone watching her, waiting for her to speak.

'There is always the option, vampire, to try to run,' Judge Harker said softly. 'If you do not agree to these terms.'

Run?

'No, Leo,' Minna whispered in her ear. 'Remember what Ulf said: if we go now, the ghosts will follow us back to the castle! I bet it's all on that paper of Judge Harker's – legally they *have* to give you a trial. While we're here, co-operating with them, they can't crash the vampire banquet! That's something, right?'

It made sense. The Ghostly Realm *did* seem all tangled up in rules and regulations.

Leo also knew that no matter how terrifying the three tests may be, they paled in comparison to what would happen if their worlds collided at Castle Motteberg.

Trembling, she lifted her chin. 'I'll take your tests,' she said. 'I'll complete your trial.'

She jumped back as Judge Harker shot forward through the desk, a swoosh of air making the bodies of the watching crowd flicker. Before Leo could shy away, Judge Harker was *right there*.

'Then we shall begin,' she said, and seized Leo by the wrist.

THIRTEEN

THE MIRRORED CAVE

With deceptive strength and a sound like creaking crystal Judge Harker yanked Leo's arm. Leo yelped as the room spun and the floor rushed up to meet her face. She screwed her eyes shut, expecting a crunch . . .

But there was none.

When Leo dared to look, they were falling. They had passed through the dusty floorboards of the clocktower and were plummeting down into the frozen ground.

All around them, layers of wormy earth flashed by, striped with veins of stone as they flew deeper. Held tightly by her wrist, Leo couldn't pull away; Judge Harker urged them onward, descending deep below Otto's End. Behind them, Leo's prosthetic leg flew, barely keeping up. It was closely followed by a waterfall of silvery bodies.

The townsfolk were eager to see the killer vampire take

her first test. At the forefront of the stampede, Minna was hot on Leo's heels. She had drawn her poker.

'Where are we going?' Leo tried to ask, but her voice was lost to the rushing earth. She stared at Judge Harker as they went, but the judge didn't acknowledge her.

For a fleeting moment Leo couldn't help but feel there was something familiar about this woman – but she couldn't quite put her claw on it.

There wasn't time to examine the thought, as they flew through a thick seam of rock and emerged into . . .

Leo gasped as they came to a halt upside down.

They were in a wintry cavern.

Icicles hung from the ceiling and the floor was dusted with powdery snow. The walls, crystalline-cold and polished to mirrors, stretched out around them before converging on an opening up ahead. Countless years of melting and refreezing had sculpted the ice into geometric shapes, some large and some small, all reflecting the cave back at her.

She rolled, turned upright by a business-like hand on her ankle.

'This is the Mirrored Cave,' Judge Harker said, by way of an explanation. 'Welcome to your first test.'

If she had had her body, Leo would have shivered. The Mirrored Cave? She had never seen a place like this before; she hadn't known that such caverns even existed beneath the Dreadwald. Dad had never mentioned them – though he wasn't exactly a subterranean scout. There was certainly no mention of underground caves in the Castle Motteberg library, either. In the hundred years since her death Leo had read every book on the forest (or, at least, she thought she had).

Above her head, the townsfolk of Otto's End poured into the cavern. They congregated in a huddle as far from Leo as possible, muttering excitedly amongst themselves.

Reflected in the icy walls, a hundred versions of Leo scooted closer to a hundred versions of Minna. All of them looked extremely worried.

'Have you been here before, Minna?' she whispered.

'Never.' Minna's eyes swivelled as she looked around them, taking in the chilly scene. She appeared to be counting the townsfolk, probably wondering how many of them she could fight.

'The first test commences,' Judge Harker announced, floating forward. A hush descended over the crowd. 'Through that passageway, vampire, is a maze of mirrors. To pass, you must find your way out – before SOMETHING finds you first.'

'Something?'

Leo didn't like the sound of that. What was in there?

'Escape the Mirrored Cave,' Judge Harker continued, undeterred, 'and return to Otto's End. It's very simple. We will await your arrival by the clocktower.'

Minna raised the poker. 'I'm coming with you,' she told Leo.

'Me too!' Ulf chipped in, flexing his muscles. His tiara glinted heroically.

'And us!' Minna's mum roared, making Minna's dad jump.

'I'm afraid that's not possible,' Clemens said from behind his clipboard. 'The test is for your vampire friend alone – she must undergo the challenge by herself. Remember that *she* is the one being assessed!'

'But why?' Minna interjected. '*Why* does she have to go alone? I fought the Orphanmaster, too!'

Leo worried for a moment that Clemens's eyes would pop out of his head.

'It's . . . it's . . . it's how it is!' he squeaked. 'It's how it is WRITTEN in our law!' He turned his clipboard, pointing to a paragraph written in tiny cursive letters that no one else would be able to read without a magnifying glass. 'Right here! This is a TRIAL, Wilhelmina, not a circus! The vampire dealt the killing blow – there is protocol that must be followed!'

Minna's lip curled. 'Protocol! What even is protocol?'

'Rules! R-regulations!'

'Do you realise how ridiculous you sound? Are rules more important than someone's life?' she demanded, prompting Clemens to puff up like an angry cat.

He turned to Minna's parents. 'Are you going to let your daughter talk to me like that?'

Minna's mum shrugged. 'Yes,' she replied.

Minna's dad winced.

'Everyone!' Leo burst out, and the voices died down. She looked round at the gathering, at Minna and her family, at Ulf and Clemens, at Judge Harker.

How hard could a maze be? She had spent all her vampiric unlife racing through the Dreadwald – *that* was a real maze. If passing this test would take her one step closer to somehow proving that she was innocent – that fighting the Orphanmaster had been her only choice – then she would do it. She was clever. She was strong and quick.

It was also the only way forward and they were running out of time. Surely Marged would be looking for her by now? Leo could only hope that Lady Sieglinde herself hadn't noticed she was missing.

'I'll take your test, Judge Harker. I'll make my way through your maze.'

And go home, in my body, without a town of angry ghosts behind me, she added silently.

Floating forward into the corridor, Leo wrapped her arms round herself. It didn't feel quite as reassuring as when she had a body. She flinched when her prosthetic leg bumped into and through the back of her equally ghostly knee.

'It's okay!' she called back, catching Minna's eye and raising a clawed thumb. 'I'll see you at the clocktow—'

There was a rumbling tremor and a scraping sound that shook the whole cave. A shower of powdery white flakes fell from the ceiling. Judge Harker held out an arm, her long sleeve billowing, stopping Minna in her tracks before she could move.

Before Leo's astonished eyes, an enormous shard of ice grew up and out of the floor, blocking her path back to the others. As the quaking subsided, she was left nose to nose with her own pallid reflection.

'Minna! Ulf!' she tried calling, but the ice reflected her own voice back at her. The sound ricocheted off into the maze.

Leo winced. As alone as she felt, she wasn't the only one here. Keeping quiet was probably best.

'To *pass, you must find your way out – before* SOMETHING *finds you first.*'

There was nothing else for it. She had to make her way through. Hesitantly Leo crept round the corner, keeping her body low to the frozen ground . . .

She was greeted by another view of herself, even stranger this time from underneath.

Wow, she thought, staring. The floor itself was made of ice mirrors, too. The effect was disorienting; the longer Leo looked, the sicker she felt. She jerked her head up, forcing herself to stare straight ahead. She had come to an immediate crossroads – there were three pathways leading off in different directions.

What a mirrored maze had to do with *being a ghost*, Leo couldn't be sure. Her head felt as though it was full of slimy Dreadwald moss. Her heart was pounding – or, at least, the memory of it was, since she had left real thing behind at the bottom of the Pool of Souls.

I should go, she thought, gritting her fangs. Then, her ghostly cape fluttering behind her, Leo picked a passageway at random and was away.

'Find the way out. Easy as that. Just get out,' she murmured to herself, flying gracelessly through the zigzagging tunnels. 'Pass the test – pass the trial – get back to Mum.' Left, right, left, left, another right – she quickly lost track of which way she had come. The passageways all looked the same. All around her, hundreds of Leos were flying; her reflection chased her deeper and deeper into the frozen labyrinth . . .

From somewhere not too far away there was another rumble.

Leo stopped, ears pricked. She crouched behind a giant protruding stalagmite that jutted up from the chilly floor – there wasn't much else in the way of cover.

Another moving wall? Her floating prosthetic wiggled in what might have been a shrug. Perhaps this maze was like her beloved library up at the castle, where the bookshelves moved and retracing your steps didn't always lead to the exit. Oh, what Leo would give to be back in the library right now, happily lost with the books. In fact, she would rather be ANYWHERE else than here . . .

'Hang on!' she blurted before she could catch herself. She was losing her mind, *talking* to her own ghostly leg. Shaking her head, Leo focused on her own spectral reflection in the wall next to her.

Mirrors. This test was about the MIRRORS, not the maze. Minna always travelled back and forth through them, like the Ghostly Guidelines said! *First-class travel.* Mirrors were the phantom passageways between worlds. As Minna explained it, they were all connected to each other across the different realms. When you were a ghost, all you had to do was picture your destination.

'What if . . .' Hesitantly Leo touched a finger to the wall. Where her ghostly claw met its reflection, a white light rippled out over the surface of the ice. Her clawtip sank right through.

Yes! A victorious grin split her face in two. She beamed at her floating leg, not caring who might be watching.

'Follow me!' Leo whispered. She thought hard about Hollowhome with its mysterious wall of reflective ice. Minna appeared through there all the time, to meet up with Leo in the forest. Leo would fly back to Otto's End and complete her test.

Rearing back, Leo pushed face first into the wall.

There was no resistance. Her vision swam with white for a split second, and then she had stuck her head and shoulders *through the ice mirror* and was looking out on to . . .

Leo frowned. This wasn't Hollowhome.

She was poking out of a mirrored wall identical to the one she had entered. It was another corridor, frosty-cold and almost certainly still part of Judge Harker's underground maze. All around Leo, reflections of herself were looking about in confusion. Then, all at once, they zeroed in on a hulking shadow.

It was so large it sucked in the spectral light, making the tunnel feel stiflingly narrow and dark. Matted fur hung from its muscled body. Great claws scored deep scratches in the frozen ground. Two jutting teeth, each as long as Leo's forearm, dripped with saliva.

A feline eye opened, fixing on Leo's reflection above it. Its gaze darted from one image of Leo to the next, over and over, until it locked eyes with the real thing.

'Oh,' Leo said.

The giant ghostly cat-beast opened its fanged mouth, strings of drool flying as it let loose a bone-rattling roar.

FOURTEEN

A MAZE OF MIRRORS

'**U**WAAAAAGGGHHH!'

Exploding back into the corridor through the ice mirror, Leo rolled backwards. She scrambled aside with only a second to spare; her prosthetic leg sailed away, batted by a paw bigger than her head. The phantom beast was squeezing its body through the wall with aggressive determination, swiping for Leo with its claws.

She flew.

Behind her, the stalagmite was obliterated. Ice splintered as the creature barrelled through it, snorting and snarling. Saliva splattered. Four hairy, muscular legs took off at a loping gait, thundering after Leo down the frosty tunnel.

The thing was fast and it was HUNGRY, its shadowy body stretching and coiling madly with each stride. It certainly wasn't like any wolf or bear – large beasts native to the Dreadwald. If anything, it looked like Button's older and more ferocious cousin, right down to the vertical slits of its pupils and its smoky black fur.

Flying as fast as she could, Leo scoured every inch of her mind. She desperately grasped at any thread of a thought that might save her. At her back the sound of the creature's panting mouth drew closer and closer. It was closing the gap.

Pulling in a steadying breath that her misty lungs couldn't hold, Leo braced herself. They were coming to another crossroads. Identical passageways crisscrossed away in each direction.

'Wait . . .' she told herself. 'Wait for it . . .'

NOW!

Soaring upwards, Leo turned a somersault backwards over the creature's head. It skidded, claws screeching in the ice. Jaws snapped at Leo as she sailed past.

Landing clumsily, Leo wasted no time. Like an arrow shot from a bow, she zoomed straight through the mirrored ice next to her and into another passage of the maze.

From somewhere far away, there was an enraged howl, loud enough to make the frozen cavern shake. With a ringing sound a few icicles fell and smashed. The animalistic cry petered out with a mournful note and was gone.

Leo was safe. For now.

She paused, her wispy body wavering. With a long sigh she drifted down on to her one remaining knee and lowered her forehead almost to the cold floor. In every mirror was the image of a relieved vampire ghost curled up into a ball. Her prosthetic leg shivered at her side.

THAT had been far too close. The beast had smashed the giant stalagmite like it was nothing. If it had caught Leo, it surely would have torn her limb from limb.

Swaying upright, she couldn't help but chuckle. It was a thin wheeze, beginning somewhere behind her translucent ribs, then spreading outwards until her whole body was shaking in mirth. If she didn't laugh, she would cry.

She was *supposed* to be at the Blood Moon Banquet right now, dressed up and pretending to giggle at Mum's Council friends' jokes. She was *supposed* to be dancing and mingling and playing games with the other vampire kids. She was *supposed* to be sitting down to the feast and gobbling as many popping eyeballs as possible.

Instead, Leo was in the Ghostly Realm . . . She was stuck in an underground maze of death . . . She was fleeing a ghost cat-creature that wanted to EAT her . . . She could hardly believe her misfortune.

'Hahahaha!' Leo laughed, tears springing to her eyes. She wrapped her spindly arms round her belly. '*Aaaa*hahaha!'

She was so busy giggling madly, she didn't notice the dark snout emerging from over her shoulder.

More obvious, however, was the thick glob of drool that fell straight through her, splattering on to the ground beneath her foot. Leo slapped a hand over her own mouth. She held very still even as her ghostly body flickered, disturbed by a puff of phantom breath behind her.

Turning her head, Leo stared up the sloping nose of the beast. Its pointed ears swivelled forward. The left one twitched once, twice . . .

And pounced.

Leo gasped as she was knocked to the ground, pinned by a very solid paw. There was a sound like the grinding of glass. The shadowy cat-creature crawled from the wall, its tail lashing and great fangs glinting in the light. Its growl rose higher into a malevolent hiss.

'No!' Leo burst out, striking out with her claws. They went harmlessly, uselessly through her attacker. 'Ugh!' She wasn't even half the ghost Minna was; if Minna was here, she would have skewered the beast already, with an epic battle cry.

The creature screamed. Its body puffed up and its hairy back arched into a striking position. Smoky wisps curled off its form, but it was as heavy as a rock on Leo's chest.

Leo pictured Minna's hand: short and slightly pudgy,

as see-through as the rest of her. In her mind's eye Minna's hand closed into a fist, ready to fight. Leo mirrored the motion with her own hand, feeling the sharp prickle of her claws in her palm . . .

With snapping fangs the creature lunged.

Her eyes closed, her whole body bracing for crushing jaws, Leo threw the hardest punch she could.

Her suddenly solid knuckles connected with the beast's nose.

The creature howled in pain, jerking back. For one precious moment it was stunned, sneezing and shaking its head.

Leo heaved the crushing paw off and rolled to the side.

There was no time to dwell on her newfound power. She dropped down through the mirrored floor, finding herself floating in yet another part of the maze. Her reflection stared at her from every angle, before whirling round to search for an exit.

What do I DO? she thought desperately, speeding away. *Where do I GO?* Behind her, was a slam and a CRUNCH of claws on the ice – she knew that the predator was hot on her heels.

Veering through a mirrored wall led to another icy corridor. Flying through the ceiling led to even more mirrors. Mirrors led to mirrors led to mirrors; there was no escaping this maze. That was, if it even was a maze at all.

It was a PRISON, Leo realised. A prison for a malevolent beast, and she was trapped with it. She had come to a dead end in the corridor, skidding up to her wild-eyed reflection. Next to her, her prosthetic leg bobbed like a fish on a line, carried by the momentum. She could keep on running – fly through the ice mirror and continue on – but the chase would never end.

Crashing round the corner, the terrible creature loomed. It screamed a shrill, reverberating cry. Frozen splinters rained down from the ceiling, falling through Leo to plink on to the ground.

As the cat began to sprint, its heavy paws pounding towards her, Leo reached out a desperate hand. She focused her mind again on the image of the ghost she knew best; in her imagination Minna was grasping for the prosthetic leg . . .

She could have sobbed in relief as she felt the gnarled ankle beneath her claws. The leg was as heavy as the real thing when Leo took its weight – as heavy as it had been the night that Dad had crafted it for her.

Her ghostly heart leapt. She could do some damage with this. The leg bent on its jointed knee when Leo swung it back over her shoulder, braced in front of the icy wall.

Following the mirrors had only brought her deeper and deeper into the labyrinth. No matter where she went, Judge Harker's monster would find her. Every inch of this place was covered in a layer of ice. There was nowhere Leo could go where she wouldn't be followed by her ghostly reflection – and by the cat.

Unless she *didn't* think like a ghost at all.

It was time to think like a VAMPIRE.

The prosthetic leg flew in a heavy arc as Leo swung it with all her strength, aiming right for the mirrored wall. Behind her, the cat-creature sprang up in a soaring leap. Time slowed to a crawl, each fraction of a second spinning out into a small eternity. The beast was suspended in

mid-air, bounding at its prey . . .

There was a piercing CRACK as the leg connected, sending fissures spidering through the wall. The ice held fast for one electrifying moment and then – just as Leo felt wiry whiskers touch her back – it all came shattering down.

Ice fell in thick sheets, smashing to the floor and exploding into tiny pieces. Close to Leo's ear, the cat yowled in alarm. It shied away, rubbing its face on the backs of its great paws.

Bare rock was exposed, dark and weathered smooth. Behind it, she knew, was miles of solid earth and stone. It was more than enough to crush Leo's vampiric body into dust, were she still inhabiting it.

Right now, though, it was Leo's way out.

Clutching the ghostly prosthetic close to her, Leo showed all her teeth in a big grin. She braced herself. *Goodbye, cat*, she thought. *I'm passing the first test!*

Without another glance behind her Leo flew through the rocky wall and zoomed towards the surface.

In Otto's End, the ghostly townsfolk had gathered again outside the clocktower, which loomed over the scene like a giant headstone. The moon was red tonight in Leo's world, but it looked sallow here in the Ghostly Realm, seeming to grow paler as time ticked on.

The night air was filled with jubilant chatter. Everyone had something to say about the murderous vampire – everyone except for the girl called Minna, who was quiet. She folded her arms round herself, scanning the clocktower steps for any sign of movement. The dozing town was almost completely still. Every now and again, something caught her eye – but it was just a leaf or a twig or an errant sock caught on the breeze. The laundryman chased after it, the washing line flapping behind him.

Minna sighed. The handle of the poker felt comforting in her hand. Whatever had been behind that icy wall, in that icy maze . . . Minna was convinced it had to be BAD.

She had never heard of this trial before. Apart from the Orphanmaster, there hadn't been any ghost murders since Minna's arrival in phantom Otto's End – and, apparently, since a very long time *before* her arrival, too. She itched to interrogate Judge Harker again, to demand to know the exact point of this test.

Please, Leo! Minna thought, trying to send her a secret message with the power of her mind. *Please be all right!*

Then, in the middle of the square, the crooked well began to glow. Its lopsided stones shuddered. On its rope the bucket started to rattle, sloshing water. Someone gasped.

'Look!' Translucent faces turned curiously. The hubbub of the crowd took on a hushed air.

A white light winked from deep within the well, growing brighter and brighter as its source sped up towards the surface. A tall spindly figure shot clumsily up into the air, limbs waggling like a nectar-drunk insect. Its raggedy cape billowed. Behind it, one leg lagged behind, detached from the rest of its body.

The crowd groaned in disappointment.

'Leo!' cried Minna.

'LEOOO!' cheered Ulf and Minna's mum, chest-bumping so hard it nearly knocked Ulf's tiara off. Minna's dad was doing an embarrassing dance. Minna thought for a moment that she saw Clemens crack a tiny smile, before he hid his face behind his clipboard.

Judge Harker's expression, however, was carefully blank. She floated over the wintry cobblestones, leading the crowd to where Leo was hovering unsteadily in front of the well.

'I was so worried!' Minna blustered, pulling Leo into a fierce hug. She cleared her throat. 'I mean, you're such a *dunce* on your own; I thought you were doomed for sure.'

'I thought so, too!' Leo's eyes bulged at the memory. 'Minna, there was this HORRIBLE GHOST MONSTER down there in the maze! Like a great big hairy—'

'Sabre-toothed cat,' Judge Harker finished. She scanned Leo up and down, searching for any clues as to what might have happened, but Leo was exactly the same as before: spindly, gangly and translucent. 'He is an ancient and noble hunter from a time very different to now. The rest of his kind are extinct – as, I suppose, is he.' Judge Harker's brow twitched. 'You didn't hurt him, did you?'

The crowd murmured disapprovingly, shaking their heads. The vampire, hurting a CAT?

'How barbaric! I would *never* harm an innocent cat!' the old woman piped up, her wrinkly mouth puckering.

'That's a lie!' Ulf said far too loudly into Clemens's ear. 'We all know what goes into her pies, WAHAHA!'

Clemens looked a bit sick.

'Hurt *him*?' Leo spluttered. 'No! Judge Harker, I had to smash the ice mirror to escape! The cat tried to EAT me!'

'Well . . . yes, that sounds about right.' Judge Harker shrugged her shoulders beneath her robe. Her graceful posture slumped slightly; she seemed tired of explaining facts to criminal children. 'Just because a creature has been dead for millions of years, it doesn't mean he has lost his instincts. Prey is prey. It is natural for a predator to seek its next meal, and YOU were running around in his hunt— In his h-hunting ground . . .'

Judge Harker curled in on herself, hacking another

powerful cough into her handkerchief.

The girls looked away. It was probably rude to stare.

Judge Harker sighed, delicately wiping the corner of her mouth. Her inscrutable expression returned. 'Hm. Regardless, vampire, here you are again. Congratulations. The first test is complete.'

Pocketing the handkerchief, she turned and began to glide back to the clocktower. Her gown flowed around her bare feet. The crowd parted respectfully to let her through.

'Wait, but did she *pass*?' Minna called after her. 'Leo escaped the maze, like you asked. She passed, didn't she?'

Judge Harker didn't turn round. 'The first test is complete,' she said again over her shoulder. 'Follow me. We still have two more to go.' The townsfolk closed in behind her and she was lost in the drifting crowd.

Leo and Minna shared a look of bewilderment.

'Test number two it is,' Minna murmured. 'Are you ready?'

'Can't be any worse than test number one . . .' Leo mumbled back, prompting Minna to throw up her hands in despair.

'Don't say that! Are you *trying* to curse us?'

FIFTEEN

THE BLOOD MOON BANQUET II

Back at the castle, the Blood Moon Banquet was kicking off, Von Motteberg-style. The foyer had been transformed into a dancefloor, whipped up by the zombie quartet who were now playing a lively waltz.

'My goodness me!' Dad shouted, bopping to the beat. 'I'm not exactly a dance machine – but I think I've got it!' His fluffy hair moved independently to the rest of him and he nearly bounced Leo – or, Leo's body, at least – off his big belly in his enthusiasm. Moving stiffly, arms pumping robotically up and down, Leo's empty brain had fallen into something of a trance. Lulled by the movements of the crowd around her, she stomped her slippered feet in time with the rhythm. Rodrigo hung on for dear unlife as he was jostled on top of her head, clinging to the wild strands of hair.

'Did you see where your mother went, Eleonore?' Dad asked. 'I'd rather hoped she might fancy a dance before the meal is served!' He could only just be heard over the din – the whoops from the crowd were a little *too* enthusiastic for the music, but then there were more empty glasses of blood wine than full ones. Next to them, a vampire lord in a bright fuchsia suit was doing a complicated dance move that apparently involved dislocating his own elbows.

Leo said nothing, stamping her feet like Emmeline squashing ants. Distantly she felt hungry for more eyeballs. Marged and the platter had disappeared some time ago. The knight had to prepare the rarely used ballroom for the actual banquet, since it was the only space vast enough to fit the table.

The crowd parted for a moment, allowing a brief glimpse of Lady Sieglinde. Rather than dancing, she was deep in conversation with Lord Ayman. He was smiling brightly. Her eyes were dark in her expressionless face as she stared down at him, like a stalking cat watching a bird, awaiting the right time to strike. All of a sudden, she burst into laughter, her lips peeling back from her fangs. Holding Lord Ayman's pillow, Nesh the butler visibly flinched.

Dad sighed. 'Oh dear . . . I had rather hoped . . . that we wouldn't be straight into business matters tonight, but what can you do? The Council waits for no one.'

His pudgy face was reflected in Leo's vacant black eyes when she turned to look at him.

'I am Leo the Vampire,' she told him.

'Oh, Eleonore – you are every inch your mother's daughter!' Dad gave her a somewhat sweaty kiss on the forehead. He smelled funny – he had probably been tinkering with chemicals in his lab in between mingling with the guests. 'I'm sure she will be free to dance soon – go on and have fun! She'll be very proud to see you having a nice time.'

'Yes.' Leo stomp-walked off into the crowd, her arms lifting up over her head. She dodged the thrashing limbs of the dancers, making her way towards a rare space clear of bodies.

'What kind of dance move do you call *this*?' Rodrigo piped up, sensing the swoosh of sharp claws as Leo pistoned her hands towards the ceiling. 'Ah!' he squeaked as one came too close for comfort. 'Be careful with those, Leo!'

'Leo!' someone called. Leo turned instinctively towards the sound, still dancing.

It was another vampire girl of about Leo's age. She had grey skin and sleek black hair that reached her waist. Her dress was a dark, intricately patterned green that reminded Leo absently of the Dreadwald in the summer. It glittered at the waist with a gold chain, artfully draped, matching her many bracelets.

'I wondered where you were!' the girl said by way of a greeting. Her gaze flickered between Leo's waving hands – first one and then the other, still moving frantically – but she didn't mention them. 'I, um . . . *Florian* said that you would be hiding away in that dusty library, but I thought you'd make an appearance. It *is* your mum's party, after all.'

'Yes.' Inside Leo's head, she pictured a box of cards – like the ones they kept in the library to direct a researcher to the section they needed. Mentally rifling through them, she came to a name. 'Anjali.'

Anjali tucked her long, straight hair behind her ear. The lobe was pierced, glinting with a large and expensive-looking emerald. 'It's been a while since the Blood Moon Banquet came to Castle Motteberg,' she commented, looking around the draughty foyer. 'I can hardly remember the last time I was here. It's . . . quaint.' She wrinkled her nose for a split second before remembering her manners. 'I . . . like your dress?'

'I like your dress,' Leo parroted, her voice completely flat.

'Thank you,' Anjali said primly, starting to bob in a less

violent version of Leo's dance. 'Dad had Madame Kinkatch make it for me. She's the best of the best, you know.'

They danced together for a while. Anjali lifted her knees in a more fluid interpretation of Leo's stomping moves. The quartet sawed away at the strings, suddenly joined by three more zombies, this time wielding trumpets. They opted for a rousing number that was half funeral dirge, half upbeat polka.

'Anjali!' a haughty voice called over the music. 'I said – *Anjali!* Hey!' Another vampire squeezed through the crowd towards them, knocked back and forth by the swarm of bodies. It was a boy – about as tall as Leo, with auburn hair coifed into a perfect bouffant on top of his head. He had just reached Leo and Anjali when he tripped on his dramatically flared trousers and fell down. 'Oof!'

'Florian . . .' Anjali groaned. 'Leo, help me, would you?'

Leo obediently bent down and the two girls heaved him up to stand. Florian dusted off his frilly blue and green shirt, adorned at the lapel with lavish feathers. His eyebrows wiggled as he looked up, as though he could see his own hair to straighten it. He shouldn't have worried; it was as solid as a rock and not a single strand had moved.

'Where did you go?' he demanded, whirling on Anjali. 'I turned my back for TWO MINUTES to get us some blood punch and then you had gone! You abandoned me in this horrible place! Oh,' he said, appearing to recognise Leo for the first time. He showed his fangs in an insincere smile. 'Hello, Leo.'

'Hello,' Leo said, already dancing again. She moved her arms up and down like a praying mantis.

Florian looked her over with a disdainful scoff. 'What is this? Some sort of . . . primitive *Dreadwald* dance?'

Anjali sniffed. '*I* think it's rather good, myself,' she said, with the air of someone who had been putting up with Florian's snootiness for a while. She joined Leo in dancing. Florian looked around for a moment before tentatively joining in, too, moving his arms and legs in jerky motions.

'Mummy says we won't be staying for long,' he said. 'We only brought enough luggage for one night. The air here doesn't agree with me – it makes me ill. Daddy says it's all the mushrooms in the forest. They release SPORES at night.'

Anjali rolled her eyes, looking away. Florian didn't seem to notice.

'I don't know how you can stand it, Leo. It's so damp and cold and crawly! Although I suppose you must be used to it by now. I bet you don't even have any allergies!' Florian shuddered, touching a hand to the back of his own neck. 'Did I tell you that some vile insect BIT ME during the drive through the forest? It's barbaric if you ask me!'

'You're a *vampire*, Florian,' Anjali pointed out. '*You* bite things all the time.'

Florian went a bit green. 'That's disgusting – I do NOT. I prefer to use the fine china, thank you very much.'

'Well, you *will*. When you complete your Hunt of the Waxing Moon like me and Leo. Isn't that right?' Anjali nudged Leo in the ribs.

'Yes,' Leo said, only half listening.

Anjali eyed her curiously, though her smile was still fixed in place.

Florian didn't reply, grumpily moving to the music. He tried a few times to get closer to Anjali, but she kept scooting away. A few of the guests around them had also adopted the stomp dance, which was quickly becoming all the rage.

One song rolled into another and they were joined by Vasily and Vlada, a burly brother and sister from the frozen North. They both had bluntly cut tawny hair that had been half wound up into elaborate topknots, making their pointy ears stick out somewhat. Their identical robes were lined with fur.

'It is good, Leo! The party!' Vlada chirped, beaming toothily. She had also sampled the popping eyeballs; there was one remaining, speared on the claw of her thick pinky finger. Leo's gaze tracked it hungrily.

'Have you chosen it? The penalty game?' Vasily asked eagerly. He flexed his muscles beneath the sleeves of his robe. 'We are ready!'

Vlada gave a cheerful flex, too, her biceps bulging. 'Ready!'

'We haven't decided on this year's game yet,' Anjali

said. There was a glimmer of wickedness in her eye, befitting the group's ringleader. 'Something will come up. Something *fun*.'

The young vampires' games had always verged on the dangerous, possibly because the group so seldom met. Some excitement was in order when you only saw each other once a year.

Their made-up challenges inevitably involved some sort of family heirloom or priceless artefact that would land the unlucky victim in big trouble if things went wrong. They called them the PENALTY GAMES, as refusal to take part usually led to punishment. Sometimes the punishment was more of a game than the actual game itself.

Leo privately wasn't sure how she felt about all of this, but she always went along with it. Tonight, however, Leo's mind was not present. There was only her body: the hungry dance machine. She took no notice when Florian looked at her slyly.

'It's *Leo's* castle,' he piped up. 'I think *Leo* should be the one to play the game tonight!'

'You backed out last time, Florian,' Anjali reminded him serenely.

Florian balked. 'It was *Mummy's best gown*!' he spluttered, his grey face darkening as he stared rapidly from one vampire to another. 'You wanted me to . . . to—' He shook himself. 'I did the penalty! That's the rule! I found a beetle in my bellybutton THE NIGHT AFTER we played!'

'I'm sorry, Leo,' Anjali said, though reluctant to admit it. 'He's right. He did the penalty – and it *is* your turn.'

'Yes,' said Leo, still busy watching the popping eyeball skewered on Vlada's claw.

'*What?*' Rodrigo whispered from Leo's hair. '*What are you agreeing to, girl?*'

'Did you hear that? A voice?' asked Vlada, tilting her head. Leo wasn't listening. From behind Vlada's waving claws she vaguely noticed Dad. He was doing the stomp dance over in the corner of the room, where the contagious moves had managed to spread. There was also Madame Kinkatch, stamping her feet with a sloshing goblet in her hand. She would probably have been lost in the crowd if not for the extra height of her poofy hair, which now glimmered with embedded jewels. The rest of the guests were giving her a wide berth – or perhaps they were avoiding Socrates the giant beetle, who was bobbing his horned nose to the beat.

Florian shook his head. 'We should hurry up and play!' he complained. 'It'll be time to EAT soon! This is BOR—'

'*Ladies and gentlemen, if I may have your attention!*' someone called.

'—ing,' Florian finished meekly, ducking behind Leo.

At the doors to the grand ballroom, Marged held herself upright and proud, clutching her sword. Her armour, polished to perfection, shone in the candlelight. 'Your host, Lady Sieglinde, speaks!' she announced.

The sea of lavishly dressed bodies parted as Lady Sieglinde swept forward, gliding across the foyer to hover before the crowd. Her eyes flashed as she looked out over her adoring subjects. The music died down and all was deathly silent.

The crowd shivered in anticipation . . .

'Honoured guests of Castle Motteberg!' Lady Sieglinde boomed, as loud as a thunderclap. Her black gaze roamed, raking over the watching partygoers as she raised a gnarled hand glittering with opal rings. 'The Blood Moon Banquet is about to begin!'

The crowd leapt and murmured. Another rash of applause spread from the far corner of the room, possibly started by Lord Dietmar, who was staring adoringly at his wife.

Unseen, Leo leaned forward, as quick as a flash, and gobbled the eyeball off Vlada's clawtip.

The ballroom doors swung open, pushed by shambling zombies. All at once, the foyer was aflutter with the shuffling of cloaks, the whisper of ruffles and the clicking of heeled feet. Like the River Mothling running downstream, the colourful crowd began to drift through and take their seats. They were led by Lady Sieglinde and Lord Ayman, already deep in conversation once more. Leo's body walked absently beside her vampire friends, following the flow of guests through the open doors.

Though seldom used, the ballroom was one of the grandest rooms in Castle Motteberg. It was enormous, with a great domed ceiling from which strategically placed spiderwebs dripped. All around the room, statues of Von Motteberg ancestors had been draped with velvet sashes in royal purple, green and Lady Sieglinde's signature grey. An elaborate chandelier loomed overhead, each of its five arms heavy with tinkling crystal and flickering candles.

The table, made of polished oak, dominated most of the space. Long enough to accommodate all the most powerful and important vampires in the world, it was only ever brought out for such occasions. At its head one chair was larger than the others, with a tall dramatically pointed back. With a sweep of her long skirt Lady Sieglinde sank into it. Her wicked claws tapped on the chair's arms that were carved with the heads of snarling beasts.

Filing through, Leo felt a brush of frilly lace on her shoulder.

'Hey,' Florian said, licking his lips nervously, 'I was thinking . . . Seeing as it IS your family party tonight, perhaps . . .' He glanced over at the others – specifically at Anjali and Vlada, who had their heads together, perhaps already hatching a plot for tonight's game. Vasily stared back, unimpressed. Florian cleared his throat. 'P-perhaps you and I should sit together, Leo? Away from the others, I mean. I was going to say – you don't look *too* bad tonight.'

'What?' Rodrigo hissed, hidden atop Leo's head. He clicked his fangs. 'Not too bad? Who *is* this young ruffian?'

'I hadn't really noticed before, but . . .' Florian blushed. 'Your dress is quite lovely. In a plain sort of way. But I rather think that, stood next to someone plainer, it can bring out one's OWN beauty even more, don't you think?' He preened, fluffing his feathery collar.

Leo turned to look at him with blank eyes.

Florian gave her a wide smile.

'No,' Leo said.

'What?' Florian spluttered. His chin disappeared into his neck when he leaned his head back in surprise. 'What do you mean, *no*? You've been saying *yes* all night!'

'We're all sitting together, Florian,' Anjali said, swooping to the rescue. Her bracelets clinked when she took Leo's arm. 'Come on, Leo.'

The group took their places at the long table: Leo, Anjali

and Florian on one side, the twins opposite them. To Vlada's left, there was already a ball of scowling lavender ruffles.

Apparently Madame Kinkatch had added even MORE frills to Emmeline's gown.

'Oh!' Emmeline glowered at Leo across the table. 'There you are! I was wondering when you would make an appearance.'

'Hello,' Leo said, already inspecting the plate in front of her. It was sadly empty. She lifted it up in case any eyeballs were hiding underneath.

Emmeline's nose crinkled. 'I thought you had slithered off into the forest again,' she said, watching her little sister suspiciously. 'You . . . I thought . . . What *are* you doing, bat-breath?'

Leo's plate clunked down on to the table. A few of the guests looked sideways at her, but no one said anything.

'Weirdo worm,' muttered Emmeline.

'Oh, Emmeline!' cooed Vlada, noticing her adorable neighbour. She touched Emmeline's puffy shoulder. 'I love it! Your dress!'

Emmeline slapped Vlada's hand away. 'Paws off!' she snapped.

Finally the guests were all seated. Everyone looked to the head of the table, where Lady Sieglinde was lazily reclining. There was a long pause while she swirled a

goblet of blood wine in her hand. Then, with her other,
she clicked her bony fingers and the feast was
underway.

All around the ballroom, a flurry of Nesh's skeleton
waiters burst into life. They hefted mountainous
platters of food, shuffling everything around on the
table to make room for the feast. Though they tried their
best, Marged's zombies were
struggling to keep up;
they were always
one step behind,
too slow to find
room for their
offering before
another dish
was deftly
slid on to
the table.

'Eyeballs!' Leo exclaimed as a worried zombie shuffled
past, a ginormous brass plate balanced on its arm stumps,
piled high with tasty treats. She greedily reached out and
took her prize.

'Aaaahhh,' groaned the zombie, relieved. Leo set the
huge plate on top of her own. It was so heavy, the table
beneath it creaked.

'Thank you, Miss Leo,' someone said at her shoulder; it was Marged, gently scooting the plate out from Leo's claws. Marged tipped a more reasonable number of eyeballs on to Leo's original plate, placing the rest within reach on the table. 'Are you having fun?'

Leo squelched in reply; her mouth was already full of eyeballs. Marged ruffled her hair fondly, oblivious as Rodrigo was squeezed by her metal hand.

There were cauldrons bubbling with steaming blood soup. There were skewers of grilled ears, deliciously chewy. The selection of finger food – actual fingers, of course – was also very popular; the towering displays were pulled apart by hungry claws as the partygoers all tucked in.

'Mmm!' hummed Vlada appreciatively, chewing on what looked to be a whole hand, grilled until it was crispy.

Vasily grunted in agreement, taking a big bite of wiggly brain.

Florian sipped delicately from his goblet. 'So,' he began, with a hint of a sulk, still stinging from Leo's rejection, 'about our penalty game. *Leo's* penalty game.'

Anjali dabbed at her mouth with a napkin, though it didn't cover her wicked grin. 'I may have an idea,' she said enigmatically.

'Anjali!' Vlada squeaked, delighted. 'I knew it! You are up to something!'

'What is it?' Your idea?' Vasily asked, straight to the point.

'Leo, pass me an eyeball,' Rodrigo hissed, unaware of the IMMINENT DANGER he found himself in.

'Tonight's game . . .' Anjali said, keeping her voice low so as not to alert the grown-ups round the table. Even Emmeline wasn't listening – she was too busy gnawing the head off what might have been a roasted rat. 'Tonight's penalty game . . . will be to retrieve one candle.'

'A candle?' Florian complained. 'That's TOO EASY! Ouch!' He winced as one of the twins – or perhaps both – kicked him beneath the table. He dropped his voice to a hiss. 'There are candles everywhere! That's not *really* a game, is it?'

Crossing his thick arms across his chest, Vasily frowned. 'Whiny boy has a point. It *does* seem a little easy.'

Florian gasped, offended. 'Hey—'

Smirking, Anjali sat back in her seat. Then, without saying another word, she turned her gaze pointedly upwards to where the great chandelier dangled above the table, swaying oh-so-slightly in the breeze from the arched windows. Flames danced on its many arms.

Florian smiled with nasty glee. 'Oh. Yes. I suppose *that is* a challenge!'

SIXTEEN

THE LIBRARIAN'S LOCKET

The first test of the trial of Leo the Vampire was over, and the second wouldn't wait. Voices echoed up the long neck of the Otto's End clocktower, twisting and mingling into an indistinct clamour as everyone was seated. The hands of the great clock face counted out the precious seconds. Floating pensively in the middle of the room, Leo was a ball of worry.

Lady Sieglinde would be stalking across the dancefloor by now. She would be laughing insincerely with Lord Ayman over a goblet of blood wine . . . She would be taking her seat at the head of the banquet table . . .

Or maybe she was wondering where her missing daughter was. While Lady Sieglinde herself was unlikely to notice, the other vampire children would definitely realise something was up. If Lord Ayman had made an appearance, then his daughter, Anjali, would too. She wouldn't fail to spot Leo's empty seat. And if Florian and the twins were at the castle, too, that would mean the whole gang was there without her. There would be a conspicuous Leo-shaped hole in the group, especially if they were planning a penalty game tonight. Leo jiggled her leg and stared up at the ceiling, feeling a bit ill.

'Leo?' someone asked, making her startle. 'You okay?' Minna's frowning face appeared at her shoulder.

'I'm okay,' Leo said, trying to smile reassuringly. Her long fangs poked over her lip.

Minna's frown deepened. Minna really was very different to the vampire kids. She was the type to stand up for herself for one thing – she wouldn't be playing any sort of pointless penalty game. Leo had only known her for a short time, but Minna was the best friend she'd ever had. Even if Leo had accidentally caused her death.

And now, becoming a ghost and meeting Minna's family and seeing the Ghostly Realm, Leo was learning more and more about *Minna's* world, too. It was a shame that the circumstances were so . . . so . . .

Leo's thoughts were interrupted as Judge Harker swept to the front of the room, beckoning to the two townspeople accompanying her. They hefted a long shape between them, which was covered in a billowing sheet that dragged behind, sprinkling flecks of dust. Leo and Minna hopped aside as they flew past and heaved the object on to the head desk.

'Yes, yes, prop it up there – that's great. Thank you.' Judge Harker nodded to her ghostly assistants, who went to join the rest of the congregation. The crowd shuffled to let them in, squeezing into the wooden pews that crowded the cramped room. 'All right, everyone. Settle down. Let's not drag this out all night.' She turned to Leo again. 'This, young vampire, is the second test. I should tell you . . . according to our records, most do not make it this far.'

Leo swallowed, feeling her misty throat bob around nothing. She wanted to demand a pause, a chance to ask questions, but time was so rapidly trickling away from them.

'Judge Harker,' she croaked. 'I'm ready.'

The judge inclined her head. 'Well, your resolve is nice, but I rather think that's for the test to decide,' she said, grasping the edge of the sheet. With a SWOOSH she swept it on to the floor, revealing a long mirror set in an ornate frame.

Despite the state of everything else in the room – the weathered benches, the scuffed floorboards, the stained-glass windows covered in dust – this mirror had been lovingly shined. There wasn't a single smudge on it. Creeping closer, Leo realised that the frame was carved with coiling vines, dotted here and there with blooms. In one corner the little face of a curious wren peered down at her.

Another mirror. Where are they sending me now? she wondered.

'For your second test,' said Judge Harker gravely, 'you will steal into the home of a human and bring back a token of your victory. You must retrieve the locket of the Otto's End librarian.'

There was a crystalline chiming sound as the crowd shifted, their ghostly bodies clinking together. Behind his clipboard, Clemens's quill was moving frantically. Had Leo heard that correctly? The second test . . . was to pinch a locket? That was it?

Judge Harker nodded solemnly. 'This is the test before you. What say you, vampire? Will you rise to the challenge?'

'A locket . . .' Leo murmured. 'A necklace? *This* is the second test?'

'Keep your guard up, Leo,' Minna hissed. 'I'm sure there must be a trap . . .'

'No trap,' Judge Harker said pleasantly, making them both jump. 'The mirror will lead you to the home of the librarian, in the Realm of the Living and the Undead. Find the locket. It is small and silver. It's engraved with a tulip; it's about this big . . .' Judge Harker gestured with one hand, before her brow furrowed and she seemed to shake herself free of some unknown thought. She stood a little straighter. 'Find it and bring it to me. The test will be done and then you're one step closer to going home. What could be simpler? Apart from the Mirrored Cave, I mean.'

The Mirrored Cave hadn't been simple AT ALL; Judge Harker knew that, didn't she? Leo felt as though she had entered a world of opposites, where up was down and down was up. And all the while, back in her world, the red moon was moving over Castle Motteberg, time slipping away . . .

'Of course, you can always decline,' Judge Harker added silkily. 'Should you wish to run instead. You have the option.'

Why do you keep saying that? That's really not *an option at all!* Leo thought. She looked uneasily at Minna.

One hand on the poker handle, Minna gave a tight-lipped shake of her head and then nodded at the mirror.

'Okay,' Leo said, more to herself than to anyone else. 'Don't worry, Judge Harker. I accept your test. I'll find that locket for you.'

Approaching the mirror, her trusty leg floating at her side, Leo tried to take a calming breath. Though her lungs refused to inflate, she puffed her chest out anyway and felt a little braver. In the glass the vampire ghost girl had a look of determination about her.

The home of the Otto's End librarian . . . She had never been there before. She couldn't help but expect a catch, no matter how much Judge Harker might deny it.

As Leo pushed through the mirror's cool surface, she

caught a glimpse of the room behind her – of the twin figures of Minna and Judge Harker – and then the second test was underway.

Stepping out of the mirror, Leo found herself enveloped in tranquil, comforting darkness.

She was in the hallway of someone's house, with floorboards underfoot and walls adorned with peeling wallpaper and various small paintings in rounded frames. A squat table bore a vase of half-wilted flowers.

Even with the lack of light, there was a vibrancy here: a richness to the deep shadows that hadn't existed in the Ghostly Realm. Looking down at her own hands and floating body, Leo saw she was still made of the same spectral light as she had been before. But now the world around her was very real. She really had passed into the next realm. *Her* realm.

She gazed around. At the end of the hallway a door was ajar. It called her closer, drawing her in with the sliver of a view into the next room. Flying up to it, Leo was about to touch the door handle, her hand outstretched to inch it further open, like she might do if she was creeping around Castle Motteberg . . .

You're a GHOST, Leo! she imagined Minna's voice telling her off. Leo stifled a snort and peeked her head through the wooden panel.

Cast in red moonlight from behind the drawn curtains, a modest living room greeted her. It appeared a lot smaller than its actual size due to the bookshelves that were crammed in from wall to wall. Every surface was piled high with the librarian's personal collection of books – and there was even a teetering stack on the floor, threatening to topple over with the slightest breeze.

Do you not have enough at the library? Leo thought, floating past them. Then she considered her own library, up at the castle, and couldn't help but sympathise. There were *never* enough books.

In the centre of the room an armchair and matching footstool faced a potbelly stove, in which the last embers of a fire were smouldering down. A pile of lumpy floral cushions took up most of the space in the armchair, making Leo wonder how a human would even fit in there to sit.

If she were a librarian, where would she keep her locket? Mum kept all her jewellery in a special chest with different compartments, where she stored her brooches and a ring for each pointed finger. Dad had a drawer for his bow ties to keep them nicely laid out. But Emmeline's room and wardrobe were an absolute disaster, no matter how much poor Marged tried to keep them tidy. The floor was a sea of bonnets, booties, ribbons and little collars with lacy frills . . .

Perhaps this was the wrong room in which to be looking for a locket. There wasn't a dressing table to be seen. Leo was about to drift back into the hallway when the pile of lumpy cushions stirred and groaned.

Hair standing on end, Leo zipped behind the armchair. Peeking over its plush back, she looked down at what was, in fact, not cushions at all.

It was the librarian.

She was an older lady, stout of build, with grey hair piled on top of her head. She had a wide wrinkly face in which her small features seemed lost. She wore a long flowery nightie and her feet, done up in pink slippers, were propped up on the footstool to relieve the veins in her legs. Round her neck . . .

Oh no.

The tulip locket reflected the red light of the moon, winking at Leo in the dark.

The librarian mumbled something in her sleep, her eyebrows scrunching together. Her mouth downturned unhappily.

Pinching from an old lady's jewellery box was one (probably, *definitely* wrong) thing, but stealing the locket from ROUND HER NECK was entirely another. Floating over the librarian, Leo leaned in to take a closer look.

It was a simple trinket with square corners and a tarnished clasp, engraved as Judge Harker had described with a tulip motif. The sight of it touched on something at the back of Leo's mind – just for a moment, as though she had seen it before but couldn't quite place where . . . It was also hung on a chain made of something Leo did NOT want to touch.

Silver, she knew, burned vampire skin like touching a red-hot iron. It was right there in the Vampiric Laws. *The Vampire will not touch the purest silver*; everyone knew that.

But then she had left her skin attached to her body, sunk at the bottom of the Pool of Souls. Right now, she had no skin to burn.

'Mhhhrgh . . . no . . .' the librarian mumbled in her sleep. She shook her head so sharply that her crinkly cheeks wobbled.

Leo pulled back, peering down as the human woman settled again with a snort.

Humans really were terrifying. Leo grimaced, nose to nose with the slumbering creature in the chair. Gingerly she reached out a ghostly claw, leaning over the librarian's face to touch the tulip on the locket . . .

Her fingertip sank clean through the metal, through the flowery nightie and harmlessly into the skin beneath it.

'Hurrk!' The librarian coughed around what must have felt like an icy prod to her neck. Leo cringed, shaking her hand. She shrank back behind the armchair, squeezing her eyes shut, praying the human wouldn't wake . . .

The librarian cleared her throat: a horrible rattling sound not unlike a Dreadwald bullfrog in the spring. Then, after what could have been enough time for three Blood Moon Banquets, a deep rumbling snore signalled that she was still mercifully asleep.

I need that locket! Judge Harker had requested it. What *this* had to do with proving her innocence, Leo wasn't sure, but she couldn't fail – not when she had come so far. She gritted her fangs, floating round the side of the chair to get a better look at her target.

The chain had a twist fastener. It lay against the floral fabric covering the librarian's throat, beneath which her human blood was beating steadily beneath her skin . . .

All at once, a queasy feeling came over Leo.

The last time she had been this close to a human's neck, she had been about to bite Minna – back before the fire that had killed both Minna and the Orphanmaster, starting this whole mess.

It would be so easy for Leo to bite this lady. To fulfil her Hunt of the Waxing Moon, for real. The librarian's throat loomed closer as Leo leaned instinctively in, lulled by the promise of fresh blood. She braced a clawed hand on the armchair and . . .

Wait. Leo's eyes widened. *What am I doing?*

Her spectral hand glimmered in the darkness: a reminder that she was no longer in her vampiric body. And even more urgently the locket – Judge Harker's prize – was right under Leo's nose. This wasn't the time for distractions.

Willing herself calm, Leo reached out again. She

focused all her energy into her clawtips – if she could only *touch* the fastening, she would be able to twist it free and take the locket. It would need the gentlest of touches. Gentler than Dad in his lab, handling some dangerous chemical, or Marged holding a butterfly.

There was a soft *clink* as her clawtip touched the chain. The sound sent a zing up and down Leo's spine, but no pain came. For her newly ghostly form silver was no problem at all.

Hah! Leo thought, victorious. She squinted, inches from the librarian's chin, as she carefully began to unscrew the clasp holding the chain together—

'CHILDREN!' the librarian shouted, right into Leo's horrified face.

'Ungh! Argh!' Crinkly eyelids still closed, sitting bolt upright in a move not unlike Lady Sieglinde awakening from her coffin, the librarian gasped. She clutched her chest and shivered violently, having been swept right through by a startled vampire ghost.

Leo spied a flash of grey hair and head-to-toe floral fabric – a split-second glimpse before she flung herself backwards and sank her ghostly body down beneath the floorboards.

Under the floor, a black rat squeaked in alarm, disturbed by the commotion. It scuttled away into the darkness beneath the house, where a hollow foundation kept out the damp of the earth. Leo trembled, listening intently.

'Yes, come in,' she heard the librarian mumble on a wheezy sigh. 'Have you come to exchange your books? Come in, wipe your feet . . .'

The armchair creaked and brisk footsteps moved across the room.

'You're in luck! 'We've had some new tales delivered this morning.'

Who are you talking to? Leo wondered, shivering. *Who's there?*

Leo peeked up from the floorboards. As far as she could see, they were the only ones here. The librarian's back was turned, and she was busy grabbing books from a teetering stack, turning them clumsily over in her hands. An old hardback with a worn cover fell down, pages flapping, to thud on to the floor.

The sound made the librarian pause. When she turned her head, the locket glimmered.

Her eyes were only half open, staring into nothing.

'Oh dear,' she said to no one in particular. 'Never mind. Would you be so kind as to pick that up for me? My back is playing up again.'

Are you . . . sleepwalking? Leo thought incredulously, emerging up to her chin. Leo crept closer, watching intently while the librarian fussed with the books. Every now and again, the old human lady would mutter to herself, her head turning this way and that as though addressing invisible children there to borrow a book.

Gingerly and focusing fiercely on her misty hand to give it form, Leo lifted the fallen book. It was heavy as she held it aloft, rising out of the floor.

'Ah,' the librarian said pleasantly, talking to the wallpaper. 'Thank you, my dear.' She took the offered book from Leo and set it on top of the pile, which was now beginning to lean dangerously to one side.

Definitely sleepwalking, then. Leo wasn't sure whether this was good fortune or not.

She floated up, hovering behind the librarian. The clasp had twisted round and was barely visible, peeking out from beneath the collar of her nightgown.

Please! Leo thought desperately, reaching for it. *Please! Let's get this over with!*

Her clawtip solidified beneath the chain, lifting it cautiously away from the flowery fabric—

'Of course!' the librarian blurted, so loudly that Leo's foggy form was blown aside. 'Over there in our Sciences section!'

Reaching for the clasp again prompted a sudden laugh and a dash to the other side of the room, where there were more books to mindlessly sort.

Twisting the clasp triggered a lecture on proper book care, sending Leo cartwheeling to avoid the librarian's waving arms.

If Judge Harker *really* wanted this locket, Leo considered with a grimace, then she would have to send someone with extra hands. If only Rodrigo was here to get the job done – Leo could have used his eight limbs. Hovering determinedly behind the librarian, turning this way and that to stay glued to her back, Leo struggled to prise the locket's clasp free.

This was her trial. No matter what, she couldn't go back empty-handed.

Out in the hallway, following the librarian's unconscious journey around her house, they passed the mirror. In it, ghostly faces peered curiously out; Leo could feel their eyes on her, watching. There was Judge Harker and Minna. Behind them, the townsfolk crowded in, hungry to see the vampire fail.

Pustules! Leo thought. This wasn't working. Her hands went clean through the chain in her frustration, fading to a cloudy mist and losing their grip. The librarian paused by the front door, brushing imaginary dust off the handle. The locket remained securely fastened round her neck.

'I had rather expected this,' someone sighed quietly, and Leo turned to see Judge Harker's tired stare reflected in the mirror. 'The Living librarian never takes that thing off; many have tried and failed to remove it, but her sleepwalking makes it impossible . . .'

'An impossible test?' Minna whispered at Judge Harker's side. 'But you said it was simple! How is this fair? What does this prove?' She paused, her eyes darting from side to side as she pieced together a thought. 'Wait, Judge Harker . . . you're running this trial based on ancient records. You said it yourself: there hasn't been a ghostly execution in Otto's End for more than two hundred years. The librarian isn't *that* old. Humans don't last that long!'

'Not now, Minna. This isn't the time.'

'How is it that so many have tried to retrieve this locket, unless you mean outside the trial?' Minna's eyes narrowed suspiciously. 'Have you *changed* this test for your own—'

Judge Harker held up a hand. 'The test calls for a token to be retrieved from the Living world. The locket is my chosen token.' She frowned down at the interfering ghost girl who had far too many questions. 'Minna, I am the judge of this town. I am the judge overseeing this trial.'

'But—'

'That's quite enough.' Judge Harker turned back to Leo, undeterred by Minna's questioning. 'Are you giving in, vampire?'

Frustration bubbling up, Leo felt herself waver. She

felt like she might cry; her eyes were burning hot beneath the sneering stares, beneath Minna's helpless anger. What did a locket have to do with what she'd done to the Orphanmaster?

Worse still, thinking back on it, the third Ghostly Guideline had plainly read: *For your safety, do not interact or interfere with the Living.* Leo was pretty sure that stealing a locket counted as interfering.

Why was she being asked to do this?

'The test is complete,' Judge Harker said gently, stepping back from the mirror. 'It's okay. You can come back now.'

Leo barely heard her. *A token of my victory . . .* she thought, staring at the back of the librarian's head. *Judge Harker wants this locket. She's in charge of this trial. We're playing by her rules, whether we like it or not.*

'Vampire!' Judge Harker hissed. 'Return to us so we can get this wrapped up.'

Black smoke fogged the mirror as Minna blew out an irritated breath. 'Judge Harker, I really don't think—'

'No, Minna. Not another word from you. Time is up; the test is over. Come now, vampire! You won't retrieve the locket while the librarian sleeps; it can't be done.'

Frozen in place, Leo thought she felt her ghostly heart lurch behind her ribs.

A truly mad idea came to her.

'Leo?' she heard Minna call out, hushed.

But Leo's mind was made up. She raised a hand, balling it into a fist. It took all her concentration to give it solid presence, willing it into reality.

Turning away from the shocked faces in the mirror, Leo knocked three times on the door next to the librarian's head.

There was a gasp from the mirror.

'Interfering!' someone uttered.

'Lawbreaker!' another voice spat.

The ghosts fell silent, drawing back from the mirror's surface until it reflected only the dark hallway back to itself. Nodding, the librarian's wrinkly eyelids fluttered open and she gave a muffled snort.

A ghostly statue, Leo was stuck in place as the librarian looked back up the hallway, blinking in confusion. By some miracle she didn't turn round. If she had, she would have come face to face with a ghost equally as terrifying as it was *terrified*.

Rubbing sleep from her eyes with one hand, the librarian reached for the key to the door with the other.

'Now, who is that at this hour?' she grumbled aloud, squinting at the lock.

Now! Leo's brain supplied, making her limbs jerk in panic. *Go! Now!*

Following the VERY-MUCH-AWAKE librarian's every

move, staying firmly behind her, Leo gripped the clasp of the locket. There was a KER-CHUNK as the bolt slid open and then a snowy gust was pouring into the house.

'Hello?' the librarian called, shielding her face with her hand as she leaned out of the front door. Upside down, Leo almost fumbled, but managed to keep her grip. Her clawtips delicately twisted, trying to pull the two ends of the chain apart . . .

'Oh, for goodness' sake . . . REALLY? AT THIS TIME OF NIGHT?' the librarian yelled down the lane, shaking her fist. 'Disturbing old ladies while they sleep!'

Jostled by the movement, Leo hung on. She felt the chain pull tight round the librarian's neck for one incriminating moment, before she hastily slackened it.

'Well, I never. Someone's idea of a joke, I suppose.' The librarian sniffed, turning back into the house. Unseen above her head, Leo rotated round, her leg waving in and out of the wall as she went. She was so close; she just had one more twist and . . .

Yes!

There was another CLUNK as the librarian locked the door, at the same time as the clasp clicked apart in Leo's hands.

There was a chorus of ghostly gasps from the mirror.

The chain, and the locket, slid free.

SEVENTEEN

A FINAL TEST

merging from the mirror, back in the ghostly clocktower and equally ghostly Otto's End, Leo gripped the locket like her unlife depended on it. It took every effort not to drop her prize. A strange thought came to her as she considered it, solid in her phantom claws: right now, this locket felt more *real* than she was, despite them both having come from the same realm.

'You did it!' someone cried, and there was a glassy squeal as a small body collided with Leo's own. Minna held Leo's hand triumphantly aloft, leaning in to examine the locket. 'Yes! There it is! I can't believe you snagged it!'

'Minna,' Leo whispered urgently, 'what you said back there, when I was on the other side of the mirror . . . Do you think Judge Harker is—'

Behind them, someone coughed.

The girls turned, shrinking smaller. Judge Harker's

shoulders quaked as she covered her mouth with her handkerchief. She held up one finger, doubling over as the convulsions wracked her body.

'Vampire,' she said hoarsely, when they had subsided, wiping a smudge of black from the corner of her mouth. 'You have something for me.'

Straightening up, standing taller, Leo nodded. She held out the locket for inspection, wincing when she lost her nerve and it fell through her claws – but Judge Harker's slim hand was there to catch it.

'My locket,' Judge Harker murmured, drawing it towards her heart, turning it this way and that. 'I . . . thought it was impossible. Until now, no one has been able to get close to it. She never takes it off. She moves around in her sleep.'

'Your locket?' Leo stared, watching as Judge Harker rubbed the pad of her thumb over the locket's tulip detail. 'I thought this belonged to the librarian?'

'Perhaps so. But before that, it was mine. And now . . . it is mine again.'

Deftly, delicately, Judge Harker opened the locket, revealing the tiny hidden compartment inside. Leo and Minna subtly tried to lean closer, curious . . .

Judge Harker bowed her head. 'Of course,' she said quietly, looking down at the empty space. If there had been anything inside once, it was gone now. Judge Harker cleared her throat and snapped the locket closed. 'Well. It seems, despite my doubts, that the second test is indeed complete. There is one FINAL TEST before deliberations will begin.'

The Otto's End townsfolk muttered amongst themselves, leaning their heads together. From the pews their ghostly white eyes threw Leo into a terrifying spotlight.

'Did I . . . did I pass the second test?' Leo asked Judge Harker haltingly, trying to ignore the scrutiny of the crowd. 'You have your locket. I brought you what you wanted.'

'Whether you pass or not is to be judged by the court,' Judge Harker said curtly. The crease of a frown crossed her translucent brow as she looked Leo up and down. 'You . . . are brave, vampire. But also presumptuous. Our laws have been in place since long before you were born. If you keep asking questions at every turn – if you *both* keep asking questions . . .' She shot Minna a serious look. 'I'm afraid it will only lead to trouble.'

Leo lowered her head.

At her side, however, Minna drew herself up.

'Just because something is old,' she told the judge, 'it doesn't make it the only way! Why is it wrong to ask questions? We have a right to know!'

'Minna, the law is complicated. You are certainly very bright and your inquisitiveness is admirable – but you need to trust me.'

'No! I've had enough of all this! I think that this law, this *trial*, ought to be changed!'

Leo was sure she felt her heart seize. She gaped at her friend. The ghostly townsfolk fell into scandalised silence and Clemens dropped his clipboard.

'W-Wilhelmina!' he cried.

Minna threw up her hands. 'Judge Harker, please! What do ice caverns or giant cats or lockets have to do with the death of the Orphanmaster?'

'I've been *very patient* with you, Minna,' Judge Harker bit out. Her gaze flitted around the clocktower, at the people all watching her, waiting for her to get the court under control. Her face glowed brighter white across her cheekbones and the tips of her ears, spreading down her neck. 'I told you – I am in charge! This trial ultimately comes down to ME!'

'Then you should be the one to tell us WHY, at this supposed trial, we haven't been given a chance to properly speak!'

Leo had known Minna was brave, but this . . . felt like a different sort of courage somehow.

Judge Harker's jaw tightened and her slender shoulders

shook. Her impassive mask was cracking. She was so much taller than Minna, looming over her.

'I *understand* that we have laws,' Minna continued, undeterred. 'I *understand* that you want to protect all of us in Otto's End. But when WE KILLED the Orphanmaster,' she added, grabbing Leo's arm, 'it was for a good reason! There was something very wrong with that man! He was scheming to HURT children – he was going to go after my friends and turn them into ghosts, too! He would have broken all your Ghostly Guidelines ten times over!'

Judge Harker squeezed her eyes shut. All around them, the clocktower seemed greyer. Exhausted. It was as though all vibrance had been sucked from the scene, the brickwork turning crumbly and dry, the beams breaking out in cracks. Above them, was a rusty grating sound as the great gears ground to a halt. Leo leapt in alarm as Minna's grip on her arm tightened.

When Judge Harker stared them down again, her gaze was colder and harder than ever. 'There is a difference,' she spat, 'between what you INTEND to do and what you ACTUALLY do.'

'I agree!' Minna retorted angrily, uncowed by the scene around them. 'But what would have happened if we had failed to act? If we'd let the Orphanmaster murder us both and then rampage through town? The Living children are here, too – my old friends; they deserve to be safe! You can't deny that Otto's End exists in the other realm as well. It's not *just* full of ghosts like us!'

Judge Harker's brow pinched. She looked to the crowd again, to Ulf and Clemens, to the watching townsfolk. When she glanced down, next to her elbow in its floaty sleeve, the gavel and block sat silently on the head table.

Her expression hardened. 'You're speaking of things that we *cannot know*,' she said tightly. 'We don't *know* that the Orphanmaster would have hurt the children, no matter what he said. The court deals only with FACTS, Minna.'

'But I DO know,' Minna insisted. 'I knew, Judge Harker. He would have brought his evil to the Ghostly Realm, too – *that's* a fact. That's why I fought so hard to stop him. It's also why I needed Leo's help.'

There was a tense pause. Judge Harker and Minna, with Leo in tow, were staring each other in the face. Behind them, the crowd burst into an uproar of outraged voices:

'Change OUR LAWS? Who does this girl think she is?'

'Plotting murder with a vampire! I think that says it all!'

'That's my daughter!' Minna's mum shouted, shaking a fist. 'And she's right! Why shouldn't the stuffy laws be changed if they're not working any more?'

Silence fell.

'We should broil them both!' the old woman said decisively, prompting a cheer from the crowd.

'Babette,' Minna's mum growled, 'I know we are neighbours, but I will fight you myself if you don't be quiet!'

'EVERYONE needs to be quiet!' Judge Harker boomed, holding up a hand. From it the locket dangled. She looked hard at Minna, and then at Leo.

For a single heart-lifting moment Leo wondered whether Judge Harker had changed her mind. Perhaps she would hear them, after all. Perhaps she would allow them to explain the terrible circumstances that had led to their final battle with the Orphanmaster.

All around them, the clocktower groaned, wind rushing up its long neck as though it was taking a breath. The splintering cracks closed up and disappeared. The rust receded from the gears and cogs and the clockwork began to tick again. Judge Harker's pinched expression relaxed and the lines of her face smoothed.

'The third and final test is upon us,' she said quietly and calmly. 'We've lingered too long as it is; we should finish what we have started.'

The townsfolk drew steadily closer, flying through the benches until they were squashed shoulder to shoulder. The blue-white lights of their bodies flared, sparking in a way that seemed . . . *eager*. Ulf, Clemens and Minna's parents were caught in the push, looking round at their neighbours in confusion as they were nearly squeezed out of the clocktower walls.

Finally letting Leo go, Minna met her gaze helplessly. She seemed to be about to say something, when Judge Harker beat her to it—

'A battle to the end with a champion of ghostly kind.'

The clocktower fell into deathly stillness.

A battle? Judge Harker wanted Leo to *fight*? Leo froze. She looked instinctively to Ulf; he was a huge man, with the body of a warrior. Would he not be an ideal choice for a ghostly champion? He had probably fought a great many in his swashbuckling career . . .

'I . . . I'm not . . .' Leo began, shaking her head. 'I don't want to *fight*, Judge Harker – isn't that what I'm on trial for?'

None of the trial had made any sense to Leo, but this was surely madness.

'A test of your ghostly combat skills,' Judge Harker continued, ignoring her plea. She reached for the gavel, turning it idly over in her hands. 'An arena from which only one will emerge – and the other will languish for ever in eternal darkness, never to return to the world they knew.'

Judge Harker looked Leo in the eye.

'You will fight *me*.'

'Wait! Wait! Hang on one minute!' Clemens was frantically rustling papers. He slapped the clipboard into Ulf's hands while he scanned over two fistfuls of ghostly documents. 'This is . . . Are you sure, Judge Harker? This . . . seems quite irregular. I'm not certain this is right? Ah . . .' He spotted something at the bottom of one of the pages. 'Hm. Oh dear . . .'

'It's my responsibility,' Judge Harker replied, as though a BATTLE TO THE END was somehow the simplest thing in the world. 'The third test *must* go ahead if this trial is to conclude.'

A knot of fear and confusion crawled up Leo's ghostly throat.

'I don't want this,' she said. 'I d-don't want to fight you. I don't want anyone else to get hurt!'

'Me neither.' Judge Harker placed the gavel back on its block, making everyone jump. 'That's why we have to go, vampire. One of us will fall to justice, and then the trial will be finished. Let's not put off the inevitable.' She flew through the desk, her hand outstretched towards Leo. 'Come with me. Everything will become clear.'

There was something compelling about her stare. Leo drifted forward a floating step before she could think to stop herself, her own hand lifting. It was as though Judge Harker somehow had the mesmerising Will, the power that vampires use to hypnotise their prey.

'Leo, don't—' Minna began – a warning, but it was too late.

Judge Harker's hand gripped Leo's own, as smooth and cold as glass. The judge smiled, though it didn't reach her eyes. A phantom power thrummed from her, rattling through them both until Leo's fangs began to chatter.

'Good girl,' Judge Harker murmured.

'Wait!' Leo heard Minna call out. When she looked back, Minna was surrounded by the townsfolk of Otto's End, blocking the path between them. 'Hang on! Where are you going? Get out of my way! LEO!'

Ulf threw Clemens's clipboard through the wall. Next to Minna, crowded in by ghosts on all sides, Wilhelm and Willa bowed their heads.

Holding tight to Leo's hand, Judge Harker dragged the killer vampire through the clocktower wall and into frosty Otto's End.

EIGHTEEN

A. H.

Before Leo's astonished eyes, the Dreadwald was shifting.

The silvery trees were muted, looking greyer and greyer in the Ghostly Realm's half-light. As Judge Harker and Leo flew, once-bright branches withered and shrivelled, bark flaking away as they became gnarled and dry.

'What is this?' Leo seized up as her beloved forest seemed to sicken and age in an instant, eaten from the inside out by a creeping rot. 'Judge Harker! What are you doing?"

But Judge Harker said nothing. Her hold on Leo's hand didn't falter even as Leo tried to pull away. Together, the two ghosts soared through the forest. There was nothing Leo could do but follow, her mind awhirl with fear – until, finally, they came to a clearing that she recognised.

'Oh no,' Leo whispered.

Before her, Hollowhome was being steadily petrified in dull, lifeless stone. The great tree was eerily still. Her life force, usually beating away anywhere her giant roots spread, was dwindling – Leo could sense it.

Judge Harker finally released her grip and Leo sped to the tree. Lying her cheek against the trunk, she knew that tears were welling up without being able to feel them.

'What have you *done*? Judge Harker, why are you doing this?'

'This is the conclusion of the trial,' Judge Harker said behind her. 'I told you: this is the final test.' When she drifted closer, the frozen earth cracked and blistered beneath her bare toes, drawing a ruined trail across the forest floor.

Why was it, Leo wondered, that whenever there was trouble with ghosts, it was the forest that always seemed to suffer? It had been the same with the Orphanmaster – he would have destroyed the whole Dreadwald if not for Leo and Minna.

'I don't mean the test!' she burst out. 'I *mean* whatever you're doing to the forest! You need to stop – this tree is special! She's important!'

The white moon hung low above them, reflected in the sluggish stream of the River Mothling. Thick scum floated on the surface of the water, gathering around the rocks and winter rushes that were rapidly turning black.

To Leo's dismay Judge Harker was unmoved. If anything, she only looked as worn out as she had done since the trial began.

'Are you prepared, vampire?' she sighed. 'I don't know about you, but I am ready for all of this to be over.'

'No! No, I'm not ready!' Leo blurted, rearing back. 'Plea—'

There was a grinding crunch as she was slammed by a wall of ghostly force. She flew backwards, her ears ringing from the impact, and skidded to a halt on the other side of Hollowhome. Judge Harker sailed straight through the tree, advancing on her.

Leo staggered upright. She had DEFINITELY felt that. She tried to brace herself, gnashing her teeth when Judge Harker sent her flying again with a sweep of her long sleeve. Leo was certain she felt the horrible ringing sound right down in her non-existent bones.

'One of us is getting out of this!' Judge Harker called. 'Who will it be? You or me?'

'I won't fight you! I won't do it— Aaarghh!'

Her foot flailed as they clashed. She grabbed Judge Harker's arm, battling fruitlessly to pull free. She couldn't have expected this. Judge Harker was slim but she was STRONG; her phantom hold on Leo was like being clamped in the jaws of a bear.

'What are we *doing*?' Leo shouted desperately. 'Ghosts can't DIE – not like this! You n-need the ghost-killing ingredients!'

Judge Harker's eyes were sombre as they stared into Leo's face. 'Oh, Leo. Do you think that dying is *really* the worst fate?'

With an almighty shove Leo broke away. She zipped for the treeline, trying to run . . .

There was a horrible, sick feeling as she approached the edge of the clearing. Something was repelling her, holding her back. When she looked down, a thick sludge of black ooze had spread out in a ring round Hollowhome, enclosing the clearing in a sticky, inky circle.

She was trapped in a ring of dark power.

'As the test demands,' Judge Harker intoned behind her, 'a battle to the end. I realised shortly after my death that my abilities are . . . somewhat unusual, as YOU will find out first-hand!'

Leo tried to fly for the piney canopy, but there was no way out. She bumbled along like a beetle caught beneath glass in Dad's lab.

The judge and the accused hovered opposite each other high in the branches of Hollowhome. Leo sagged, her head full of fog. She felt as though some illness had taken root, perhaps thorny throat or toad tummy. But there was no Marged to tuck her into bed with a warm cup of blood.

Marged was up at the castle at the Blood Moon Banquet in another realm entirely. None of Leo's family knew where she was – *again*. Minna had been held back by the ghosts of Otto's End. No one was coming to help.

There was only Judge Harker, floating amongst the twisty Hollowhome branches.

'It's pointless, Leo,' she said calmly. 'You're right – killing a ghost is a tricky business. An oversight on the part of whoever first wrote this trial, I will admit.'

'Then . . . let's stop this and head back to Otto's End!' Leo tried. 'We can go back and look over the evidence. Finish the trial. All go home!'

Judge Harker smiled. 'Wouldn't that be nice? Unfortunately those ancient lawmakers didn't count on a judge like *me*.' There was a creaking, popping sound as the Hollowhome branches twisted painfully tighter, the stony grey colour creeping further and further up. 'Death isn't the only option, Leo, not while I'm in charge.'

Tears welled again before Leo could steel herself. 'No . . . Please . . .' When she reached out to touch the bark, it crumbled like dust beneath even the gentlest brush of her misty clawtips.

'Living things don't tend to survive between realms,

Leo,' Judge Harker was saying. When Leo looked tearfully up at her, the judge had wrapped her arms round herself. 'I wondered for a long time, why me? Why is that *I* can rip reality open? Every ghost has their gift, but is this not more of a curse?'

'I . . . I don't . . .'

'I thought maybe it's because of my indecision. Maybe it's . . . because of the kind of person I was, in two minds about my path, about what I wanted to do.' Judge Harker sighed. 'I didn't know myself yet, when I died. Maybe I was still too young. But perhaps it was all leading up to this moment – to this crucial decision, right now! Do you understand? One of us will remain here for ever, between worlds. Unable to touch or hear or feel. Locked away for all eternity.'

'Who *are* you?' Leo blurted, wiping her face on her spectral sleeve. Maybe she could buy some time, some room to think, to find a way out. 'Who are you really? I feel . . . I feel like we've met.'

'We haven't. We've never met. You've been lucky.'

'Lucky?' Leo shook her head. Her vision swam, wavering at the edges with the motion. She focused fiercely on Judge Harker's bright form. Perhaps she had a weak point somewhere.

'Had we met when I was alive, Leo, I'd have staked

you where you stood, the first opportunity I had.' Judge Harker's mouth quirked at the corners, as though she was recalling a faraway memory. 'Believe me when I tell you: I wouldn't have missed. I didn't need ghostly powers back then.'

Drawing back, Leo tried to tuck herself behind the stony branch. It was useless, she knew. 'You . . .' Her voice cracked; she shivered and tried again. 'You were a *vampire hunter*?'

If Leo had had any blood in her, it would have turned to ice.

'I was,' Judge Harker confirmed. 'Or I *am*. It's impossible to leave the hunting life behind, no matter how much I try or how dead I am.' She gave a rueful half-smile. 'I suppose you might say that killing monsters is my calling – but really, it's the only thing I'm good for.'

Round her neck, the locket floated. The tulip reflected the ghostly light, glimmering. Through the nauseating sickness that gripped her, Leo clutched at invisible threads, trying to tame her spiralling thoughts.

She *had* to get out of here. She had to get back to Minna.

'You never met me, but did you ever meet the Orphanmaster, Judge Harker?' she asked suddenly, fearing that the judge would attack again if she stopped talking. 'Did you know him?'

'Did I *know* him . . .' Judge Harker inclined her head, looking at Leo with wide eyes. Her shoulders hitched beneath her floaty robe, creeping upwards, before she came back to herself, blinking. 'Why, yes. Yes, I did, once. Better than anyone.'

'H-how?'

There was that feeling again. Her face . . . it was definitely one Leo had seen before.

In a portrait.

With tulips.

In the Orphanmaster's room, the night of the fire at the orphanage.

'Well,' Judge Harker said, taking the locket delicately between her fingertips, 'because I am Agnes Harker. I was Bill's wife.'

'You're . . . you're *Agnes*?' Leo pointed a shaking claw before she could stop herself. 'Minna told me your story – you died looking after sick children . . . Your death drove the Orphanmaster to madness.'

'That was a long time ago,' Judge Harker sighed. 'My Bill . . . He lost himself to hatred.' Her mouth trembled and then set into a grim line. 'It's why I left my dagger on the driveway, for the children to find, in case they should ever need to protect themselves from him. It was all I could do for them – and even that was illegal. It's forbidden for us to interfere in the world of the Living.'

The dagger? Leo had entirely forgotten. Fumbling with the pockets of her cape, she found a familiar item; it was indeed the tooth-shaped dagger, rendered now in the same misty glow as the rest of her. Leo always brought it with her, so of course it had been on her when she'd entered the Pool of Souls. She drew it out and her hands shook as she looked down at its leathery covering.

'This . . . this is YOURS?'

Slowly Leo drew the dagger an inch from its sheath. She already knew the inscription on the blade – A. H. – though it still made her shiver to see it.

A. H. Agnes Harker.

Wife of the Orphanmaster. Guardian of orphans.

Vampire hunter.

'It was mine, yes,' Judge Harker said. 'Although it rather looks like it's yours now. Convenient to have a Spirit Anchor that fits in your pocket. Not everyone is so fortunate. I think Ulf holds the record for most unwieldy Anchor.'

'I can't believe it,' Leo rasped, only half listening. She looked wildly from the dagger to Judge Harker. 'I can't believe you're here!'

'I had unfinished business. My work wasn't over so I remained as a ghost. I still had children to protect. I just never thought . . . I would be trying to protect them from *him*.'

'You . . . Ah, gosh, you must be so angry with me . . .' Leo fretted. 'I mean, for killing your husband.'

'Leo, I laid Bill to rest years ago. There was none of him left in what the Orphanmaster became.' The judge fixed Leo with a serious stare. 'Do you think I don't know what had to be done? Do you think I don't know of his misdeeds? You and Minna did the RIGHT thing. Your actions protected the children of Otto's End.'

'Then . . . then why . . .' Leo clutched the dagger tightly as she stared around them at the rotting clearing. 'Why the trial? If you're not angry – if you *really* don't blame me – then what are we doing here? I don't want to hurt you!'

The sick feeling surged. Leo bent double, coughing into her hand. When the fit subsided, her palm was stained with black.

Ugh . . . She grimaced in disgust, gritting her fangs. What was happening to her?

'The Orphanmaster was far from the only monster in this forest,' Judge Harker said, oblivious to Leo's increasing distress. Either that, or she didn't care. 'After his death . . . I thought I would move on – I *should* have moved on – and yet here I am. Still trapped in the Ghostly Realm, with this horrible ghostly power, good for nothing but causing harm. Why do you think that is, Leo? Doesn't that seem unfair?'

Leo coughed weakly, feeling more black slime burbling up. She gripped the dagger hard enough to make her knuckles creak.

'There must be something else out there for me,' Judge Harker continued. 'Another evil I have to defeat before I can be at peace.'

She turned her face skywards, towards the mountain and Castle Motteberg.

'Our laws have prevented me from hunting like I used to. Vampires are foul beasts, that much is true, but you *still* inhabit the Realm of the Living and the Undead.' She drew herself up taller, fiercer, whirling back round to loom over Leo. 'I am the judge of Otto's End. I have a duty towards my people. I uphold the law; I do not break it. To *interfere* in another world without due cause would be illegal.

'But now, with you here, Leo von Motteberg . . . there is indeed a way for me to finally reach the monster you call LADY SIEGLINDE.'

For a long moment Leo couldn't speak. Her chest heaved, her throat clogged with something horrible.

'You . . . you *want* to go to the castle?' she gasped out. 'You *want* to fight the vampires – t-to fight Mum?'

'Of course I do. I told you, Leo: I am a hunter. My family has tracked Lady Sieglinde's movements for generations.'

'But—'

The branches of Hollowhome creaked in defenceless alarm as Judge Harker floated through them, advancing on Leo.

'Lady Sieglinde has taken countless innocent lives,' Judge Harker said plainly. 'But it's clear to me that there is no malice in you – *you* aren't a typical vampire at all. Your resolve, your bravery, your loyalty to your friend.' She paused, staring Leo down as though she was a particularly difficult puzzle. 'Yet you're not a ghost, either, not a proper one.'

Leo couldn't argue with that. She'd known that from the beginning.

Judge Harker huffed a small breathy laugh. 'A true ghostly citizen wouldn't have smashed the ice in the Mirrored Cave. Or managed to take the locket. You have *impressed* me, Leo. You are not the conniving creature I thought you to be.'

I'm . . . I'm not?

'But no matter.' Judge Harker straightened her flowing sleeves. 'It was inevitable that we would wind up here, you and me. A final battle, then your ordeal will be over and my work can begin!'

Quaking, Leo lifted her see-through hands. They were now bubbling with black sores, tight and painful. She screamed as Judge Harker took hold of them, folding them into her own grasp, squeezing round the sheathed dagger.

'Prove, Leo the Vampire, that you can defeat a ghost again!' Judge Harker said breathlessly. She was suddenly energised, a hint of madness overtaking her. 'Leave me here and Otto's End will arrange for your execution. Or if you cannot, if you could not POSSIBLY fight another ghost, your innocent soul will remain trapped for eternity. Lady Sieglinde will face your consequences for you, as the TRUE source of this evil!'

'That's not *fair*!' Leo cried. 'You *tricked* me! There's no way to win! If this is true, then I can NEVER g-go home!'

She didn't wait for a reply. As she wrenched her stinging hands free, the dagger fell, bouncing harmlessly away. There wasn't time to spare it a thought; Leo zipped towards the earth, trying to fly through the frozen ground and escape beneath the surface. Pockets of ooze bubbled up like geysers, exploding on all sides as she rolled clear of them.

'Come on now!' Judge Harker called, somewhere overhead. 'I've fought PLENTY of vampires – I know you have more fight in you! What would your MOTHER say?'

Stumbling, coughing and covered in sores, Leo was a

limp scrap of fabric, blown in the breeze. Whatever awful power Judge Harker had – this ghostly sickness – it was draining her. Her one remaining leg stuck in the phantom sludge and she tumbled head over heel.

'Oh dear . . .' Judge Harker said. When Leo looked up, her attacker was hovering over her. Judge Harker's face creased in what might have been sympathy. 'This was less interesting than I'd hoped, but perhaps it's best. I had rather hoped to slay Lady Sieglinde before the dawn.'

Something was drawing Leo down into an inky darkness. All around her, the trees bent and warped. Hollowhome wavered madly. Up was down and down was up – and Leo herself was turning inside out, watching as the pale moon spun across the sky.

One of us will remain here for ever, between realms.

Reality was splintering. Colours burst from nowhere, then streamed and ran backwards like dripping paint. *This* was Judge Harker's true ghostly power.

'LEO!' someone shouted.

There was a white blob emerging from the trunk of Hollowhome. Its features swam on its round face.

Something streaked towards them, whistling through the air. There was a reverberating ringing sound and Judge Harker gasped, struck through with a long hooked spike. It jutted out of her shoulder like a giant thorn – the POKER,

Leo realised, blinking. The clearing slowed, bringing its crazy dance to a close. The trees straightened. The black rot retreated enough for Leo to worm a hand free, clear of sores.

'Minna!' she gasped. Her claws curled round the ankle of her ghostly prosthetic; she swung the leg, smacking Judge Harker in the chest and knocking her backwards.

Minna, as usual, meant business. She grabbed Leo by the scruff of her neck, hauling her up. When she held her left hand skywards, the poker pulled free of Judge Harker's body with an unpleasant crunch, darting faithfully back to its owner.

'How are you *here*?' Leo cried. 'Judge Harker, she's—'

'We need to go – follow me!' Minna said, snatching the poker out of the air.

They both looked back to where Judge Harker was floating on her knees, her head lowered. She was wracked with another coughing fit, her ribs quaking with each powerful burst.

I've failed, Leo thought, squeezing her eyes shut. Minna pulled her along, through Hollowhome's grey bark and inside the great tree.

What would they do? What *could* they do?

'New plan!' Minna told her, as though reading her mind. She pushed something into Leo's hand: the fallen dagger.

'Here, take this. We need to get your vampire body back.'

'But how? Minna, we can't leave! Judge Harker has put s-some sort of CURSE on the forest; there's no way out!'

With the tip of the poker Minna tapped the icy mirrored coating on the inside wall of Hollowhome.

'How do you think I managed to reach you here?' she snapped. 'HH *is* our secret base, isn't she? She's on our side!'

Leo's eyes widened. Her mouth wobbled before she could pinch her lip between her fangs. 'Minna, I—'

'Yes, yes!' Minna flapped a hand. 'Let's cry later – come on! Before the judge follows us!'

With one last look around her beloved base Leo let herself be squeezed through the mirrored ice portal, and then Hollowhome was gone.

Water rushed past Leo's ears. Far away, a weak, red light filtered down in undulating beams. Tiny bubbles floated upwards as pockets of air were disturbed around the bottom of the pool.

'—here!' Minna was shouting, her voice muffled by the water. 'It's not here!'

It was disorienting. Leo felt as though the water was

filling her ears, rushing into every space inside her ghostly head, weighing her down.

'Leo! Focus!' When Leo eyes snapped open, Minna's face swam into view. 'Your body isn't here, Leo!'

They were at the bottom of the Pool of Souls, where Leo had swallowed the splitting stone and sunk her body at dusk. Minna was right: when Leo searched frantically around her, there was nothing but old bones and pebbles and fine silt. There were no vampires to be seen.

'Oh, pox and pustules!' she gasped. Her voice sounded strange underwater. No air bubbles emerged from her mouth. She looked to Minna in desperation. 'What *now*?'

'It should be right here! You tell ME, it's YOUR body!'

'No one followed us here, did they? No one could have stolen me away?' Leo worried aloud. 'And it's not as though my body could . . . c-could GET UP and walk off without me!'

There was a pause.

Minna frowned. 'You don't think . . . ?'

'No! I really *don't* think!' Leo protested. 'I don't *want* to think!'

'Where would a vampire's body have gone in the Dreadwald?' Minna wondered. Then, perfectly synchronised, they both looked *up*.

As they emerged from the Pool of Souls, not a single

ripple disrupted its glassy surface. The two ghosts shot upwards, flying past Leo's abandoned boots, high into the sky above the pines. In the distance Leo and Minna could see the red moon starting to sink behind the jagged, twisting spires of Castle Motteberg. They could see the distant rooftops and crooked chimneys of Otto's End. Leo's phantom insides swooped and squiggled, and then her body seized up all over. Even her ghostly prosthetic, floating at her side, shivered in alarm.

'Oh no . . .' Minna whispered. 'Oh no, no, no . . .'

From their vantage point, they watched the ghostly procession flooding out from the top of the Otto's End clocktower.

The ghosts had entered the Realm of the Living and the Undead. They were advancing on Mount Moth, in pursuit of the vampire who had fled. The vampire who had broken the ghostly law and refused the trial.

The vampire daughter of the Great and Terrible Sieglinde von Motteberg.

NINETEEN

THE BLOOD MOON BANQUET III

Leo's body had no idea of the peril her spirit found itself in; she was on a quest entirely of her own.

Far below where she clung spider-like to the ceiling, the Castle Motteberg ballroom seemed to roll. The long table, crammed from end to end with colourful figures, swayed queasily.

There was Mum at one end, with Dad at her side. She was turned away from him, leaning on one pointy elbow to talk with Lord Ayman. The current Head of the Council was in the lap of a dutiful skeleton, having taken over from Nesh for the meal. Every now and again, its bony hand offered a spoon of blood soup. Between its feet, it kept a discreet bucket handy to catch every mouthful – eating was hard when you had no stomach.

There was Madame Kinkatch, with Socrates at her shoulder. There were Marged and Nesh, hovering round the edge of the table, by turns glaring at each other and doting on the guests.

There was the group of vampire children. Emmeline was digging her chubby fists viciously into her plate, loaded with squiggly intestines. The rest of the group, however, was looking *up*.

'*The chandelier, Leo,*' Anjali had said, her polished fangs gleaming. '*We need a candle from the chandelier!*'

'*Before the feast is finished!*' Florian had hastened to add with the wag of a bejewelled finger. '*Or it will be a PENALTY!*'

'*Yes,*' Leo had replied. She had long since finished all the eyeballs and her belly was finally full.

Like the beasts of the Dreadwald, Leo's friends (once-a-year friends, would-absolutely-betray-you friends) had caught the scent of blood. They all watched in gleeful anticipation as Leo crept along the ceiling, approaching the dangling chandelier. The skirt of her dress, heavier than her cape, hung down.

On her head, Rodrigo was panicking.

'Leo!' he spluttered. 'What are we doing? What are YOU doing?'

'Candle,' Leo replied.

'Candle! There are *plenty* of candles! We don't need one from – wait, are we *on the ceiling*? This is madness! Lady Sieglinde won't like this, not one bit!'

He squeaked as Leo tripped, her wooden foot scraping against the ceiling inside its slipper. A spattering of stony dust fell on to the table below – the children gasped, but no one else gave any sign that they had noticed.

'Leo! Leo, please!' Rodrigo clung on, feeling gravity's pull. 'This is crazy! Why are you up here? Did those *other children* put you up to this? Is THIS what's popular with the youngsters these nights?'

Leo said nothing, crawling closer to her prize. She was directly above the chandelier, in reach of the thick chain that bound it to the ceiling. The metal was flaky with rust when she stretched out to grasp it. It groaned beneath her weight as she crawled on head first, hanging upside down.

'Auuuugh!' Rodrigo moaned, his furry body bristling. 'Ahhh no!'

The chandelier creaked.

Slitted pupils zeroing in on the candlelight, Leo's wiry muscles flexed. She pulled herself down the chain, creeping on to one of the chandelier's arms. The whole thing tilted, candles swaying . . .

Madame Kinkatch blinked, frowning as she felt the patter of something on her head. Rooting around her voluminous poof of hair, she found nothing out of the ordinary. The drip of candlewax sizzled, cooling. Behind her, Socrates sighed.

'This is too much partying for me,' Rodrigo was muttering. 'I don't get it. Why is this fun? It's the quiet life for old Rodrigo from now on!'

TING! TING-TING!

From far below there was a ringing sound. Marged was stood dutifully next to Lady Sieglinde's chair, tapping a teaspoon against a goblet to get everyone's attention. The conversation died down as Lady Sieglinde rose to stand.

Her face split into a pleased sneer. 'Our guests,' she purred, motioning down the table with her bony claws. 'I trust that you are enjoying the banquet. It is my pleasure to announce some GOOD NEWS that has recently graced our family.'

High above the table, the chandelier was almost completely on its side as Leo reached the end of the arm, her weight unbalancing it. The candles flickered and bobbed; a few were extinguished as the wax ran over, disturbed by the swaying.

'We are pleased to declare that the Von Motteberg tradition of PERFECT first hunts has been maintained,'

Lady Sieglinde continued smugly. 'You may remember that my eldest daughter, Emmeline, completed her Hunt of the Waxing Moon on her first try . . .'

A claw lifted to indicate the end of the room, where Emmeline's enormous portrait dominated one wall, scowling down at the party. The table murmured in appreciation. Someone began to clap and everyone turned to Emmeline, who was smiling equally as nastily as Mum. She basked in the attention.

Stretching the last inch, Leo finally caught hold of the target candle. There was a squelch as she plucked it from its metal base, like removing a mushroom from a log. In her fist her prize felt soft and mushy. The hot wax burned her hand. The feeling registered somewhere on the edges of her mind, but she was far from caring.

'Leo!' Rodrigo hissed, pulling on tufts of her hair. 'This has gone far enough!'

'We are NOW proud to announce,' Lady Sieglinde proclaimed, her voice rising, 'that our youngest daughter, Eleonore, has ALSO followed in the family's footsteps! Another first-time success!'

Heads turned, looking at Leo's empty seat. A spattering of sparse applause started up again, more hesitant this time. The guests stared around in confusion. There was a worried *squeak* that might have been Marged's armour.

Lady Sieglinde's nostrils flared. Her mouth drew into a tight pucker as her shrewd eyes flickered up and down the table, looking for any sign of her missing daughter. Of course, there was none; Leo was inching her way back across the chandelier, above the eyeline of the unsuspecting crowd. The other vampire children averted their stares, almost turned to stone beneath Lady Sieglinde's glare. Leo's mum was SCARY.

After a beat, Lady Sieglinde composed herself. She cleared her throat. 'Here we have a NEW portrait, commissioned to commemorate this very special time,' she continued smoothly, glancing at Marged. Behind her chair, the knight obediently moved to stand next to the wall, where a velvet covering concealed something.

'It brings me much gratification to share this moment with YOU –' Lady Sieglinde smiled her grimacing smile – 'our friends. Our vampire FAMILY. Our Council members, to whom the Von Mottebergs are so dedicated.'

There was a great *flump* of fabric as Marged pulled the golden cord, and the velvet covering fell. The vampires *ooh*ed and *aah*ed.

It was the scene from the parlour, where Marged had painted them. Leo's face stared out from a powder-blue collar, half choked by its ruffles. Dad stood proudly at her side, beaming. Mum looked as stern and severe as ever, posing like a carnivorous insect ready to bite the head off its prey.

More applause rolled down the long table. The din covered the squeal of the chandelier as Leo reached for the chain again. Her foot slipped where it was braced on one of the metal swirls. She barely caught herself, balancing the juddering candle, and . . .

Leo lost her grip.

She fell.

There was a tearing sound and Leo OOFed as she was suddenly stopped by something, her legs pinwheeling as she tipped forward into the air. The skirt of her dress had caught on one of the chandelier's arms, tearing at the back before catching at the hem. It struggled to hold her weight as she swung from the momentum, barely managing to hold on to the candle and dangling below the tipping chandelier like a fly caught in a spider's web—

'Oh my life! Oh, Leo! What is HAPPENING?' Rodrigo shouted in her ear. 'TELL ME we're back on solid ground!'

'Yes!' Leo gasped out as the dress pulled tight round her chest and belly. 'Ugh!' She couldn't reach above her head to pull herself up; her legs kicked fruitlessly, inadvertently shaking her slipper loose from her wooden foot . . .

It fell as though in slow motion, tracked by the hungry stares of the other noble vampire children. All of them watched it go in horrified glee – except for Emmeline, who was surreptitiously tucking into her meal while no one was looking.

The silk slipper made an audible *slap* as it dropped right into Emmeline's curls, rolling down on to her forehead.

Emmeline's eyes crossed.

Everyone turned to stare, looking at the peculiar slipper that had appeared from thin air.

Then, all at once, everyone looked up. High above, dangling with her long bloomers on full display, Leo was upside down.

The sight of her was so alarming that no one noticed the two ghostly faces peeking down through the ceiling.

TWENTY

BATTLE AT THE BANQUET

Leo and Minna couldn't believe their eyes as they took in the scene below them.

The banquet table was crammed full of food and drink and lined with the extravagantly dressed guests. At either end matching Waxing Moon portraits looked down on the scene: one of Emmeline, sneering proudly, and one of Leo, reluctant in her hideous dress.

Above it all, directly below where Leo and Minna were peeking down, there was a bundle of black fabric. Skinny arms and legs stuck out, waving like an overturned beetle. In one hand, a short candle was almost burned out.

It was Leo's body.

'Oh, pox and pustules!' Leo cried into her misty hands.

At the head of the table Lady Sieglinde's face froze over as she stared at her dangling daughter.

'Leo!' Minna hissed. 'What do we do? We don't have time for this!'

She was right. They had barely managed to outrun the ghosts of Otto's End; they hadn't had much of a head start.

'My . . . my b-body . . .'

My body is hanging upside down from the chandelier! she wanted to scream. *Above the ballroom!*

How has this happened?

There wasn't a chance to voice any of this, however, as with a sudden RIIIIP, the black fabric tore and Leo's vampiric body began to fall.

Leo's soul zoomed earthwards.

Her vampiric body flipped in mid-air.

There was an unearthly burst of blue-white light and the feeling of suddenly being enveloped in warmth, like gulping a warm cup of blood or sinking snugly into bed.

The crowd of vampire nobles gasped and reared back as Leo's feet slammed on to the table, her knees bending to absorb the shock of the fall. Knives and forks rattled. Platters of appetisers flew. A steaming pot of blood soup was overturned.

Back in her body, Leo felt her heart pounding away,

so hard that it was coaxing her usually dormant vampiric blood to move. Her ears rushed with it as she slowly looked up, taking in the scene around her.

The vampires were statue-still, staring in amazement. There was Emmeline, who had a black slipper on her forehead. There were Anjali and Florian and the twins. There was Madame Kinkatch, open-mouthed, and Socrates, who looked distinctly unimpressed in his own beetly way.

Lord Ayman and Dad both turned to stare at Mum – at LADY SIEGLINDE, who was quietly boiling at the head of the table. There was a twitch in her eye and a curl in her lip. Her glare threatened to liquefy Leo's insides and shiver her brain to mush.

Suddenly, feeling her belly jolt, Leo heaved. Curling over, her ribs wrenched and a hard slimy lump moved up her throat . . .

HURK!

SPLAT!

The splitting stone bounced, pinging off a brass ladle and splattering goo. It squelched down the table before finally sliding to a sticky stop in front of Lady Sieglinde. There had been no room for it inside Leo any more, having been squeezed out by her soul.

'Hah!' Florian barked, grinning at the slushy mess of an extinguished candle, splattered on to the table at Leo's feet.

A familiar voice chimed in from atop her head. With a jolt Leo recognised the scratch of Rodrigo's spidery legs. 'Oh! You've *really* done it now!'

'Miss Leo!' Marged squeaked.

'Leo!' Emmeline snarled under her breath.

'LEO.' Lady Sieglinde's voice cut across the ballroom like the sharpest of blades. The candles flickered on an ill wind. The faraway beating of wings grew louder and louder until Leo could feel it slamming through her.

She couldn't move. She couldn't speak. Lady Sieglinde would surely turn her to dust right there, stood on the table like a dismal party decoration . . .

In the end, however, the wrath of even the Great and Terrible Sieglinde would have to wait.

Above the ballroom, screaming down on to the vampire guests, an army of ghostly townsfolk swooped in.

It took only a second for the world to erupt into chaos.

All around where Leo stood, the vampires reared back, hissing furiously. Chair legs screeched on the flagstones. Fangs were bared, claws flashed, strings of saliva flew.

'CHAAAARGE!' Old Woman Babette roared, brandishing her rolling pin at the forefront of the ghostly deluge. The ghosts plummeted, diving on to the crowd.

Caught in the downpour of misty bodies, the table rocked. Leo stumbled, unused to the sudden weight of her body. Her wooden foot caught in a bowl of chopped lungs. Gazing around in horror, she saw Madame Kinkatch pull two fistfuls of pins from her hair, wielding them like extra claws. She saw the ghostly laundryman lasso two vampire guests. She saw Anjali, handed an onyx bow by a skeleton servant, swiftly drawing a flaming arrow that sparked with green fire . . .

Anjali smirked as the ghosts scampered aside, spooked by the flame. She was flanked on either side by Vasily and Vlada, who had each produced a pair of viciously curved hand axes.

'What is this? GHOSTS! Argh!' Vlada repelled a swipe by one of the townsfolk, deflecting them away with her muscular arm.

'In the north we eat them for breakfast!' Vasily roared, headbutting the ghostly beekeeper so hard his beekeeping hat spun around his head.

Staring into the fray for any sign of gappy teeth or messy hair,

Leo realised with a sinking feeling that Minna was nowhere to be seen. For better or worse, neither was Judge Harker.

Lady Sieglinde, on the other claw, had exploded into a furious storm of furry grey moths, swirling like an ominous hurricane above the battle. Her GRIMWALK was a terrifying sight to behold, even for the other vampires. Occasionally a ghostly attacker was picked off and dragged into the storm, only to vanish with a shriek.

'LEO!' someone called, and Leo whirled to spot Ulf only a few feet away. He had three vampires hanging off him, trying to chew on his arms.

'Ulf! You— aaahh!' Leo cried as she was knocked backwards off her perch by the swarm of ghost bees. They surged towards her, buzzing furiously.

Crawling beneath the table to get away, Leo found herself nose to nose with a cowering Florian.

'Help!' he blurted, spooked. His perfect quiff had a dent in it and his feathers were bent.

'Florian! What are you doing down here?'

'What am *I* doing down here? What are YOU doing down here?' Florian blinked. 'Wait – there are GHOSTS, Leo! Why would we be OUT THERE when we could be hiding!'

'He's right!' someone piped up from Leo's head. 'We should definitely hide!'

'Rodri?' Leo gasped, remembering her stowaway. 'There you are! Again! Don't you realise how dangerous this is!'

'Sp-sp-sp . . .' Florian stammered. 'Sp-*spider*!'

Leo and Rodrigo watched as Florian reversed down the table, crawling rapidly backwards.

'What's wrong with him?' Rodrigo asked.

Leo sighed. 'Rodrigo,' she said sternly, 'you shouldn't be here.'

On the other side of the table, vampire feet clad in high heels and stompy boots clomped back and forth, chased by dangling ghostly toes. There was a scream and someone's bejewelled arm fell to the floor, sliced cleanly off.

'Someone had to keep an eye on you!' Rodrigo argued, while Leo was busy shrinking back in terror. 'You should be thanking me! THANK you, Rodrigo, for keeping me safe! THANK YOU for accompanying me to the party!'

'Stay down! And stay quiet!' Pushing Rodrigo back into her wild nest of hair, Leo tried to summon her bravery. She crept out of the other side of the table, stumbling upright to run to Ulf.

'Hey!' she gasped. 'Have you seen Minna?'

Ulf turned. His darting eyes were roaming even more madly than usual beneath his bushy brows. With one gigantic fist he extracted Clemens from the grip of an elderly vampire guest. 'Ah! There you are again!' he boomed, noticing Leo. 'Uh. No, no, I haven't seen the small warrior. Wasn't she with you?'

'I must have lost her when I got my body back!' Leo cried. She looked around in despair. Everywhere she turned, there was carnage. Ghosts tore at the vampires, lifting them into the air. Vampires swiped at the ghosts, sending them flying with their vampiric powers. Even gentle Socrates was caught up in the heat of battle; the great beetle stampeded through the ghostly horses, sending them skittering away, mouths foaming.

'Leo! Focus!' Clemens's back end said – or Clemens himself said, when Ulf turned him round. He gripped a bugle tightly in his fist. 'Listen closely. Judge Harker is after your mother! If I know Wilhelmina, she'll have tried to distract her. But . . . YOU! Do you realise what you've done?' He gestured madly at Leo. 'YOU aren't in the Ghostly Guidelines! There's NOTHING in the records about what to do with vampires that are—'

'There probably is, though,' Ulf said helpfully, setting Clemens down. 'It probably says to DESTROY THEM ALL or something like that.'

Clemens glowered up with him. 'There's nothing, *Ulfricsson*, about what to do with vampires that are secretly GOOD!' He prodded Leo in the shoulder with the bugle, still glaring at Ulf. 'If you would let me finish, then you would know that!'

'Clemens,' Leo said. 'Thank . . . you?'

'Don't thank me! I'm saying I DON'T KNOW WHAT TO DO!' Clemens shied away when a hissing vampire crawled up behind him. It was promptly sent flying by Ulf's boot.

In truth, Leo didn't know what to do, either. But there was one place to start.

'Let's look for Minna,' she said. 'Please be careful! I don't want anyone to get hurt!'

It seemed, though, that it was too late, as someone's eyeball went sailing overhead. Mum could certainly stick up for herself. But Leo worried for the rest of her family – especially Dad, since he wasn't exactly a martial arts expert.

'Stick together!' she told Ulf and Clemens, already scampering back into the skirmish.

In the end, she found her family first.

'AHAHAHA!' Emmeline cackled. Her skin was as white as porcelain, cracking and crumbling as she activated her vampiric strength. She had stolen the ghost boys' toy hoop and was perched on top of it, her chubby arms outstretched as she wheeled after them on a wave of telekinetic power.

'Evil baby!' they cried, fleeing. 'Evil baby!'

Dad and Marged were back to back, battling the ghostly barrage. Marged's sword sliced with masterful ease. Dad bonked a ghost less gracefully on the head with a heavy leather-bound book.

'Look out, my lord!' Marged cried.

Spinning, Dad ducked as Marged's sword sailed over him, slamming its rounded pommel into another phantom attacker. 'Phew!' he blustered, wiping his brow. 'That was close!'

'Stay close to me, Lord Dietmar!' Marged said. 'We need to find . . . Miss LEO!'

Leo found herself abruptly caught in Marged's metallic embrace, half crushed against her metal breastplate.

'Ohhh, Miss Leo! Oh, thank goodness you're all right!'

Dad's lenses pinged atop his goggles, snapping into place to further magnify his eyes. He blinked owlishly around them. 'I'm not exactly a ghost-hunter,' he said, 'but I believe we're under attack!' He rooted in his pocket, producing a small phial of purplish liquid that bubbled inside its glass prison. 'Eleonore, take this – it's only to be used in an ABSOLUTE EMERGENCY, and ONLY when you are up in your room! Grab your sister and get to safety!'

Over his shoulder, Emmeline was still laughing madly, riding the spinning hoop up the wall and on to the ceiling.

Leo looked down at the phial in her hand. She tucked it into the pocket of her skirt. 'What about you? What about Marged?'

'We'll be *fine*, Miss Leo,' Marged said. 'Please, little one. You should do as your father says!'

Dad was preoccupied with the ghostly hand suddenly grabbing at his leg through the floor. He flapped at it with his book.

'Will you look after someone for me?' Leo whispered urgently to Marged, and the knight made a strangled sound as Leo produced Rodrigo from her hair. Rodrigo clicked his fangs anxiously, wiggling his eight legs.

'What are you up to NOW?' he complained. 'Honestly!'

'Honestly!' Marged agreed, her plume bristling. 'Miss Leo, really, now—'

'You're getting mixed up with GHOSTS again, aren't you—'

'—ghosts are EXTREMELY DANGEROUS, Miss Leo, and if they're here at the castle it has to be for a REASON—'

'—there's no WAY that Lady Sieglinde will turn a blind eye to this!' Rodrigo concluded. 'Even *I* can't, and I'm *actually blind*!'

'Please! Both of you!' Leo cried. 'I need to find my friend. I need to find Minna. I think we're ALL in huge trouble!'

Above them, Lady Sieglinde's GRIMWALK twisted. The moths whirred a deep resonating sound of warning. Leo's heart was in her mouth. Minna had been there alongside her, hiding in the ceiling only minutes ago. Was she still up there? Had Judge Harker trapped her somehow?

'Please!' Leo said again. She held Rodrigo out to Marged.

Marged raised her visor. Inside her helmet there was only an empty space, as always; it was perfect for a spidery passenger. Taking Rodrigo gently from Leo, she helped him crawl inside where her face should have been.

'That phial, Miss Leo, that Lord Dietmar gave you,' she said, closing the visor again, 'I've seen that before, only the once. If you are to use it, you MUST go to your room first, and bolt the door tightly. It's—'

But Leo didn't learn the precise nature of the phial – at least, not at that moment. Lady Sieglinde's GRIMWALK reared up, forming a vicious needle of winged bodies that stabbed down at the crowd. A skeleton fell to bits beneath the assault. Ghosts wailed and scrambled out of the way.

'Get Lord Ayman to safety!' Nesh was ordering,

waving a bandaged hand to direct the skeleton waiters to the door. 'Castle Motteberg is under ghostly attack! Lady Sieglinde has lost her marbles – she can't protect us! The Von Mottebergs are mad!'

'Wait!' Lord Ayman's voice rang out. 'Anjali! My daughter!'

Anjali was busy across the room, skewering ghosts with impressive marksmanship. Her bracelets jingled as she drew back her arm, firing a flaming arrow at the ghost lady with the book, hitting her squarely in the bottom.

'Go and help them!' Leo told Marged. 'I'll be okay. I *promise*.'

'Miss Leo . . .' Marged wavered. Her armour rattled when Lady Sieglinde's moths split the table in two with an almighty CRACK, shards of wood blasting off the Von Motteberg statues. 'Just –' she held Leo's hands tightly, her sword dangling between them – 'please, be *careful*!'

'I will,' Leo assured her. 'Marged, don't worry about me.'

Still holding Leo's hands in one gauntlet, Marged used the other to shove a howling ghost away from over Leo's shoulder, barely missing a beat.

'I *always* worry about you.'

TWENTY-ONE

CHANGING THE RULES

Running up the outside wall of Castle Motteberg, her legs pumping frantically to keep her momentum, Leo's throat was tight with terror. The freezing air bit at her. She stumbled over the woody stems of the ivy. From their alcoves the stony eyes of the gargoyles watched her as she passed, skittering like a spider while the ballroom within was rocked by battle.

A hundred scenarios crowded Leo's mind. Images of Minna sprang up before she could push them away. She pictured her friend turning faded and ill, or covered in sores, or coughing up black slime – suffering Minnas whirled around Leo's brain like the hurricane of moths still humming inside the ballroom. Leo ran, retracing her path to the sloping tiled roof above the ballroom.

Even out here on the wall, with only thin air at her back, she could still hear the struggle inside. There was the glassy shriek of ghostly bodies, the metallic clang of weapons and the occasional rattling of skeleton bones. Every now and again, a phantom arm or leg poked through the wall before being whipped back into the fight.

Reaching the lip of the roof, Leo skidded to a halt. Her torn skirt and messy hair were blown about by the wind.

The red sky bled down, the colour streaming towards two figures.

Judge Harker and Minna grappled in the middle of flowing, shimmering wings of bending reality, the Castle Motteberg turrets warping madly around them. It was as though they were in the fold of a piece of parchment that was closing round them . . .

'STOP!' Leo roared.

Judge Harker looked round, startled, and it was the opening Minna needed to yank her down.

'Leo!' she shouted, pushing Judge Harker into the tiles. The poker glimmered, stuck out of the roof a few feet away. 'I've got her! I couldn't stop the others – are you okay? Where's your mum?'

'Minna! Wait! Please stop!' Leo went to grab Minna's shoulder, but there was a cold rush, like dipping her hand into the River Mothling, and she phased right through her. 'Ack, Minna, please! Judge Harker! We need to end this!'

'She wants to KILL all of you, Leo!' Minna protested,

wild-eyed. 'We *can* end this right now! And this is how! Look! She's opened up a tear between the worlds – we can seal her away there!'

'It's not right!' Leo had to shout to be heard; there was a rushing sound and a pressure that built up in her ears. 'None of this needs to happen! No one else needs to get hurt!'

'You don't know who she is! You don't realise! She's—'

'She's AGNES! I know! I *know* she's the Orphanmaster's wife!'

'The *Orphanmaster*,' Judge Harker snarled, 'wasn't MY Bill!'

Her mouth agape, Minna stared at Leo. 'You know? How did you know?' she demanded, ignoring Judge Harker's thrashing. 'Even *I've* only just got it!'

Leo's shoulders crept up towards her ears. 'We . . . we *talked*! We talked it out!'

'Was this before or after she tried to trap you in a prison dimension for all eternity?'

'I . . . erm . . .' Leo blinked. 'I suppose it was before AND after, but . . . that isn't the point, Minna! I'm sure we can put a stop to all of this! Our people are fighting. Mum is angry. If we don't end this now . . .' She pressed her fists desperately over her eyes.

A small scared part of her considered that it was

probably too late to save herself now – Lady Sieglinde was a ticking clock, counting down to oblivion. Her precious party, her Blood Moon Banquet, was now in tatters. Any hopes of scoring favour with the Vampiric Council had been viciously dashed. Leo had ruined everything.

But all those vampires and ghosts . . . Their fate was much more uncertain.

'There hasn't been an attack like this on Castle Motteberg since before I was born,' Leo gritted out through her fangs. 'Th-this is the Blood Moon Banquet; Lady Sieglinde *won't* let this go! If we don't put a stop to this, it *will* lead to another vampire-ghost WAR!'

Judge Harker stopped struggling. Minna's grip on her loosened, enough for her to pull herself out of the crazily wavering vortex of tiles. The ghosts both stared at the vampire.

'Yes,' Leo said grimly. 'I know you think you can take on Lady Sieglinde, but this will NEVER END if she loses control. She will never stop coming after you. And even if you do slay her – which is HIGHLY UNLIKELY – you can't take on all of the Vampiric Council. They'll hunt the ghosts of the Dreadwald to the ends of the earth!'

Reality settled. The world around them returned to black tiles and creeping vines, stained glass reflecting the blood moon and the jutting shapes of the towers. Slowly, eyeing each other suspiciously, Minna and Judge Harker broke apart. Despite the ferocious battle raging beneath the very roof they were standing on, the air felt suddenly quiet.

'Leo, Minna . . .' Judge Harker rasped. 'My family, the Harkers . . . we have hunted the Great and Terrible Sieglinde for generations. Tales of her kept me awake at night when I was young. I KNOW how dangerous she is. It has to be why I'm still here. I haven't moved on into the afterlife . . . because *she still exists.*'

An inky black well bubbled up from the roof tiles beneath Leo's feet. Before she could leap away, a viscous glob of sticky ooze shot up, gripping her in its slimy hold. It reached up her body, immobilising her.

'You SLY, SNEAKY—' Minna burst out. The poker flew into her hand. Before she could finish her insult, Judge Harker threw out her arm and sent her careening away.

'I'm sorry, Leo,' she said, floating forward.

Leo struggled, gasping, squeezed by the slime. It smelled like rotting decay. 'Judge Harker! Please, listen to me!'

'*You* need to listen.' Judge Harker's misty eyes loomed close. Her irises swirled like smoke trapped in glass. 'Why wouldn't you get out of my way when you had the chance?

It seems we must finish the third test, after all. Then I can do what has to be done.'

'NO!' Minna yelled.

A piercing shriek of ghostly bodies rang out. The two spirits clashed, inches from Leo's nose.

The ooze was tightening. Inside her skirt pocket, something was digging uncomfortably into Leo's hip.

'You need to let this trial go!' Minna snapped. 'It's irrelevant! Out of date!' She shook Judge Harker, trying to pull her back, trying to make her listen. 'How can that be good? If we don't challenge things that are written, does that mean we have to stay the same for ever, even when it puts EVERYONE IN DANGER? It's RIDICULOUS!'

'Minna!' Leo gasped. She felt like a blood sausage encased in a skin that was far too tight.

Judge Harker frowned, staring at Minna from over their grasping arms. 'You don't know what you're saying, Minna! I'm not . . . It's not that easy! I can't change any vof this . . . !'

Leo groaned. She could feel her bones being rearranged.

'You CAN! You're *choosing* not to!' Minna shouted. 'You're not a vampire hunter any more! Why did you even become a judge if it wasn't to help Otto's End? THIS is how you can help: by being a proper leader!'

Looking at Minna, then at Leo, Judge Harker's face fell.

'I . . . I'm sorry it has to be this way. I truly am.' Her

eyes pinched shut, her brows knitting together. 'I only wish I could make you understand.'

Behind Leo, the sky ripped open, sucking in all colour and light. Something in Leo was splintering – maybe it was her ribs or her spine.

Or—

Well, THIS isn't good! was all Leo could think, as the phial of purple liquid inside her pocket burst.

The liquid never touched Leo's skin; it turned to vapour, wafting from Leo's pocket and through the rotting ooze with ease. It billowed up into a thick purple cloud, spilling out around Leo's shoulders and floating above her head.

Before her astonished eyes, the cloud BREATHED, swelling and shrinking . . .

And then tendrils went coursing off, winding down through the miniscule cracks in the tile, sinking into Castle Motteberg.

There was a harsh quaking tremor, a shift from deep within the mountain's core. Right from its foundations to the tip of the western tower, the whole castle shuddered. Far below, where Mount Moth met the Dreadwald, a flock of winter birds took flight, disturbed by the commotion.

Lurking in their spiked alcoves, the stony faces of the gargoyles all turned to the intruders.

TWENTY-TWO

CASTLE MOTTEBERG BITES

The tiled roof rushed to meet her and Leo dropped to her knees. Around her, bubbling down, the inky sludge vanished as Judge Harker's hold loosened and broke.

Minna had the poker raised in a defensive posture. 'Leo!' she shouted over the thunderous din. '*Please* tell me this isn't another horrible vampire-castle thing!'

One of the gargoyles took a step towards her, its feet scraping, stony dust falling from it. It shook a frosty spiderweb from its wings. Beneath its gravelly skin, its muscles stretched and flexed. Its jaws, full of sharp fangs, opened on a snarl—

KRR-CHUNK!

Leo flattened herself against the roof, twisting to look behind her. Standing over her was a ghostly figure. She was clad in a gown and robe. Her sleeve billowed behind her hand, clasping the fist of a second gargoyle before it could slam into Leo.

'Judge Harker!' Leo cried. She rolled on to her back, coiling her body to strike. The gargoyle screamed a long furious note, straight into Judge Harker's face. It was cut off as it caught the heels of Leo's feet in its rocky belly, sending it careening off the edge of the roof.

'What's going on?' Minna cried, parrying a punch. The first gargoyle swiped for her, growling as she dodged deftly aside. '*Why* are they doing this?'

'The castle defences!' Leo gasped, flat on her back. 'I don't . . . I've never . . .'

She had never seen this in action before, but she had *read* about it in the library. Dad's wards, woven from science and magic, could only repel so much – and they certainly didn't work against GHOSTLY INVADERS, as Leo had found out the hard way.

But Castle Motteberg was an ancient place, with primeval vampiric sorcery in its walls. Older than Leo. Older than Dad. Older even than Mum (and she was *extremely* old). Leo hadn't known there was a way to trigger the defences any more. But they had indeed been activated by the phial Dad had given her – and they recognised even the youngest Von Motteberg lady as a THREAT. No wonder Dad had warned her to go to her room . . .

'On your feet, Leo!' Judge Harker barked, pulling Leo up. 'What do you mean, castle defences?'

'Hold that thought!' Leo shouted. She turned to hiss at the gargoyle attacking Minna.

The rocky beast was caught between the three of them, Leo and Minna and Judge Harker. They attacked it from three angles, dodging its thrashing wings and viciously spiked tail.

'Powerful vampire magic!' Leo gasped out, deflecting a blow with her forearm. 'The castle won't stop until all the intruders are gone!'

'What do we do? How do we stop this?' Judge Harker pushed her misty hand through the gargoyle's shoulder and pulled it down on to her very much solid knee. With a bitten-off howl of pain, a crack spidered up the beast's belly and chest.

'"WE"?' retorted Minna. 'We're NOT working with you! You were trying to KILL Leo only a second ago!' The poker flashed and three stony claws fell, sliced clean off. They bounced away on the tiled roof.

'Minna,' Judge Harker said, 'you don't understand—'

'I understand that you're a COWARD!' Minna socked the gargoyle in the face, batting it towards Judge Harker. 'This isn't about what's right! 'You've twisted everything to fit your own agenda – even though you *know* it's wrong!'

Judge Harker punched the gargoyle back. Her mouth pursed and her nostrils flared with the effort, her gown flowing behind her. 'Justice is complicated, Minna! In time, you'll come to realise I was trying to protect you all!'

BANG! 'You're not protecting anyone! You only care about yourself!'

BLAM! 'You don't *know* vampires like I do, Minna! They're not your friends! They're a scourge that needs to be wiped out!'

'So you WERE twisting the trial! You've only wanted to get at Leo's mum all along – you admit it!'

'BOTH OF YOU!' Leo cried. 'Please, stop!'

The ghosts froze, mid-battle. Minna's poker was poised. Judge Harker had her elbow halfway to the monster's maw. Even the gargoyle itself paused, with one of its horns and half its claws now missing. It blinked at the vampire girl.

'We need to stop arguing and get it together – yes, *all of us*!' Leo exclaimed. 'There won't be any ghosts – *or* any vampires – left to protect if we don't—'

Surrounded by enemies, battered and broken, the gargoyle finally spotted its opening. Raising what was left of its fists, it summoned all its strength.

There was an echoing BOOM that ricocheted off the towers and turrets of Castle Motteberg. Roof tiles cracked and exploded into shards. Beneath them, there was the ear-splitting shriek of splintering timber.

Leo tried to stumble back. Beneath her feet, a hole opened up in the roof, which was weather-worn and half rotten from countless winters high on Mount Moth. The gargoyle tumbled in faster than it could flap its wings. Tiles slid, falling in clumps down to the ballroom below, where a swirling storm of furry grey bodies was a whirlpool waiting to suck Leo in . . .

Lady Sieglinde's GRIMWALK.

Scrambling, leaning backwards, Leo's claws grasped at thin air.

She plummeted.

Her vision blurred, obscured by beating wings. She hung in place, suspended. The sound of the moths was deafening, rattling through Leo's head and crashing down on her body. Every now and then snatches of the chaotic ballroom below were visible; vampires and ghosts were locked in battle, joined now by a massive stony gargoyle. All round the edges of the room, the statues of Von Motteberg ancestors began to twitch . . .

'LEO! THERE YOU ARE!' a voice thundered, and Leo's heart tried to crawl up her throat. Mum's enormous disembodied face emerged from the moths, pinched with fury.

'Mum!' Leo gasped. 'I—'

'Not another word!' Lady Sieglinde grimaced, showing her sharp teeth. Her eyes, dark as black pits, were narrowed suspiciously. 'I don't know WHAT you thought you were doing, falling from the ceiling like some FERAL CREATURE, but it seems we are under ATTACK!'

'We are, Mum!' Leo said desperately. 'We are! The castle, it's—'

'You will GO TO YOUR ROOM!' Mum snapped. Her gaze was like a hundred needles, sticking Leo all over. 'You've done QUITE ENOUGH damage here tonight! Whatever silly games you children have been playing, it's time for the ADULTS to handle this now!'

'No, Mum, I—' But before Leo could finish her plea, she was dropped, falling in a clump on to the ruined table. She managed to get her legs underneath her in the nick of time, landing unsteadily on her feet. She stared up in dismay at the silvery GRIMWALK, and then around at the pandemonium.

This was worse than bad, Leo thought, watching as a vampire guest was hoisted up by his ruff by the statue of Great-Aunt Millicent. Her sister, Great-Aunt Claudia – also a statue – was busy stomping on the ghostly beekeeper, her stony stiletto heels going straight through the terrified ghost as he crawled away.

Lady Motteberg the Second was swinging Madame Kinkatch around like a doll. Lady Motteberg the *Third*, on the other claw, was climbing the wall on the opposite side of the room, swiping at Emmeline and the fleeing ghost boys.

Great-Uncle Bertrand was facing down Vasily on one side and Vlada on the other. Great-Grandma Armandine was rampaging through into the foyer, her long braid whipping behind her, chasing those who were trying to flee. The gargoyle had been lassoed by Minna's mum and was trying to throw her off its back.

More gargoyle friends joined the fray, pouring in past the jagged roof tiles that stuck out like broken teeth. To Leo's horror they were chased by the ghostly sabre-toothed cat from the maze of mirrors, its shadowy body stalking across the ruined ceiling. It must have followed the scent of blood after Leo had unleashed it by breaking the ice.

'WAHAHA!' Ulf roared in delight, staring madly around. 'What's this now? A REAL challenge! Excellent!'

'No! Hey – absolutely *not*!' Clemens said, aghast, clicking his fingers to try to get Ulf's attention. 'Not "excellent" at all! Terrible! Dreadful! It's— *DUCK*!' He tugged Ulf down by his beard as a green-flamed arrow went sailing over their heads. Clemens whipped round, lifting his bugle to his mouth. A shockwave of sound blasted out of the end, sending Anjali and Florian flying.

Lady Sieglinde's GRIMWALK surged down the back wall and on to the floor like a crawly carpet, pulling in victims indiscriminately. A vampire lord yelped and vanished under the rolling wave of moths, leaving behind a puff of feathers and a glittery sapphire earring.

'Daddy, no!' Florian yelped, before Anjali dragged him away.

'Ulf! Clemens!' Leo gasped, sprinting to them. She crouched to avoid Old Woman Babette as she zoomed past. 'Are you all right? Has anyone seen the judge?'

'The judge? Who's that?' Clemens sneered sarcastically. 'No, we haven't seen her! Have *you*?' He waved his arms – and the bugle – wildly. 'We followed her here! We need SOME direction – this a disaster! She's disappeared! She's abandoned the town!'

'No, no, she's here – but we lost her!' Leo shook her head. 'Listen! You need to leave! We ALL need to leave! It's the castle defences!'

Behind her, a bright figure swooped down to join them.

'Yes!' Minna jabbed the poker towards the door. 'Leo's right, we need to get everyone out! No one's LISTENING to me, but we need to go! Now!' She whirled round to blow a great blast of smoke into the face of an attacking vampire lady, sending her scurrying for cover again.

Ulf's mouth downturned. 'But . . .' He pointed to Lady Motteberg the Third, now upside down on the wall and being hit in the face by the ghostly hoop, which Emmeline was swinging around her frilly waist. 'But,' Ulf continued sadly, 'giant moving statues? Gargoyles? Where's your FIGHT, young warriors? This is a REAL BATTLE now!'

There was a rumble.

It started far below the castle, so quiet as to be nearly unnoticeable, a tiny vibration through the floor. The fallen tableware began to rattle. The remains of the discarded furniture began to judder, strewn around like fallen soldiers.

The rumble became louder and stronger and more violent. Somewhere underground, Castle Motteberg was rearranging, its guts moving and reshaping, reforming around new passageways that snaked their way up towards the surface. Through them a distant rattling was drawing closer and closer . . .

Everyone paused. On one side of the ballroom were Dad and Marged and Emmeline, the vampire gang and their families, and Madame Kinkatch and Socrates. On the other were the ghostly townsfolk of Otto's End and the snarling sabre-toothed beast. Through the foyer doors Nesh and Lord Ayman were looking around in alarm, surrounded by startled gargoyles.

The moths crawled upwards, spinning into a tall thin

knife-like shape in the middle of the room. Lady Sieglinde emerged from her GRIMWALK, her eyes glinting malevolently. In her wake her battered, dishevelled vampire victims got uneasily to their feet. The captured ghosts now floated upwards, clutching their heads in confusion.

In all four corners of the room flagstones scraped and sank. They each slid away to reveal a spiral of stairs drilled deep into the castle innards. Shouts of alarm echoed from the foyer, where similar stairs had been uncovered. From below snarling and hissing and clattering rose to a deafening cacophony.

An army of vampire skeletons – Von Motteberg ancestors, long dead – poured up from the crypt in a geyser of clacking, clashing bones.

Screams went up amongst guests and invaders alike as Castle Motteberg was flooded with skeletal vampires. Fangs gnashed and claws flashed. Those trying to flee were cut off at the great doors.

No one was exempt.

'Oh, pustules!' Dad cried, extracting his book from the jaws of what might have been his great-great-great-grandfather. 'Ugh! Marged, what the devil is going on?'

'This was YOUR PLAN, my lord!' Marged kicked a screeching skeleton away. 'The castle defences have been sprung! What do we do NOW?'

'I had rather thought we would all be out of harm's way at this point! I'm not exactly a battle strategist!'

'Dad!' Emmeline yelled, sailing down to them. Her red eyes narrowed and she swept away three advancing skeletons with a wave of her chubby hand. 'Where's Leo?' she demanded, dribbling with evil joy at the thought of her little sister's doom. 'I KNOW she's behind all of this!'

In the middle of the ballroom, Lady Sieglinde was busy decapitating the bones of her predecessors. She flashed back and forth in a rush of needling moths. Her gown swept dramatically behind her as she reappeared, her claws piercing through a skeleton's ribs. She threw the screeching creature up and over her head as though it was made of parchment.

Dad gulped.

Emmeline grinned.

Marged swung her sword, battling back Von Mottebergs she might have once served, a very long time ago.

'So sorry!' she squeaked as the skeletons collapsed into pieces. 'Pardon me, my lady!' A fanged skull rolled away, still hissing. 'A thousand apologies!'

The ghostly townsfolk were fighting back, too, pulling out all the stops to defeat their new foes. The ghost bees swarmed around the beekeeper's hand, forming a gigantic fist. The laundryman whipped the washing line back and forth. The ghost boys, having recovered their hoop from the crazed vampire baby, were running underfoot, tripping their bony attackers.

Leo's group of unlikely allies scattered, broken apart as the vampire skeletons surged. Leo and Minna ran in one direction, Ulf and Clemens in another.

'Not AGAIN!' Leo gasped. She nimbly dodged one skeleton's grasp, dropping down to kick another's legs out from underneath it. She looked desperately around for Judge Harker. 'Where did she go? Where's Agnes?'

Minna shook her head, skewering two skeletons at once on the poker. She shoved them back towards Leo who, with a powerful swipe of her claws, sent them shattering. But there was no time to celebrate; more advanced, their fanged jaws clicking . . .

Over Minna's shoulder, across the room, Old Woman Babette was held aloft by a particularly tall skeleton. Her little feet kicked, trying to fight back. Somehow, despite her ghostly body, she couldn't escape its grip.

'What?' Leo heard Minna mumble. 'How . . . ?'

There was a whooping war cry and Minna's mum charged in, riding one of the ghost horses. Minna's dad, sat behind her and hanging on tightly with one hand, reached down and yanked Babette from the skeleton's grasp. As she was pulled to safety, Babette gave the offending creature a resounding BONK on the head with her rolling pin.

Leo hadn't thought that it would be possible to grapple a ghost. From the look on Minna's face she was equally as confused.

'Ancient magic!' a tinny voice exclaimed, making Leo jump.

'Marged!' she gasped.

'Yes, little one – AH!' Marged stuck her sword point-down between the flagstones, deflecting a rib that had been thrown like a boomerang. 'This is OLD VON MOTTEBERG POWER! Your ghost friends need to be careful! Oh, hello again, Minna! I'm glad you're okay!'

'Hello, Marged,' Minna said with a shade of awkwardness. Leo shuffled her feet.

A spidery face peeked out from behind Marged's visor.

'Why are we still here?' Rodrigo cried. 'Let's *go* – Lady Sieglinde will handle this!'

All around them, the ballroom was teeming with scrawny bodies crawling over each other and climbing the walls. A vampire lady screamed as fangs pierced her shoulder. A ghost was swarmed and pulled down into the thrashing mass of bones.

'He's right, Marged – grab Dad and Emmeline and go!'

Leo said desperately. 'It's the only way to . . . to . . .' She trailed off, staring.

She couldn't believe her eyes.

From Emmeline's Waxing Moon portrait, a shimmering mass began to emerge. The carved face of a mermaid came first, cast in ghostly white. Behind her, the bow of an enormous ship came next, cutting through the writhing mass of bones, skeletons bouncing off it. Sails billowed on their masts. A rippling flag was hoisted proudly, sticking up and out of the ruined ceiling.

The enormous ghostly galleon ploughed across the ballroom. At its helm stood Ulf.

'WAHAHA!' he laughed, spinning the wheel. His beard bristled joyfully. 'How's THAT for a Spirit Anchor?'

The actual anchor dropped, its ghostly weight smashing heavily down on to the heads of growling, grasping Von Motteberg ancestors, pounding them into dust. Clemens peeked down from the deck, hanging on tightly as the ship veered and came to a halt. Emblazoned on the side of the ship in shining lettering was the name *MAGPIE*.

Marged nodded, taking Leo firmly by the arm. 'Right you are, Miss Leo!' she squeaked, already hoisting Leo off her feet. 'Time to go!'

'Marged, no. I can help!'

'Miss Leo, you can *help* by getting to safety! I . . . if

something happens to you, I don't . . .'

Leo clapped a hand on to Marged's metal pauldron. 'I *need* to fix this,' she said, staring stubbornly up into her butler's visor. Rodrigo looked blindly back at her and Leo's heart squeezed. 'You round up the vampires!' she insisted. 'We'll get the ghostly people out of here. Marged, *we all need to work together*!'

'WAHAHAHAHAAA!' Ulf roared overhead, using both hands to lift his beard and vest up out of the way. A thousand phantom rats were pouring out of a hole in his belly, skittering down the sides of the ship.

'There'll be no castle LEFT at this rate!' Leo twisted round. 'Minna, let's—'

A gentle metal hand turned Leo's face back towards Marged.

Marged's free gauntlet clenched and she rattled where she stood, only for a moment, before she held it together again. She smoothed down Leo's wild hair and tried to straighten her tattered dress.

'Stick with your friends now, Miss Leo.' She gave Leo what was probably a very serious look. 'I'll meet you over the other side of the bridge!'

The ballroom was rocked by the battle. The walls creaked and groaned with the impact as the war at Castle Motteberg raged on – vampires and ghosts, skeletons and statues, gargoyles and rats and a sabre-toothed cat, all embroiled in a fight worse than the Dreadwald had seen for centuries. Colourfully clad figures began to flee across the drawbridge, led by Nesh and urged on by Marged, directing the vampire guests to the edge of the castle wards. A few were picked off by divebombing gargoyles before they could make it, and more still fought against the Von Motteberg statues that stood watch over the bridge.

In the middle of the frenzy were two girls – a vampire and a ghost. Above them, a towering ship fired cannonballs into the fray, explosions loud enough to make the ears ring and the eyes water. The ghosts, without direction from their leader, would not leave. No matter how loudly Minna shouted, they refused to budge.

'This is ridiculous!' she yelled, losing her temper. 'Have you all lost your minds? Do you want to DIE AGAIN?'

'Minna!' someone called, and Minna's parents came to a skidding halt on their ghostly horse. Minna's mum held out her hand. 'Come on! Girls, let's go! Both of you!'

'B-but the people, Mum!' Minna despaired aloud. 'What will we do? They won't listen!'

'You've done all you can, my dear!' piped up Old

Woman Babette, peeking out from behind Minna's dad. 'You were right! This is madness! Grab your vampire friend and let's go!'

The horse stamped his feet impatiently, tossing his head. Another series of shattering bangs exploded above them. A bony arm, severed at the elbow, clattered to the flagstones and crawled away on its fingertips.

Watching it go, Leo caught sight of a figure across the battlefield.

She was tall and slender, with a cloud of hair around her head and a broken chair leg in her hand, held like a makeshift stake. She was advancing on Lady Sieglinde, whose back was turned, occupied with pummelling another enormous wave of skeleton attackers.

It was Judge Harker. Agnes Harker, vampire hunter.

'We'll be back!' Minna told her parents desperately over the sound of their protests. Her mum seized her by the wrist before she could slip away. Leo, on the other claw, was already running.

'AGNES!' she shouted, stumbling over the rubble.

But Judge Harker couldn't hear her – or, perhaps, she didn't *want* to hear her. She kept on gliding, moving single-mindedly through the wreckage towards her vampire foe.

'*Agnes!*' Leo finally caught up with her, trying to catch

hold of her sleeve. It wafted through her grasping hands. 'It's over! Come with us!'

Judge Harker paused, glaring at her. 'This is FAR from over, Leo the Vampire. I meant what I said. I'm sorry that it's come to this, but it doesn't change what you *are*. What SHE is.' Looking to Lady Sieglinde, Judge Harker's face creased with grief and rage. Her hand, the one holding the stake, began to tremble.

'I *am* a vampire, Agnes,' Leo said desperately. 'I can't . . . I can't deny who I am. But you know I'm right – you know that doing this . . . it will only lead to more pain. If you attack Lady Sieglinde, you *will* trigger another war. Is that what you want to leave behind, after you are gone? The other ghosts have to suffer so you can find your peace? You're the leader of Otto's End!'

When she reached out again to grasp Judge Harker's hand, she was surprised to find she could actually touch her – Judge Harker's misty form was cold, but her hand was solid beneath Leo's clawed one. Leo held on tightly, feeling the stake dig into her palm.

They both jumped as another chunk of the ceiling fell in behind them, shattering in a rain of dust and broken tiles.

'I won't let you do this!' Leo cried. 'I'm not running away!'

'Then you are a fool indeed.' Judge Harker stared hard

into Leo's eyes. 'You should go – and consider yourself lucky! It's too dangerous for you here.'

'And for you! And for your people!'

'My people . . . Hah . . .' They would have seen you killed, Leo!' Judge Harker's voice lowered to a hiss through her gritted teeth. 'They would have *delighted* in your death! They want your head on a spike! Your body roasted in the sun! Why do you care about them so much?'

'Why care about anyone else at all?' Leo insisted, hanging on. She could feel her pulse rising up her neck, filling her ears like a war drum. 'Why did YOU care about the children of Otto's End? Because it's the right thing to do! Because underneath I *know* you are good!'

'That's different!' Judge Harker shouted. She shook her head despairingly. 'Ugh. What would my family think of me now, talking in circles with you? We are a line of HUNTERS, Leo! THIS is what's right!'

With a sudden anguished scream, Judge Harker raised their conjoined hands, the stake clutched between them. The pointed end jerked towards Leo's chest and stopped short, right over her vampiric heart.

'Why can't you leave this to the grown-ups?' Judge Harker demanded, baring her teeth. 'Are you not afraid? I could stake you where you stand, VAMPIRE!'

Somewhere behind her, Minna's shout burst across the

ballroom. It melted away into the cacophony of the battle.

In Leo's mind, however, all was still.

'Agnes, I . . . I believe it's possible for vampires and ghosts to exist together.'

Leo lifted her chin. She stared into Judge Harker's eyes, willing herself not to blink. Beneath her hand, the deadly stake was frozen.

'What?' Judge Harker hissed.

'Minna and I are proof. It can be done. We don't have to be enemies until the end of time. Or the best of friends. We could just . . . be. As we are.'

'That's ridiculous. You are young and naive.'

'Maybe. But I'm not afraid.' Leo's claws dug into the broken chair leg, gripping it tighter. 'I think . . . maybe *you* are afraid. Afraid of what you've done. Or that you haven't done enough. I don't think you really want to put it all right, as much as you're trying to run away! Kind of like me. I'm still trying to hide from my mistakes, too.'

'Leo . . .'

'You think,' Leo continued, 'if you kill Lady Sieglinde and escape into the afterlife, that'll be that. But the ghosts will all remember you, Agnes. It matters what you do now! What do you want their memory of you to be?'

With a wrenching pull Leo yanked the stake free of Judge Harker's misty hands. She tossed it behind her, away into the wreckage, ignoring Judge Harker's startled gasp.

From behind them the phantom clip-clop of hooves drew closer and closer. Minna and her family raced up to them, Old Woman Babette in tow.

'Leo!' Minna cried, drawing her poker. 'Are you okay?'

Leo brushed her hands free of splinters. 'We're okay. We're ready.'

'I'm . . .' Judge Harker blinked at Leo, then round at Minna and the ghosts. 'Th-this isn't over!' she cried. 'We're here to slay Lady Sieglinde! Join me! This is our chance!'

Her sleeve billowed as she jabbed a finger over at where Lady Sieglinde was ploughing through vampire skeletons, their skulls popping off and rolling away into the rubble.

'No,' Minna's mum said, looking down at Judge Harker from astride the ghostly horse. 'We're here to make sure *the children* don't get hurt. Hasn't it been about them this whole time? I thought that was your mission – to protect them?'

'From the Orphanmaster, Willa! And . . . I couldn't do anything to help the children in the end. You know that. We all know that.' Slowly Judge Harker lowered her hand. Her glassy, faraway stare looked off into nothing. 'My work here . . . it's all been pointless. Nothing has mattered.'

Leo wanted to speak – she wished she could find the words, anything to put this right.

Before all this, she couldn't have imagined the hopeless frustration of being a ghost. Now, though, she'd had her glimpse of the Ghostly Realm. She was beginning to understand.

'If I may,' Minna's dad said gently, flying down from the horse's back, 'I rather think that the *children* would disagree with you, Agnes.'

Judge Harker looked up at him. More ghostly cannon fire exploded above their heads, but amidst the raging battle the ghosts were quiet. Leo was quiet.

'I think the children know that you did everything you could,' Minna's dad continued. 'I think they know that even your death . . . though a terrible, senseless thing . . . it was in service to them.'

He put his hands on Minna's shoulders, holding her tight.

'I think the children are extremely grateful for everything you did for them, Agnes,' he said firmly. 'Just like everyone in Otto's End is grateful to you now. I'm not sure it is your purpose to hunt vampires, not any more. You left that life behind. I think there must be something else for you, work that still needs to be done to make things better for our town.'

Held in her dad's embrace, Minna nodded.

Judge Harker looked round at everybody. Her mouth

opened and then closed again, as if she was unable to speak. She lowered her head, clutching her hands to her chest. The tulip locket floated up to nudge against her cheek.

Then—

'LEO.'

Heels clicked on the floor behind them. The bones of half a vampire skeleton rattled as they were flung aside.

A long, thin shadow fell over Leo as she looked up into the ice-cold fury on Lady Sieglinde's face.

TWENTY-THREE

THE BLOOD MOON SINKS

'GHOSTS, Leo. At my Blood Moon Banquet.'

Lady Sieglinde's voice was deceptively calm and even, like the way a predatory beast will allow its heartbeat to slow before it lunges to strike.

'Ghosts . . . in my castle.' She cast a baleful glance over the ghostly congregation, making them all shrink back. Lady Sieglinde's presence alone was enough to make everyone age one hundred years in an instant. Any optimism or hope was extinguished in the flap of a moth's wing. 'Ghosts at my event. And MY daughter . . . has brought them here?'

There was an icy spike of terror in Leo's belly, stretching all the way up between her ribs to pierce her throat. She couldn't move. She felt her eyes begin to bulge as the words wouldn't come – anything, she thought, any excuse to get out of this, anything to make Mum less angry with her . . .

Then, through the tingling numbness that had set in, she felt a ghostly grip adjust to close round her wrist.

'*Play along if you want to survive!*' she thought she heard someone whisper, the tiniest breath in her ear.

She cried out as she was wrenched forward and up, held in the iron grasp of Judge Harker. Beneath her tattered skirt and flailing feet, a whooshing tear opened in the air under them, swirling with a cascade of colours. The ruined rubble of the ballroom stirred and ran, starting to be pulled in through the gap between realms. Lady Sieglinde reared back and so did the ghosts, the horses bucking with a whinny of alarm.

'Lady Sieglinde!' Judge Harker intoned above Leo's head, sparking with a sudden phantom power. Her gaze was unblinking, unflinching as she drew herself upright, meeting Lady Sieglinde's frosty glare with a manic grin. 'Finally we meet. Oh, it has been a LONG TIME COMING!'

What? Leo thought, her veins freezing over. After all this, Judge Harker STILL wanted to fight Lady Sieglinde? Had she heard nothing they'd said?

'I have no time for this, GHOST,' Lady Sieglinde spat. 'You will LEAVE my castle, or you will perish!' Leo couldn't believe what she was seeing. Mum was *taken aback* by this strange ghostly woman – the one who was staring her down with such confidence, holding her youngest daughter aloft between them.

Leo had never seen Mum like this. The way Sieglinde looked at the madly warping and wavering space between realities, it could have been fear – if Leo didn't know better. The Great and Terrible Sieglinde feared nothing. This was . . . something she'd never encountered before. That was all.

'I should think, Lady Sieglinde, that better security should be put in place for an event such as this,' Judge Harker said mockingly. She looked down at Leo and her lip curled in a way that would have been perfectly *vampiric* if not for her straight, human teeth. 'THIS ONE tried to fight me off, but of course she is no match for a whole ARMY of ghosts. My question is: why is your *daughter* the only one watching out for the famous Von Mottebergs?'

Leo gasped. A bluff. Ghostly trickery!

Yes, Agnes!

Crying out as she was tossed to the floor, Leo sprawled clear of where the ballroom floor was still bending into the rift, folding in on itself. She scrambled backwards, her mouth agape as Judge Harker glared down at her. Hovering above the streaming pit of light, Agnes looked like she might have risen from the Underworld itself.

'You fought well, young vampire,' she rumbled, keeping up the act. 'Though I cannot say the same for the rest of your kind.' Judge Harker sneered at the destruction all around them, her eyes lingering on the ghostly galleon that had ceased its fire. Even the skeletal Von Motteberg ancestors were staring, their empty sockets all trained on where the judge was floating. 'Castle Motteberg . . . is not what it once was. It was a waste of our time to come here.'

Lady Sieglinde puffed up furiously, her form already wavering as parts of her flaked away into flapping moths.

'You DARE to—'

Judge Harker held up a hand and smiled. 'I very much *do* dare,' she said, with a glint of some mischievous confidence that Leo hadn't seen in her before now. She shot up into the air, her robe flowing behind her.

'GHOSTS OF OTTO'S END!' she boomed, her voice bouncing off the crumbling walls. 'FOLLOW ME!'

'NO!' Lady Sieglinde shrieked, her voice carried away into the storm of swirling moths as she burst. 'YOU WILL NOT GET AWAY!'

It was too late, however. The townsfolk were, in fact, getting away; ghostly bodies zoomed upwards, flowing after their leader. A few skeletons swiped at them, snarling in surprise, but the spirits were making their escape, disappearing through the ruined ceiling and out into the dwindling night. The *Magpie* weighed anchor, and Ulf cackled madly as he steered her up and out, Clemens still clinging desperately to the railing as they went.

Minna hesitated, trying to pull back as her family urged her on to the horse. 'Leo . . .'

'Go on, Minna!' Leo urged. Out of the corner of her eye, she saw Dad bumbling over to her. 'I'll be okay. I'll see you out there!'

'HYAH!' Minna's mum flicked the reins, guiding the ghost horse up towards safety. From its back Minna turned and held Leo's gaze, her long hair streaming behind her before they vanished through the ballroom ceiling. Moths smashed into the ruined plaster and falling tiles, buzzing angrily. Their furry bodies shaped into a giant clawed hand that reached for its prey, snatching at thin air and falling back to earth.

Leo felt hands at her back, heaving her up to stand. 'Oh, Eleonore . . .' Dad brushed her down. His goggles were askew and his waistcoat was torn to shreds. 'I'm so glad you're all right – I have your sister, let's go!'

'But, *Dad*!' Emmeline complained next to him. 'I didn't see Mum turn Leo to dust yet!'

The three of them set off at a run, hurrying through the foyer. The polished floor had been churned up in the fight and the tapestries were all torn. The stage where the zombie band had played was now upended, splinters of wooden supports sticking out of cracks in the wall. More makeshift stakes, Leo thought with a shiver. She let Dad usher her out through the doors.

There was a WHOOSH as Lady Sieglinde joined them, swooping in at Leo's side to glide across the bridge. Leo felt her insides lurch. Mum looked down her long nose at Leo for a moment, considering, before looking away.

The mountain lake glimmered with a reflection of the lightening sky; morning would be here soon. A gathering of dishevelled vampires awaited them on the other side of the bridge, battered and bruised, outfits utterly ruined, cast in stony silence as the reality of what had happened began to dawn on them all.

As the Von Motteberg family reached the end of the bridge, as Leo's wooden foot inched through the protective magical wards that stretched over the castle like a dome . . . there was a collective clattering THUD from inside the castle walls. Gargoyles fell from the sky, a few crashing into the lake like falling asteroids. The statues stuttered and froze where they stood with a grinding, gravelly sound.

Then, finally, at the water's edge, all was quiet and still.

A loud raucous cheer burst out and swept through the

crowd, igniting a collective roar in the vampire guests. Feather boas were flung into the air and a few high heels went flying, too. Leo found herself jostled, grabbed round her shoulders and pulled into a sudden celebration that was equal parts mirth and sheer disbelief.

'THAT,' Anjali shouted in her ear, 'was the BEST Blood Moon Banquet EVER!'

'What?' Florian grumped. 'Are you *serious*? We almost DIED! And my . . . my . . .'

Voices called out. 'Florry!' It was Florian's mum and dad, both dishevelled, their elaborate outfits torn to shreds. They swept Florian up into an enormous feathery hug.

There was no sign of the ghosts. The zombie band started up again, though half their instruments had been smashed in the battle, and there was an impromptu dance by the mountain lake. Everyone seemed to favour a weird stomping dance move that Leo hadn't seen before, but she went along with it anyway. Even Madame Kinkatch, her puff of hair bent entirely sideways, was joining in. Socrates, on the other claw, sighed and lumbered away for a lie-down on the frozen mountain path.

'Miss Leo!' a familiar voice called, and Leo could barely look round before she was swept up into metal arms. 'Oh, Miss Leo, you have WORRIED ME TONIGHT!'

'Marged!'

'Hnnngh!' Marged squeezed Leo tightly. 'Oh, little one. Why do you do this to me, putting yourself in harm's way like that? Do you not understand how much you mean to us all?'

'I . . . I'm s-sorry, Marged. It's been a very STRANGE night!' Leo let Marged fuss over her, cupping her face in her gauntlets. 'I don't like to worry you.'

'What about me?' Rodrigo's voice grumped from inside the helmet. 'You worry me ALL THE TIME!'

'I'm sorry.' Leo hung her head. 'I'm so sorry.'

'We will *talk about this* later, Miss Leo,' Marged said, suddenly serious.

'Yes,' cut in an icy voice, and Marged's plume sproinged. She stepped aside as Lady Sieglinde approached, her face a hard, cold mask. 'There is *much to discuss*, Leo.'

'Mum, I—'

Lady Sieglinde raised a deadly sharp finger and Leo's words died.

Mum looked her over and paused, her sour gaze alighting on the moth brooch pinned to Leo's chest. There was a beat, and her fangs clicked shut. She rumbled a low sound that could have been a growl or a sigh or both.

Leo's soul tried to leave her body again as the weight of Mum's clawed hand came to rest on her shoulder.

'Later,' Lady Sieglinde said. 'For now, the sun is coming up. We must return to the castle.'

As she spoke, there was a groaning sound from Castle Motteberg behind her – and then the spilling of rubble as the side of the ballroom collapsed into the lake. Emmeline's portrait, her sneering face glaring out from the canvas, sank beneath the surface and vanished with a blub.

Mum hissed through her teeth, letting Leo go and already gliding away to speak with Lord Ayman.

Leo stared after her, blinking hard. Her thoughts folded up, small and quiet in her mind, far away from the partying crowd while Marged fussed with her hair and scrubbed dirt from her cheeks. She peered out from under the gauntlets, looking to the castle.

Above the twisted turrets, ghostly figures were looking back at her as they boarded a giant glimmering galleon.

One by one, the ghostly townsfolk stepped aboard. Ulf waved everyone on, his tiara glinting majestically in the very last of the moonlight. Next to him, Clemens was spectacularly sick over the side, his phantom vomit splattering before vanishing into nothing.

Minna's parents stepped up, and Minna's mum extended an arm to help Old Woman Babette over the railing. Babette batted her hand away, but Leo thought that she was probably smiling. They were joined by the ghostly boys, who immediately sent their hoop spinning and ran around the deck after it. The sabre-toothed cat batted it away like a giant kitten.

Two ghosts lingered for a fleeting moment before boarding. There was Minna, waving. Next to her, the taller figure of Judge Harker was statue-still, gazing down at Leo and the vampires.

'Time to go, Miss Leo,' Marged said gently. 'It's not safe out here. Let's get you to bed.'

Ulf weighed anchor and the phantom ship sailed over Mount Moth and disappeared, bound for the Ghostly Realm.

TWENTY-FOUR

TROUBLE

The moon rose over Castle Motteberg and the Dreadwald below, comfortingly ordinary.

In the wake of the Blood Moon Banquet – the most chaotic banquet that the Vampiric Council had ever seen – the castle was feeling its effects. A fortnight had passed and restoration efforts were in full swing, aided by the loan of butler Nesh's *non-vampiric* skeletons. They were handy for a lot of the lifting, as long as there wasn't anything heavy enough to break bones.

Every night, the castle was bustling with the construction efforts, guided mostly by Dad, while Emmeline flew around and barked orders at everyone for the sake of it. From what Leo had heard Lady Sieglinde had retreated to her coffin shortly after seeing the last of the guests off on their journey home. She apparently hadn't been seen since.

And, high in the western tower, the youngest lady of the house . . .

Was grounded.

'Ugh! This is TORTURE!' Leo groaned, face first on her bed. She kicked her leg agitatedly back and forth, crumpling the blanket. 'It's been *for ever*. You're so lucky, Minna. You get to go wherever you want. Whenever you want!'

Inside the dagger – Agnes's dagger – which was propped up against Leo's pillow, Minna's translucent face peeked out from the Ghostly Realm's Hollowhome.

And rolled her eyes.

'It's been barely two weeks, Leo. I wouldn't call that for ever,' she said. Behind her, the Hollowhome fireflies buzzed in what might have been agreement. Leo tried not to feel too offended at their betrayal. She was glad that Hollowhome herself was alive and well after her ordeal.

'A *lot* can happen in two weeks,' she insisted, wriggling on her belly to get more comfortable. 'Go on, what am I missing? Tell me everything and spare no detail! I'm so bored. I need to know.'

A cloud of black smoke filled the dagger's shiny face before Minna wafted it away. Her mouth twisted. 'Well, you know. Ghost stuff,' she said awkwardly.

Leo sighed wistfully. 'I *love* ghost stuff. How's Ulf? How's Clemens?'

'They're fine. Still arguing. And you shouldn't love ghost stuff, not after everything we've been through!' Minna shook her head. 'Leo, I'm starting to think we're—'

'Cursed?' Leo cut in.

'Y-you said it!' spluttered Minna.

'You were thinking it?'

Minna cracked a tiny smile. 'Yeah, I suppose I was. You might be grounded, but I'm glad you're still here. I'm glad we're ALL still here.'

'We are. So tell me,' Leo said, propping herself up on her elbows. 'Has Judge Harker accepted your idea? Are they going to rewrite the rules of the trial?'

'She's considering it,' Minna said. 'Stop it, Leo. I said she's *thinking* about it. These things, they take time, so . . .'

'I'm really proud of you.' Leo wiped at her eye, smearing away an inky-black tear before it could fall. She gave Minna a watery smile. 'You've done something really great. You are an excellent ghost. I bet Ulf is glad to have you as his apprentice!'

'Well . . . it's not set in stone,' Minna said, though there were two bright points on her cheeks. 'But it's a start. I'm not sure Otto's End – GHOSTLY Otto's End, I mean – can go back to the way it was. I think you've . . . er, caused some confusion.'

'Me?'

'These people have never met a vampire like you. You're . . . *weird*, Leo. The weirdest vampire in the world. Weird enough to change Judge Harker's mind a little bit.'

Leo was about to reply, when the sound of clanging and clattering wound its way up the spiral staircase.

'Butler alert!' Leo hissed, shoving the dagger unceremoniously under her pillow.

The crashing footsteps came to a halt and there was a dainty knock at her bedroom door.

'Miss Leo?'

Rattling into the room, Marged set a steaming cup down on the bedside table. The fragrant smell of warm blood reached Leo's nose, making her stomach growl before she could remember to complain—

'Marged!' She threw a dramatic arm over her eyes. 'Marged, really! How long is Mum planning on keeping me here?'

'Well, little one, Lady Sieglinde was *very specific* in her instructions!' Marged said diplomatically, already drifting over to tidy Leo's desk. She had been itching to fiddle with it for a few nights now, and was finally caving in to her fussing habits. 'You are to stay put until the spring—'

'The SPRING! Marged, you *can't* be serious!'

'Until the *spring*, Miss Leo,' Marged continued firmly, 'at which point . . . ah . . .'

Looking down at her gauntlet, Marged paused. Gently she set the *Encyclopaedia Silva* – Leo's most beloved of books – down on the desk, smoothing over its cover.

'What's wrong, Marged?' Leo asked. She scooted over to make room as Marged left her books alone and approached the bed.

'Miss Leo,' Marged began, taking a seat. Her armour rattled as a sigh filled the empty space in her helmet. 'There is something I've been meaning to tell you.'

Leo sat up straighter. What was going on? From across the room Leo's top drawer slid open and a worried spidery face peered blindly out.

'Marged, you can tell me,' Leo said, feeling her insides roil like a nest of centipedes.

Marged's armour creaked. 'Well . . . you see, Miss Leo, your parents are very concerned about you. This whole . . . GHOSTLY BUSINESS at the banquet . . .' Marged nervously chuckled, downplaying the bloody battle that was still very much fresh in everyone's minds. It was a miracle that no one had actually died, though a few were now missing body parts. Knowing what they knew about ghosts, and what they knew about Lady Sieglinde . . . this was very irregular indeed. Ordinarily any vampire-ghost battle would be to the second death.

'They're worried that, should such a thing happen

again, you and your sister are at risk,' Marged continued. 'You are young, after all. There is much you do not yet know.'

Shaking her head, Leo touched Marged's metal arm. 'Trust me, Marged, that *won't* be happening again.'

'As much as I hope you are right,' Marged said with a frown in her voice, 'the Vampiric Council fears it may be only the beginning. There was an emergency meeting last night. Lady and Lord Motteberg wish to take . . . just some small, reasonable precautions, Miss Leo – nothing to worry about, of course! It's understandable, given vampire-ghost history. The other noble vampire families all have similar fears for their children.'

'Wait!' Leo gasped, her mind snagging on one small detail. 'You mean, Mum's finally awake? She's out of her coffin?'

'Yes, and she's put together a plan with the aid of the Vampiric Council,' Marged said gently. With a deliberate look at Leo she pulled back the pillow to expose the dagger. 'I would say that any more *ghostly shenanigans* would be ill advised, young ladies.'

From inside the blade Minna's face blinked. She nodded.

'Is that what you needed to tell me?' Leo pressed. She worried at the cuff of her pyjama sleeve. 'You wanted to tell me . . . that there's been a meeting?'

'Miss Leo . . . in the spring . . .' Marged's plume drooped. 'Lady Sieglinde intends to send you and Miss Emmeline away. Only for a little while.'

'What? Send us away? Away *where*?'

'You will know everything in time.' Marged's fidgeting gauntlets landed on the blanket, pulling it straight. She gently set the dagger on top, propping it up so Minna could see. 'I know this must come as a shock. But it seems our enemies are still many. Your parents want you to be safe and prepared as young vampires, should an *incident* like this ever happen again. I must say . . . I agree with them, little one.'

'B-but . . .'

The Dreadwald.

All her things – her collections. Her books.

Minna.

'I know you don't want to go, Leo,' Marged said. 'But . . . I'm sure it will be fun! All the other vampire children will be there! Of course I will miss you so very much, but at least your *sister* will be there, in case you feel homesick.'

Oh, pox. Now Leo really did feel ill.

Marged patted her knee. 'Let's not dwell on it for now, little one. Come now, you haven't touched your blood yet.'

She nodded to the cup on the nightstand, which had begun to cool. 'All will come right in the end, that's what I always say. You'll have a wonderful adventure at the Ichoria Institute – and then you'll be home again and everything will be back to normal.'

In the dagger's polished blade, Leo and Minna stared at each other.

'Ichoria Institute . . . ?'

THE END

ACKNOWLEDGEMENTS

Hi! It's Alex! An enormous, heartfelt THANK YOU to you all for joining me on another adventure with Leo and Minna.

A very special thank you to the wonderful staff and students, parents and carers of school communities who have welcomed me this past year. I've met the most amazing, fantastically dedicated people. It's a complete privilege also to know such bright future talent – I am certain I will be reading your stories, poems and scripts very soon. Keep working hard. You are phenomenal.

To my friends at Oldfields Hall Middle School in particular: this is another one for you. Thank you so much. I'm very proud to have come from Oldfields. I feel so lucky to know all of you. I look forward to every time we can hang out together.

Speaking of friends, thank you to all my friends and family for cheering me on, for keeping me going, for looking after me and helping me on my journey. Having you watching for *Vampires* (and now *Ghosts!*) means so much. Thank you for keeping your eyes peeled for us in the wild.

Dad and Di, there is a lot I would miss out on without you, thank you for always being on the other end of the phone. To the Swanners and the Wall family: I don't know why you are friends with me, because you are all superstars and I am a disaster! But thank you for putting up with me and I love you a lot. I'm so excited for all you do this year. Thank you to all the hard-working and knowledgeable librarians and booksellers. You are all so brilliant. Thank you for all you do to get *Vampires* into the hands of readers. I can't wait to hopefully meet more of you in the coming year. A huge thank you also to lovely booky people online and on social media: your recommendations have been great for my heart but very difficult on my wallet (and bookshelf space!) It's clear you know your stuff. Thank you for taking the time to read *Vampires* – and I hope you enjoy *Ghosts* also!

Thank you to the University of Derby and the alumni team for cheering me on. Derby Uni was an important milestone on my way to being right here, writing this dedication for my second book. Wow, it certainly feels really strange to write that, but I'm very grateful. Thank you for everything.

An extra vampiric thank you to David Higham Associates – to Caroline, Cbel, Becca, Allison, Livvy, Savanna and everyone – for your hard work, for your expert advice and for always being there. I appreciate you so much. I'm so thankful for everything you've done for my career but also . . . I just really love seeing you all and chatting about everything bookish! I think back to Catherine's hard work, too, preparing me to go out into the world with *Rules for Vampires*; there are a lot of people who have made me, and I think about you all every time I pick up a copy of our book.

Speaking of people who make magic happen: a super GRIMWALK-sized thank you also to the team at Simon & Schuster for following me into the Ghostly Realm, for working so hard on this book and for bringing Leo's story to (un)life again! Thank you to Lucy and Katie for your dedication and patience on the edits, sorting me out and making me make sense. Thank you also to Ali, Rachel, Laura, Olivia, Eve, Fahima, Jennie, Sorrel, David, Jesse, Anna – and everyone at S&S. I know there are so many of you – you are all golden. A special thank you always to Lucy Rogers for believing in Leo, for bringing us on board and allowing me to meet all of these incredible people.

To Sara Ogilvie, who is so kind and talented and has this power to see straight into my brain and make mind-blowingly amazing illustrations: thank you so much for working with me. I feel so, so fortunate to create this weird world with you.

To all the kids who love Sara's illustrations more than they love my writing: I *absolutely* understand!

And finally a thank you to my little family at home – Tris and Mac – for always being there with a sneeze and a hug. Everything is better when it is with you.

ABOUT THE AUTHOR

ALEX FOULKES is from Stoke-on-Trent in the Midlands of England, and lives with her boyfriend and their dog, Mac, who is just small enough to sit on the back of a broomstick (very convenient!). She has worked as a teaching assistant and a school librarian. When she's not reading and reading and reading, she's writing her very own stories with chills, thrills and maybe even a talking spider!

ABOUT THE ILLUSTRATOR

SARA OGILVIE is an illustrator and printmaker. Her unique, bestselling and internationally renowned work includes *Dogs Don't Do Ballet* and *Dave the Lonely Monster* with Anna Kemp, *The Wildest Cowboy* with Garth Jennings and *The Detective Dog* and *Hospital Dog* with Julia Donaldson. Sara lives in Newcastle upon Tyne in the north of England.